Endless Circle

A Circle-D Saga

Book 1

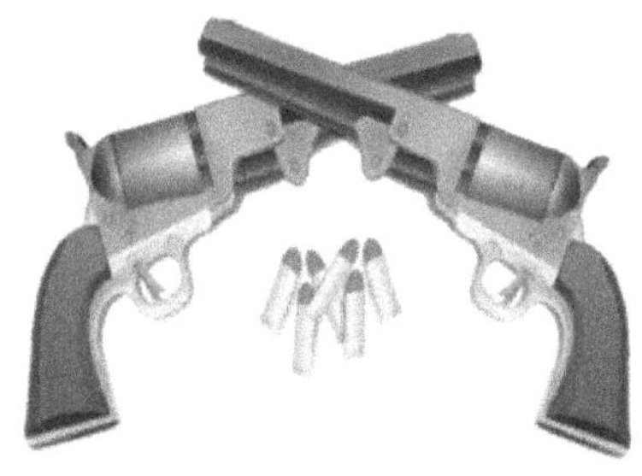

Nancy M. Wade

GARNAN Enterprises, LLC

Published in the United States by
GARNAN Enterprises,LLC of Ohio.
Copyright 2013 First Edition by Nancy M. Wade

Published and printed by Barnes and Noble Press
November 2019 - Second Edition

Published by GARNAN Enterprises, LLC of Ohio
Third Edition - 2023

ISBN-978-1737699835
ISBN- E978-1737699859
Library of Congress Cataloging #2013915529

Titles of Nancy M. Wade

Circle - D Saga

Book 1 - *Endless Circle*

Book 2 - *Moment in Time*

Book 3 – *Gun for Hire* (coming 2023)

Reflections: A Sentimental Journey

Frontier Heart

Courtship of Laura

A Meadowood Mystery – Series

Scarecrows and Corpses

Reunion with Death

Deadly Bones

Berry Little Murder

Table of Contents

ACKNOWLEDGEMENT

A huge thank you for the support of the members of the Lost State Writer's Guild of the Tri-Cities of Tennessee, especially my friends and fellow authors, Linda Dobkins and Tammy Robinson Smith. Their advice and shared wisdom have been immeasurable.

A special thank you to my husband, Gary, for his support and encouragement during all of my writing endeavors.

PROLOGUE

The red and white Cessna Skyhawk climbed into the western sun. The city of Laramie lay in miniature beneath them as the small plane reached higher altitudes on its journey home.

Suddenly the right wing dipped sharply; the single engine hammered an erratic noise. The pilot adjusted levers and throttles, pulling desperately on the controls.

"Nothing's responding! The flaps won't retract; I can't get her to straighten up!"

"Brian, do something!" Sarah screeched in a panic, gripping the arms of the passenger seat, as the plane continued to descend precariously.

"I don't understand it. Everything was perfect when I did my pre-flight. Unless ...."

Realizing they were doomed in a futile struggle, Brian grabbed for his wife's hand.

"I love you so much. God, I'm sorry I got you involved in this. Please forgive me!"

The jagged peaks of the Big Horn Mountains loomed directly ahead of them.

CHAPTER 1

A battered Ford pickup truck bounced and rattled on the gravel cemetery road. The driver paid no heed to the bone jarring bumps and ruts as the truck slowly braked to a halt. Dust swirled behind the truck, marking its passing. The dry powder settled onto the parched earth, coating everything in its path with a thin film of Wyoming dirt.

The door creaked and protested as the driver climbed down. Standing by the old blue truck with its faded white lettering on the doors that once proudly proclaimed the *Circle-D*; Andy took a minute to brush some of the grime off blue jeans and shirt. The soft felt Stetson sat low on Andy's forehead, shading eyes from the searing summer sun; eyes that scanned the horizon and searched in vain for any sign of rain clouds that would end this horrible drought.

Grave markers were lined up in crooked rows; tall and short, old headstones with weathered engravings or new smooth granite. The new stones looked out of place, too bright and too fresh, among the other century old sentinels. Grass grew high and obscured some of the lower markers; the caretaker long gone and residing now among his old comrades. Only the occasional visit of some family member showed evidence of any recent pruning. A lonely tin vase holding wilted meadow flowers stood in front of a wide, rectangular piece of marble.

Andy squatted and pulled the dead wildflowers from the container and tossed them onto the ground. Filling the vase with some water from a canteen kept in the truck, Andy lovingly arranged some fresh daisies and sprigs of sage. Memories and emotions came rushing forward as Andy pressed a tear-streaked cheek against the smooth marble and hands caressed the deep lettering.

The engraved stone linked the names for all eternity just as their mortal lives had been linked. Sarah Cummings Dunlap, born Feb. 1, 1949, and Brian James Dunlap, born Aug. 5, 1947, died July 21, 1997. Andy stood and stared sightless at the tombstone, visions of two vibrant people laughing and talking swam before her; memories of another time, happier and carefree, if she could just grasp… her hand outstretched to the ghostly images.

Noise from another vehicle coming up the cemetery road shattered the illusion, intruding on her solitude. Andy hastily turned her back to the road and quickly wiped away the traces of her mourning.

She did not move as she heard the slam of the truck door and the sound of feet crunching on the gravel path. The footsteps stopped behind her as the man's long shadow spread across the ground, mingling with her own.

"Your Grandfather said I'd find you here. How are you?"

Andy turned slowly and took off her Stetson, wiping the beaded sweat from her forehead with her shirtsleeve. Long dark brunette hair tumbled to her shoulders, released from the crown of her hat where she had gathered it up. She bent her head slightly, letting the mass fall forward, so she could again tuck it into the cowboy hat and keep the weight of it off her neck in the summer heat. Her ivory complexion was flushed from the heat, cheeks stained a pale pink.

Dove gray eyes that turned to him now were still glistening with recently shed tears.

Deputy Hartman watched the petite girl that he had known since childhood and admired the feminine woman she had grown into, possessing an artless beauty that was hers even while dressed in a cowhand's work clothes. Her fragile looks were in sharp contrast to the steel grit that she really possessed. He waited as Andrea gathered her composure and cloaked herself in that reserved manner and defiant streak of independence like a suit of armor. Her eyes darted to his, challenging him with a look, waiting for his criticism – none came.

"I'm fine Jason, how 'bout you?"

"Can't complain, I guess. I've been busy with the election coming up, running for county sheriff, you know. Gonna vote for me?" Jason grinned broadly and shifted his weight slightly on his feet, rocking from side to side and snatched off his own Stetson; his sandy blonde hair shone in the late morning sun.

Holding his hat, nervously rolling the brim between his fingertips, Jason changed the subject to the real reason he had come looking for her, "Look Andy, is there some place we can go to talk? How about we go get a cool drink? Maybelle's got some homemade lemonade on ice down at the diner."

Talking was the last thing Andy felt like doing and her exasperated sigh signaled that to Jason loud and clear, but a glass of cool lemonade did sound good, and her throat still felt constricted and raw from emotions held in check.

"All right, I'll meet you at the diner in a few minutes, but I'm not promising I can stay long. I've got to get back to the ranch."

Jason smiled a broad grin that lit up his face and made the corners of his blue eyes crinkle. The tiny crow's feet crinkling the corners of his eyes were evidence that smiling was something that J.C. Hartman did frequently. He was as easy going and open an individual, as Andy was cautious and withdrawn. They seemed to be such opposites, yet like magnets, Jason felt the pull of attraction.

The two walked slowly back to their trucks. Andy tossed the canteen onto the torn vinyl bench seat and climbed behind the wheel. The manual transmission groaned as she pushed in the clutch and rammed the gearshift lever into first gear. Shaking her head disgustingly, she made a mental note to have one of the guys service the transmission and check the lubrication. "Isn't there anything that isn't on its last leg?" Andy voiced her worries out loud.

Jason's shiny four-wheel drive Explorer purred quietly as he followed the other truck onto the road leading into town. The old cemetery had been placed on a hillside on the outskirts of Deer Springs when it had been a thriving boomtown in the late 1800's. Over the past hundred years the town had shriveled in size and prominence as neighboring cities in the state grew in importance. Now the outskirt was a good five miles away.

Glancing in the rear-view mirror, Andrea Dunlap looked at the man following her, "What am I going to do with you, Jason Hartman? I tell you to leave me alone and you still come back for more. If I didn't like you so much ... well, better not go down that road. Why does life have to be so confusing?" She reached over and switched on the radio, the only thing that still worked well in the old truck. Andy turned up the volume, allowing the mellow country singer's voice to fill the cab, leaving no room for painful thoughts.

Andrea parked in the asphalt-paved lot behind The Eatery, one of the few places in town where a person could get a simple meal for a decent price. Jason pulled in a few seconds behind Andy and parked his truck in the adjacent space, then hurried to catch up to her as she began walking around the corner to the front entrance of the diner. His long legs quickly carried him to her side, and he reached for the screen door to hold it open as Andy entered the restaurant. A few people glanced their way, then disinterested, resumed eating or talking. A couple men nodded a greeting as they recognized J.C. or Andy.

Maybelle Parker was busy pouring coffee for two men seated at the counter while her daughter Clarisse flipped burgers on the sizzling hot griddle. Both women looked up as Andy and Jason walked down the single aisle toward an empty booth near the back. A trio of paddle fans hung from the ceiling, gyrating slowly, circulating the hot air through the narrow confines of the former railroad car turned restaurant. Jason slid into the red vinyl upholstered booth and removed his hat, then laid it on the seat next to him. Andy took her seat slowly, the heat and the strain showing in her movements, if not her words. She tilted her hat back further on her head and reached for a paper napkin to wipe her brow. Andy glanced around the room with its faded black and white checkered flooring and cigarette smoke yellowed walls.

"Howdy J.C., what can I get you?" Maybelle asked as she ambled to their table, wiping her wet hands on the front of her red gingham apron. She pulled the pencil from behind her ear and waited with her order pad in hand as she looked from Jason to Andy. "Real sorry to hear about your folks, Andy. They were good people."

"Thank you; I appreciate your kind words," Andrea replied without looking up into the good-hearted face of the older woman.

She had known Maybelle all her life and knew the woman's expression of sympathy was sincere, not just polite. Maybelle was a surrogate mother to most of the kids in Deer Springs; her home or diner was always open to anyone. She was a large woman, earthy, with an ample bosom and a shoulder wide enough to cry on. And many a body took advantage of her kindness and did just that. She probably had heard most of the woes and tall tales of the entire town.

"How about bringing us two tall glasses of that good lemonade you have with lots of ice? Are you hungry, Andy? Want something to eat?" Jason turned to his companion.

Andy shook her head "no" and sat quietly staring out the window, her eyes focused on the mountains in the distance. Jason watched her for a few minutes as Maybelle returned to their table and set down two frosty glasses. He took a healthy gulp to quench his thirst while Andrea sipped hers more slowly.

Jason turned in his seat slightly to see if there were any listeners sitting close by before he quietly spoke. Watching Andy's face and trying to read her expression, he began, "What are your plans, now that your parents are gone?"

Dragging her gaze from the window, Andy forced her attention on Jason. "Gramps and I will live at the ranch like always. Why? Things will be a little more difficult, naturally, but we'll manage."

"There's been some talk, rumors around town," Jason spoke softly and hesitantly, "Word is that the Circle-D is in trouble financially. That true?"

"Maybe, but when isn't a cattle ranch experiencing some cash flow problems? Who's spreading that kind of talk anyway? What business is it to anyone but us?" Andy gave her full attention to the conversation now, her anger coloring her cheeks more than the afternoon heat. She swallowed more of the tart lemonade then pushed the glass to the center of the table, meaning to rise and leave.

Jason reached for her hand and checked her action, hating himself for bringing up the subject, "Please stay. I'm sorry Andy; I didn't mean to imply anything was wrong. I just wanted you to know that if you need any help, I'm here for you. You can count on me. Okay?" He squeezed her hand lightly, reluctant to let go, and waited for her answer.

Andy leaned back in her seat again and studied the face of the man sitting opposite from her. He was a good man, and she shouldn't take out her hurt and anger on him. Not wanting to make a scene, she forced a smile, tried to relax and quickly glanced around at the other customers.

Silver eyes looked deep into his cobalt blue ones as she leaned forward and returned the pressure in his hand.

"I know you are Jason. Believe me when I tell you that it means a lot to me too. Thanks. Now I really have to be going. Stop by the house some time."

She strode to the door, waved good-bye to Maybelle and Clarisse, and let the aluminum screen slam behind her. Jason finished his drink and paid at the counter as he saw Andy's pickup turn the corner and head west toward home.

"That man is wearing his heart on his sleeve for that gal and she just doesn't seem to notice," Maybelle told her daughter as she shook her head in pity after Jason left.

"Can't understand how any girl could pass up J.C.; wish he'd look in my direction. He wouldn't doubt my attention. I'd just like the chance, one night, that's all I'd ask," Clarisse sighed dreamily as she watched the good-looking deputy drive past on his way to the sheriff's office.

"Huh, you and every other gal in town. I reckon your husband, Bart, might have something to say about that. You just keep your attentions home like a good wife oughta and leave chasing J.C. Hartman to the single girls. One of these days Andrea Dunlap will wake up and see what a good man he is and that he'd make her a fine partner. Mark my words."

"Oh Ma, a gal can dream can't she? No harm done," Clarisse whined as she wiped the counter and stacked some dirty coffee mugs in the sink.

CHAPTER 2

Samuel Dunlap unsaddled his horse in the corral and threw the leather saddle and gear across the top split rail as Andy pulled into the barnyard. Shading his eyes from the glaring sun, the elderly man strode across the dusty yard with a gait that a younger man would be hard pressed to match. Denim Levi's and work shirt molded his lean frame, and a red bandanna was tied around his neck, just touching the fringes of silver hair that extended from beneath the black cowboy hat.

Andy watched her grandfather with a pride that swelled her heart as he walked toward her. Meeting him halfway across the yard, they turned and headed toward the rustic log ranch house. No words were needed as Andy met her grandfather's inquiring look and his eyes read the pain and sorrow reflected on the young woman's face.

The screen door swung shut behind them as Andy's feet dragged across the wide plank flooring and she flopped onto the softly cushioned sofa. Automatically propping her booted feet on the edge of the split barrel coffee table, Andy leaned her head back and rubbed her closed eyes. Grief threatened to overwhelm her and she didn't dare give in to it. Not now, when there were so many things that needed doing. She couldn't afford herself the luxury.

Pulling herself upright, she idly studied the only home she had ever known. The old sofa with its warm earth tones was showing patches of wear on the arms, but the plump pillows covered in shades of turquoise and coral were still inviting. A brown leather chair that had been her father's favorite now sat empty; the leather supple and stretched in places from many hours occupied with late night reading. Some flowers and window curtains with their ruffled edges were feminine touches her mother had tried to add to the room. The massive stone fireplace filled one side of the room, providing heat and cheer on cold Wyoming winters. Andy looked at the smiling face staring down at her from one of the framed photographs perched atop the oaken mantle. Her mother was holding a bouquet of wildflowers and smiling lovingly at her husband by her side; the sun's rays glinting on her dark hair created a halo effect as the picture had been snapped. God, how she missed her!

Andy abruptly jumped to her feet and walked briskly into the kitchen. Her thoughts and emotions were threatening to drown her in the very self-pity that she was trying to avoid. *"Better to keep busy and keep her mind off her sorrow,"* Andy decided. She opened and closed cupboard doors with a bang as she grabbed dishes and rummaged through canned goods. Setting the table quickly, she turned back to the kitchen sink then looked up guiltily at her grandfather standing quietly in the doorway with arms folded across his chest.

"I'm sorry Gramps. Guess I've been a little noisy in here."

"I understand. I miss them both too, Andy."

Throwing herself into his strong arms, Andy gave in to the tears that she had been holding at bay. Callused hands gently stroked her hair and patted her lightly on the back, offering her comfort and shared grief.

"It hurts Gramps. I never even got to say good-bye. I don't know what I would do if I didn't have you; you're all the family I have left."

"What we need is time - time to soften the hurt and heal the wounds. Nothing will ever fill the loss, but we'll survive and carry on because we have to, that's all anyone can do."

Straightening her shoulders and brushing back long hair, Andy wiped her wet eyes and reached deep within to that core of steel found in the center of all the Dunlaps. She looked up at her grandfather and saw his own pain mirrored in his eyes. Touching his whisker-stubbled cheek fondly, she asked softly, "How about some lunch? I made some tuna fish sandwiches and poured a couple of glasses of cold iced tea."

"That sounds like a good idea. Did you see J. C. in town? He called earlier."

"Yeah, he tracked me down." She hesitated a moment before broaching another worry. "Gramps, I've been thinking about moving the cattle up into the north pasture where there's more tall grass and water. What do you think? If this drought keeps up much longer we won't be able to keep feeding and watering the herd; the grasses are already beginning to burn off."

Chewing his sandwich thoughtfully, Sam stared out the kitchen window at the cloudless sky and the waves of heat rising from the parched ground. "I think we may have to sell off some head, maybe a couple hundred or so, better to get a good price for them while they're still fat. This heat and lack of feed will thin them down soon enough. Guess it wouldn't hurt though to move the herd for a while, until market prices look good."

"I'd like to do it. Take the herd up country, I mean. I need the time alone Gramps and hard work and sore muscles might just be good medicine."

"All right Andy. I don't want you gone on the trail more than two or three weeks though. That's plenty of time to move them, set up a line camp and ride back. I need you here too, gal." Gramps squeezed her hand in warm affection.

"Fine, that's settled then. Gramps? Are we OKAY, money-wise? Jason mentioned something to me today that really got my dander up but got me worrying too. He says there's been talk around town that the Circle-D is in trouble."

The elder Dunlap sat back in his seat and studied the concerned expression on his granddaughter's face. "Your father has been running the business end of the ranch for the past five years; I've been busy with breeding stock. Guess what I'm trying to say, is that I haven't paid much attention to the finances for some time, but the lawyer went over some stuff with me after the funeral. The ranch has been losing money for a long time now Andy. Brent Logan has made some offers to buy our land. Guess he approached your father a few months ago. I don't know what Brian's answer was, but the lawyer had a record of the inquiry. "

"Are we in danger of losing the ranch Gramps?" fear tinged Andy's voice.

"No. No, of course not. But we have to turn things around and this damn weather isn't helping matters. We can't afford to buy feed if the pastures dry up; we'll have to sell the stock. We can keep some to start up a new herd, but most would have to go. I don't know where else to cut corners and save on our budget. We already live on a shoestring. Whatever we decide, we'll do it together, all right?"

Selling off the herd was a sobering thought and Andy knew her grandfather had been giving that solution a lot of late night floor walking, deep thinking. A cattleman doesn't like having to liquidate an entire herd; sell some and reduce the size of the herd, sure. But sell out or give up their land?! Andy nodded to her grandfather and rose to start carrying their dishes to the sink when the jarring ring of the living room telephone interrupted her contemplation.

She stood with a plate still poised in mid-air as she watched her grandfather listen solemnly to the speaker on the other end of the phone. She strained to hear the other voice coming through the line.

Samuel Dunlap clenched the telephone receiver in his fist as the cold, bureaucratic voice told him to retrieve his son and daughter-in-law's personal effects. His face started to blotch with angry red spots as the impersonal official relayed the final message. Resisting the urge to slam the receiver down, he hung up and walked quietly back into the kitchen.

"What is it, Gramps? Who was that?"

"Some man from the NTSB says we can come get Brian and Sarah's things from the wreckage. They're done with their inspection and don't need them anymore."

Andy blanched and sat down quickly on a kitchen chair, her knees turning to water. Her mind conjured the sight of twisted metal. She looked up at her grandfather's still angry expression.

"What else? What else did the man say? Why are you so mad?"

"It seems the crash has been ruled an accident and the cause listed as *pilot error.* You know damn well that my son was a good pilot and careful! He didn't make any *errors* where flying was concerned. Brian would turn over in his grave if he knew those sons of bitches were chalking this up to pilot error! They're just too lazy to look for the real answer."

Andrea's own temper flared as her grandfather's words spilled forth. He was right, she knew, her father always checked and double-checked every airplane he flew. He would've been especially careful with her mother on board. He loved that single engine Cessna and knew every inch of it. The tragic crash that claimed her parents' lives could not be merely written off as pilot error.

"I'll go to Laramie to pick up the things, Gramps. I'll leave in the morning and drive down, and you can be certain that I'll be asking some questions when I get there too!"

"You don't need to go Andrea. I can do it."

Andy recognized the level of his agitation by the fact that he called her by her formal name. She tried to think of a plausible excuse for her to go and him to remain behind, suddenly she remembered the transmission problem in the truck and latched onto that.

"That old pickup truck might not make it as far as Laramie, Gramps. I was going to tell you about it later, the clutch is slipping I think. You need to have one of the boys check it out. I would worry about you driving real far in that old thing. I'll call Jason and ask him to take me."

His thoughts diverted to this new problem, Sam relented. "Have any trouble with it today? Why didn't you say something before this? There are plenty of miles left in that truck, you just have to learn to care for it better. I'll have Frank crawl under it and look at that clutch plate, probably just needs an adjustment. Frank is an expert with anything mechanical; man was born with grease and oil in his blood."

Muttering under his breath, Sam headed out toward the bunkhouse in search of Frank. Andy watched him cross the yard with a satisfied smile then walked to the telephone to try and get hold of Jason. The tattered telephone book in the center desk drawer held the entire listing of the ranch's frequently used numbers. Skimming the pages, Andy ran her finger down a column until she read the number of the sheriff's office and dialed quickly. The call was picked up after the second ring and a familiar male voice answered.

"Platte County Sheriff's office, Deputy Hartman speaking."

"Hi Jason, this is Andy." She sensed his surprise and could hear a muffled thud as if he had suddenly sat upright causing his propped feet to hit the floor. Andy would have laughed if she knew how accurate her imagination had been.

"Well hello! What can I do for you? Is this a personal call or is there some trouble I need to rescue you from?"

"Both actually; I wanted to ask a favor. Could you drive me into Laramie tomorrow?"

"Sure, what's going on in Laramie?" He would relish the break in the monotony and always enjoyed any time spent in the company of Andrea Dunlap.

"The NTSB called and they're releasing my parents' things found in the crash. I've got to go and pick them up. I'd really appreciate it if you could go." Andy dreaded the ordeal alone and her desperation unconsciously colored her voice.

"What time do you want to leave? I can pick you up around 9 o'clock, gives me time to get the morning chores done at the ranch, if that's all right," he offered.

Her relief was evident as she replied, "Perfect. Nine it is. Thanks a lot Jason."

"See you in the morning then. Bye." Jason hung up the receiver slowly, reluctant to let her go. He sat at his desk, staring unseeing out the front window, thinking of the emotion he had heard in her voice. It pleased him immensely that she needed him.

CHAPTER 3

Andy returned from the stable where she had spoken with Frank Costello and Bill Shultz, two of the four men who were employed by the Circle-D as wranglers. She informed them that they were going to be moving the herd up country in a few days. They would start to get the necessary gear ready. Frank and Bill had each been with the ranch since Andy was knee high and she looked on the men as dear friends, almost surrogate brothers, rather than employees. She respected their knowledge and skill with the animals and trusted their judgment.

Jason beeped his horn in greeting as he pulled onto the gravel road leading through the Circle-D fence gates and waved to the two riders, recognizing Sam Dunlap and his foreman Charlie Tucker. He drove the half-mile distance to the ranch house and parked next to Andy's blue pickup. Frank was just starting to jack up the front end of the truck and from the looks of the tool chest sitting nearby, repair work was in order.

"Howdy Frank, Andy inside?"

"Yep. Hear tell you're runnin' for sheriff, J.C. You got my vote."

"Thanks Frank, appreciate it."

"Are you two going to stand around and jaw all day long or are we going to get moving? It *is* a long drive to Laramie, you know," Andy complained as she kicked up dust with every step she took.

Throwing a withering look at Frank that said he should know better, she turned to Jason.

"And a fine good morning to you too Miss Andrea! Get up on the wrong side of the bed?" Jason laughed as he touched the brim of his Stetson in a salute and held the vehicle's door open for her.

"Let's just get going. This is one trip that I'd rather not be making."

"See you later Frank," called Jason as he climbed into the driver's seat and turned the ignition key. The motor came to life and he dropped it into gear, turning back onto the main drive.

Andy sat quietly looking out the car's window, watching the perimeter fences of the Circle-D slide past as they started onto the county road. She fidgeted with the crease of her chino slacks, smoothing the fabric under her palms. The pale yellow summer top she wore was cooler and dressier than her usual attire, but she would have preferred her denim work clothes. Dressing up to go into Laramie did not help her disposition.

Now she squirmed in her seat, uncomfortable with her own bad behavior, until she finally turned sideways to face Jason. "I'm sorry I snapped at you back at the ranch. It's just this trip that has me on edge. I never did see the plane after the crash, and now knowing that I have to face it ... well, I'm just not looking forward to it. Gramps said he would go, but between the two of us, I thought it would be better if I did. Now I'm not so sure."

"I take it you just got the call yesterday from NTSB? Must have been after I saw you. We didn't get any official report at the office since the accident occurred out of my jurisdiction. What was the outcome, or would you rather not say?"

"Gramps took the call and it upset him plenty. The official verdict is *'cause of accident, pilot error'*, but I just can't believe that and neither can Gramps. You knew my Dad, Jason. Can you ever remember a time when he wasn't careful about flying?"

"Well I can see why you'd both be upset, especially your grandfather. Andy, those people at NTSB are usually pretty thorough. I know you don't want to hear this, but if that's what the report says, then you're going to have to accept it."

"Whose side are you on anyway?! I should've known that you would take the government's word over mine." Andy crossed her arms and turned her back to Jason, once more facing the window. If that's how he thought, then she had no intention of speaking with him for the balance of the two-hour ride.

"Now Andy stop being childish! I never said I was taking any sides. I only said that most of those kinds of reports are pretty accurate. Let's just wait until we get there and see for ourselves, All right?"

"Fine!" She answered him in a huff, still intending to brood. "Let's just change the subject."

The road stretched ahead of them in a black ribbon of asphalt across the wide plain. Long prairie grasses bent in the hot Chinook wind blowing across the land, baking everything in its path until the earth was scorched and brown. Even the Lodgepole River beneath the bridge they were crossing was a mere trickle; the dried riverbed was shallow and rocky instead of the torrent that usually flowed. The summer sun beat down mercilessly on man and animals alike.

Waves of heat radiated from the prairie surface creating a rippling illusion. Jason watched a pair of buzzards circling overhead in the distance, a sure sign of something dead. The cool air conditioning blowing across his skin was in direct contrast to the temperatures outside the vehicle prompting Jason to break the silence that had filled the cab.

"Sure glad we aren't making this trip on horseback today, aren't you? As much as I like a good ride, there are some definite advantages to modern conveniences."

"Yeah, I suppose you're right. The air conditioning does feel good. Gramps and I don't miss it much at the house, but on a day like this, it would come in handy."

Andy's thoughts were wandering elsewhere as she answered Jason, her attention not really on the heat outside or the cool air inside. She casually studied her friend as he steered the Explorer with one sure hand lightly on the wheel, the same manner in which he would treat a favored steed. The heat didn't seem to bother him much; his crisp, tan uniform with its Platte County badge and insignia didn't even have a single wrinkle. Sunglasses shaded piercing blue eyes that didn't miss a thing.

"How's the Circle-D making out with this drought? Pop and I have moved some of our herd to higher ground. We've lost most of the lower pastures and we're trying not to use the bales of winter feed yet." Jason's voice broke into Andy's musing, bringing her attention back to the present.

"Most of our pastures are gone too, dried up. We were thinking of moving our cattle north in a few days. I just told the boys this morning to start getting the gear ready. I'll be leaving on Thursday."

"What do you mean, you'll be leaving? You're taking the herd up country?"

"Yes, what's wrong with that? Don't you think that I can handle trail bossing my own cattle and men?"

"Andy, I never meant to imply anything of the kind. I'm aware you can handle yourself around a ranch. It's one of the things I respect and admire about you. I just worry about you; that's all. How come you're going and not Sam?"

"I volunteered. I told Gramps that I needed the time away. You understand, don't you? Sometimes there's no place in the world better than the high country. I can't explain it, but I can draw my strength from those hills. The solitude and majesty of the mountains ...well it's just something that I feel. I suppose that sounds like a silly woman talking." Andrea was suddenly embarrassed to voice her thoughts out loud to him.

"No, it's not silly. I do understand what you mean, something a city slicker wouldn't comprehend though." Jason smiled and nodded. He was relieved that the easy camaraderie was restored between them again.

The remaining drive to Laramie passed pleasantly as Jason headed for the county airport located on the east side of town. They followed a perimeter road around the small terminal and entered a cyclone-fenced area where they found several tall hangars and air cargo offices. Next to one of the freight offices was a metal building that looked like it might have been an old Army Quonset hut with a wooden sign swinging in the wind. The initials NTSB in faded red letters were barely readable.

Jason pulled up and stopped next to the group of buildings. Reaching for his hat, he regarded his passenger. "You ready?"

"Yes, let's get this over with," Andy replied reluctantly.

Opening the car door, she slid off the seat, swinging the door shut behind her. Raising her hand to shield her eyes from the glaring sun, Andy stood a moment to take in her surroundings.

A row of private airplanes, Piper Cubs and Cessna, were parked on the ramp to her left. Men dressed in coveralls were operating a forklift, raising a pallet of wooden crates then maneuvering them into the cargo hold of a Lockheed C-130. Metal drums containing oil or aviation fuel were stacked in the shade of one hangar. Engines roared to life as a plane taxied down one runway, preparing to take off into the western sky. Above all the noise of running engines and men shouting directions was the sound of the hot, dry wind shrieking across the open field. Andrea turned to Jason and pointed to the door of the small administration building; her voice lost in the bedlam. He nodded and started walking toward the entrance.

The narrow wooden door opened into a stifling room. Two fans perched on floor pedestals at opposite ends of the office were trying in vain to relieve the oven-like interior. A trio of metal file cabinets lined one wall; the President's picture hung above one, the frame tilted crookedly. An odd assortment of framed certificates decorated the other walls. Papers littered an "in" basket and a mug of stale coffee sat on the corner of a gun metal gray desk. The sun was heating the metal building until every living thing or soul within it felt suffocated.

Dan Johnson slouched on a swivel desk chair; his short sleeve white shirt was perspiration stained and his tie hung askance, a shadow of unshaven whiskers played along his jawline. The weary inspector observed the couple approaching his desk and drew his own conclusions. Johnson noted the man's deputy uniform but dismissed him as being unimportant. He eyed the petite beauty of the woman by his side, looking her up and down in a thorough manner and enjoying the curves he saw.

"You must be here for the Dunlap case. I'm Johnson; I called yesterday."

Andrea's dry throat croaked; she could barely find her voice as she answered his query, "Yes, that's right. I'm Andrea Dunlap, you spoke with my grandfather."

Jason stood quietly at Andy's side, studying the man before him. He didn't like the bored attitude and he definitely didn't like the way he was scrutinizing Andy.

"Let's go outside. I'll just get your copy of the report and you can sign off on the personal effects' inventory."

Johnson stood and picked up a clipboard and pen then sifted through some files in the top drawer of one of the cabinets. His voice was so cold and indifferent that it made Andy inwardly seethe.

The three left the stifling office and walked into the noon sunshine. Andy and Jason were relieved to be out in the open again, at least the air moved. A pair of workers dressed in dirty coveralls watched them as they followed the aviation agent and entered a hangar located at the end of the row of buildings. The dark shade inside was almost cool and the elevated ceiling allowed the heat to rise. It took a minute for Andy's eyes to adjust from the bright sunlight to the shadowy interior. When she was able to see, she turned toward a line of tables against one side of the hangar. Resembling a gruesome banquet, broken pieces of airplane parts were arranged along the tabletops, some had tags or labels tied to them identifying the part. Larger sections of the Cessna were assembled in the center of the hangar.

Andy reached for Jason's hand for support as she slowly walked over to the wrecked plane that took her parents' lives. One wing was intact, bright red call letters GLW994 still unblemished. The tail section lay torn apart, placed on the floor in the position it would have occupied. The right wing had been reassembled, struts broken, its fragments defining the point of impact. The once white fuselage now lay in two sections, black charring evidence of the ensuing fire after the crash.

Andrea gasped as she stared at the wreckage. Waves of revulsion rocked her and she swallowed hard to keep the gorge from rising in her throat. She couldn't pry her eyes away from the sight of the small plane's cockpit; visualizing her father at the controls, her mother sitting confidently by his side.

Jason felt Andy unconsciously tighten her grip on his hand. He looked over at the shattered aircraft and back at the woman by his side. Knowing that the sight was tearing her apart like the broken fragments spread before them, he tried to gently ease her away.

"Come on Andy, you don't need to see this. Let's go back to Mr. Johnson and get the things he has ready."

She started to shake her head no, she couldn't move. But Jason kept gently pulling her backwards, insisting. Mr. Johnson was impatiently tapping his pen against the clipboard, and a look of annoyance was settling over him like a cloud. He handed Andrea an envelope and she glanced inside at some official looking documents. She drew one out and slowly started to read the findings of the board, her gray eyes darkening to the color of storm clouds.

"This can't be true! You people never knew my father. He wouldn't have done this."

"I'm sure this has been a shock to you, miss, but the findings are accurate. We don't make mistakes. Now if you will just sign for your family's things and initial the report on the bottom of the page in triplicate, I can release this."

Andrea's anger was rising in relationship to the temperature outside as she faced the indifferent inspector.

"I don't care what your report says, I say it's wrong! My father was an excellent pilot and he would never have caused that kind of malfunction. I don't care how long it takes, but I am going to prove you are wrong."

Thrusting the forms at her again, Dan Johnson lost his bored manner. "Just sign this and take your things. You think you can come in here and threaten my office because you're with some hick, small town deputy? You are talking to an agency of the United States government!" Johnson's voice got louder with each word as if he needed to emphasize his importance.

"I'll be back and you'll see!" Andrea hastily scribbled her name on the documents and grabbed the small cardboard box containing her father's belongings.

Unshed tears were stinging the back of her eyes but she was determined that the horrid man would not see her cry. She was not going to give him the satisfaction.

Jason walked her quickly to the waiting Explorer and started the engine, turning on the air conditioner and letting the truck idle. He was grinding his teeth so hard, he was certain he just lost half of his enamel.

"I'll be right back; you stay in the car and let the AC cool you down."

"Where are you going?"

"I forgot something, be right back."

Jason refrained from slamming the truck door, as he would have liked, no need to abuse his own vehicle. The anger was building in him like a pressure cooker, and it was about to blow. He walked back into the hangar where Dan Johnson was still lingering, enjoying the cool interior. The official looked up, startled at the return of the cowboy cop.

His jaw clenched and his usually smiling eyes now dangerously narrowed, Jason approached the inspector. He stopped just short of trampling on the man's toes, forcing that one to take a step backwards.

Jason spoke in a deceptively quiet voice, "That little lady is a very close friend of mine and she just lost her mama and papa. I don't take kindly to her being pushed around and treated badly. It wouldn't have hurt any if you had been a might kinder."

Jason glared at the man's flushed face and proceeded to make his point as he jabbed his index finger into the man's chest with each word. "If Andrea says your report is wrong, then it is wrong. And this hick, small town deputy is going to do everything in his power to help her prove it. Do I make myself clear?"

Jason didn't wait for a response as he strode out of the hangar and joined Andy. He would have felt better if he had belted the guy, but at least his own temper was beginning to lower in degrees. He looked out of the truck's window and noticed the same two ground crew members were inordinately interested in his and Andrea's actions. Jason's sixth sense and police training started sending him signals as he made a mental note of the men's descriptions. They weren't doing anything wrong; it was just a certain look about them. Instinct was all Jason had to go on, and he was definitely out of his jurisdiction, so he shrugged it off and decided it must be because of the confrontation he just had with Johnson.

CHAPTER 4

Jason eased the truck back onto the perimeter road, leaving the airport behind them. He kept glancing at Andrea to try and judge how she was faring and making his own decision, pulled into the parking lot of the first restaurant he saw.

"Why are we stopping? I've got to get back, Jason."

"We're both hot and you need something to eat and drink. I think it would be a good idea to take a few minutes to get your emotions under control too. That wasn't the most pleasant of experiences back there and I can see how upset you are. Don't think you can hide it from me, Andrea Dunlap, I know you too well."

Andy turned her head away from Jason's prying eyes and tried not to loudly sniff the threatening tears. The man did not allow her any pride at all. Andy hated the thought that she was becoming so transparent. She always thought her feelings were her own, to hide or share as she determined. She didn't appreciate being so easy to read.

On impulse Jason reached for the small box, intending to carry it into the restaurant with them. As they started across the open lot toward the cafe's entrance, he noticed a tan colored sedan pull in. The driver resembled one of the men he had seen at the airport. Jason slowed his pace so he could get a better look, but the occupants of the car didn't get out. His interest peaked, but it could be just a coincidence, so he didn't say anything to Andy as they entered the cool interior of the restaurant.

A cheerful waitress seated them at a corner table. She chatted on about the hot weather and how she would be glad to get back to college come fall. Jotting down their orders of ice tea and turkey club sandwiches, she promised to return in a jiffy.

"Why did you bring that box in here?" Andy asked as soon as the waitress left.

"I just thought it might be a good idea not to leave it unattended in the car. Can't explain why; just a feeling. Wouldn't you like to look through it a little?"

"I think it can wait until I get home. I've seen enough for one day." Andy shuddered inwardly, seeing again in her mind's eye the twisted wreckage arranged so neatly in the hangar.

"All right Andy, whatever you think is best."

Jason started to push the box further onto the bench seat, but when he moved it, one of the top flaps came undone. He tried tucking the flap edge under the adjacent flap to secure it, but the corner wouldn't fit. Investigating the obstruction, he found the hard edge of a book that had been shoved in at an angle. Drawing it out to try and repack it flatter, Jason showed the book to Andy.

"Look at this, leather binding on it is really old. It even looks stitched on and I know they don't do that anymore."

"Let me see that. This was in with my father's things? How strange. I wonder where he got it. I don't recall seeing a book like this before and I know all the books we own at home. I've read most of them at least twice when we were shut in during last winter's blizzard." Andy turned the book over, running her hands over the worn cover. It even smelled old. "There's no name on it, no title or author I mean."

Opening the book cover, Andy was surprised to see fine swirling handwriting on the ivory colored pages. It was a diary, the first entry dated June, 1884.

"Look Jason, it's a journal of some kind. My father must have found it during one of his visits to those flea markets and auctions that he loved. He was always collecting old books and things; he had such a passion for history. It would be just like him to carry around some old worthless book. Here, try and fit it back into the box and I'll show it to Gramps when we get home." She handed the diary back to Jason and watched as he shifted a few articles so the book would lie flat, then closed the cardboard box.

Their food arrived and they both ate quietly; Andrea absorbed in her own memories and Jason casually scanning the cafe's customers for any familiar faces. Downing the last of his iced tea, Jason stood and reached for the check.

"Want to use the ladies' room before we leave? I'll pay the bill and wait for you by the door."

"Fine, I'll only be a few minutes." Andy found the rest room located at the rear of the restaurant. The room was empty and she was grateful for the few minutes of solitude as she splashed cold water on her face. "He knows me so well," she said to her image in the mirror. "He sees my pain even when I try to hide it. Can he read my mind so well; does he see within my heart too?" Shaking her head, to give herself a much-needed mental wake up, she dried her hands and walked out.

Jason looked up as she approached and smiled warmly to her. He never tired of the mere sight of her, and his pleasure was reflected in his warm expression. A few men stared admiringly at Andy as she walked past their tables with an athlete's grace and Jason swelled with male pride knowing that she was leaving with him.

"You seem awfully pleased about something," Andy commented as she took Jason's hand and they headed toward the car.

"I'm just enjoying your company, Andy, my girl. I am glad to see you a little more relaxed though. Guess lunch did the trick."

He put the box on the back seat and they climbed into the sports truck. Fastening seat belts and a quick check for traffic, Jason pulled back onto the northbound highway. As they passed a gas station, Jason spied the tan sedan and watched in his rear view mirror as it departed and also headed north. Although the car was behind them by almost a quarter mile, Jason decided he would watch closely and see if they were truly following him or simply traveling in the same direction. He was so intent on scrutinizing his outside mirrors and observing normal traffic that he missed what Andy was saying. It was a second before her words broke into his concentration.

"Jason, I asked you about the election. Shouldn't you be campaigning or something instead of being here with me?"

"Sorry Andy, I wasn't paying attention. What did you say about the election?"

"I was asking about your campaign. The polls are open tomorrow; you do remember the election, don't you?" Andy laughed and shook her head at her absent-minded companion.

"Of course I remember the election! What a funny question. Listen, I've been a deputy for close to five years, lived in this county all my life so people ought to know me by now. I've stated what I intend to accomplish as sheriff and if that isn't good enough, then the citizens can vote for someone else. Running around campaigning the day before the vote isn't going to suddenly change people's minds; they either like you or they don't."

"Well, Deputy Hartman, I'm sure you know that you have the support of everyone on the Circle-D and I'm confident you'll win hands down. Still, I can't help feeling slightly guilty about monopolizing your time today."

"I appreciate the thought; just be sure and back it up with a nice big vote tomorrow!" Jason smiled broadly and winked at Andrea. Returning his attention to the road once more, he scanned the cars behind them for a glimpse of a tan sedan.

By the time they neared the city limits of Deer Springs, Jason had lost sight of the tailing vehicle and the remaining traffic was limited to a pair of pickup trucks and his Explorer. He waved to Maybelle standing outside as they passed the diner. She stopped her sweeping of the sidewalk and front entrance just long enough to wave a friendly hello and note just who his passenger was.

Maybelle nodded to herself in satisfaction at seeing the couple together. Tapping the bristles of the straw broom to dislodge some dirt and tumbleweed, Maybelle dusted her hands on the front of her apron and entered the empty diner. The lunch crowd had gone, and it was a few hours before her evening trade would wander in for supper. She reached for the ever-hot coffee pot and poured herself a cup, relaxing for some well-deserved minutes in a cushioned booth. The air blowing from the overhead fans felt good on her sweaty brow and Maybelle sipped her coffee while she gazed out the front window and idly watched a tan car try to parallel park along the curb. A couple of men dressed in soiled work clothes got out and sauntered toward the diner.

"Guess my break is over," thought Maybelle as she got up and once more moved behind the counter.

Dust swirled around the wheels of the truck as it came to a halt in the barnyard. Charlie Tucker was balancing the hind leg of a young pinto between his own knees as he nailed on a new horseshoe. He quickly applied a file to the rough head of the nails and released the leg. Finishing his chore, Charlie called a greeting to Jason and Andy.

"Hey J.C., where you two been all day? If you're looking for Sam, he went into town to pick up a few supplies. You probably passed him on the way."

Andy climbed onto the lower split rail and stretched across the top of the corral fence to pat her favorite mare's nose. The animal nuzzled her hand, looking for an apple or other treat. Jason stood to the side and spoke quietly with Charlie, both of their expressions solemn as they stole a quick look toward Andy. She glanced up to witness Charlie nodding in agreement to something that Jason had said before they parted and Charlie turned toward the stable.

"C'mon Andy, I'll carry your things into the house for you." Jason called over his shoulder as he walked back to the car and reached into the rear compartment. He tucked the carton under his left arm and swung the door shut.

The house was cool inside despite the lack of artificial air conditioning; the pair of tall century old elms standing sentinel next to the log structure spread their branches above the roof to form a shady canopy. Jason set the box down on the wide coffee table then moved over by the fireplace. Leaning an arm against the mantle, he studied the family photos gathered there. Sam's expression looked serious as he stood at attention in his Army uniform; the photo had a date of July 1945 scratched on the back. A second shot found Sam smiling broadly as he draped an arm about the shoulders of his new bride, Mary. Jason looked at Brian and Sarah's picture and saw Andy's eyes reflected in her mother and her smile was the same one worn on her father's face. *"Generations of Dunlaps have lived under this roof and now only a few remain",* Jason thought as he dragged his gaze from the collection of portraits and glanced around the cozy room.

Andy walked in from the kitchen carrying two glasses of cool pink lemonade and handed one to Jason, "Thought you might like something cold to drink before you head out."

She started toward the front entrance; the screen swinging shut behind her as she plopped onto the wooden swing that was suspended from one end of the porch roof.

Jason brought his drink outside and sat next to Andy; setting the swing into an easy rocking motion. They sat enjoying the silence of the afternoon until the quiet became awkward.

Jason cleared his throat slightly before he began, "Will you join me for dinner tomorrow night, Andy? I'd like to have someone to celebrate the outcome of the election if it's successful, and well ... if it's not, then I'd like to have some company too. We could go anywhere you'd like."

Andrea glanced sideways at his handsome profile, the jaw lean and hard. She watched the way his eyes crinkled when he was squinting from the sun, like now. She knew she would enjoy the evening, Jason was always good company. It was just this odd mood she was in that made her hesitate.

The smile left Jason's eyes as he saw her hesitate and misread her reasons. He got up and set the glass on a small table then adjusted his Stetson lower on his forehead, shadowing his eyes.

"Guess I'll be going. See you later."

"Jason wait!" Andy jumped up from the swing, the sudden movement sending it careening into the porch rail. "What time do you want to pick me up tomorrow? And Jason, thanks for driving me to Laramie today. I'm glad you were there." She turned the brilliance of her full smile on him.

"All right! How about eight o'clock? Should have election results by then."

Jason briskly walked back to her and leaned over the porch rail to kiss her cheek. Spinning on his heel, he practically trotted back to his waiting truck. Waving a quick farewell, he left the grounds of the Circle-D and headed back to town.

Feeling considerably light of spirit and whistling off key, Jason approached the sheriff's office on Cheyenne Avenue. As he drove past the Eatery, his thoughts were on Andy, almost causing him to miss the sedan parked outside. The car was plain and an inconspicuous model that really would not draw attention, unless you were someone that had been watching that same car follow you for close to sixty miles. That got your attention. Jason slowed as he passed and hastily scribbled the license plate number down on a small note pad that he always kept clipped to the dashboard.

"Hi Mac, how's it been going?" Jason greeted his fellow deputy as he hung up his hat on the coat tree. He went straight to his desk with its computer terminal online with the state division of motor vehicles and entered the tag number. The keyboard chattered as he quickly typed the information. Gavin McNally studied his partner waiting impatiently for the data to come across the screen.

"What's up J.C.? Got a hot one?"

"Just running a hunch. Spotted a strange car in town that looks like one that followed me from Laramie earlier today."

The computer screen glowed as columns of encoded data rapidly filled the screen. Jason scanned the information and then began to punch other function keys as he opened another database on the master menu. Mac stood next to his desk as the access to NCIC appeared and Jason began a search of the National Crime Information Center.

Within a minute the facts entered the computer's memory and transmitted to the printer for transfer to a hard paper copy. Jason stood next to the printer and began reading as rapidly as the machine spit out the file.

"Now this is interesting. Why would a vehicle registered to Diamond Bar be down at the Laramie Airport? According to DMV it's not stolen."

Jason leaned back in his chair, the computer printout dangling from one hand as he let his mind absorb the facts and roll around some new possibilities.

CHAPTER 5

It was evening as Andy began cleaning up the remnants of supper that she had cooked for herself and Gramps. She lit a lamp in the living room before leaving to join her grandfather on the front porch. The cool night air beckoned her. She found him relaxing on the same swing that she had shared earlier with Jason. Puffs of smoke swirled above his head from the pipe clenched between his teeth. The breeze carried the aromatic wild cherry tobacco that he favored.

"Come sit awhile and tell me how your day went," the elder Dunlap patted the seat next to him invitingly.

"Jason and I went down to Laramie. We found the airport OK, but that guy from the NTSB was a jerk. He was rude and obnoxious, and you probably would have wanted to punch him in the nose if you'd been there. I'm glad Jason was with me; it was terrible seeing Dad's plane in little pieces, all busted up. We brought home a box packed with Mom and Dad's belongings."

She fell silent as she thought of the small carton still sitting on the coffee table where Jason had left it. She couldn't bring herself to even lift the lid.

"Is that the box I saw in the living room?"

Andy could only nod as she stared into the night sky, the stars shimmering in the tears filling her eyes.

"Do you want to look through it together? I don't imagine there'll be much worth keeping." Gramps' voice trailed off as his thoughts turned to the son and daughter-in-law that he had loved and lost. He sat slowly rocking the bench in a gentle motion.

"Can we leave it go until tomorrow? I'm all done in, Gramps. I think I'll turn in early."

"Sure, Honey, it can wait. You go get a good night's sleep." He leaned over and kissed her on the forehead and hugged her briefly then sat back and continued puffing on his pipe. His mind was far away now, remembering the little boy who used to climb onto his lap to sit and swing on summer evenings past. A single tear traced down his bearded cheek.

Clouds filled the horizon and distant thunder rumbled but no rain came to break the heat wave. The morning sun blazed hot and gave promise of another dry, blistering day. Andy dressed for chores and was already feeding the horses in the stable before her grandfather called from the house that breakfast was ready. Wetting a bandanna in the water from the horse trough, Andy ran the wet cloth across the back of her neck. Sweat was dampening her thin cotton blouse and she could feel a tiny trickle run between her breasts. She shielded her eyes as she futilely scanned the horizon and then walked back to the house.

Cold orange juice was a welcome sight and Andy reached for it first as she joined her grandfather in the kitchen. Bowls of cereal and sliced fruit were set on the table with mugs of steaming coffee. Andy raised an eyebrow at her grandfather as she took in the breakfast menu.

Shrugging, he justified his choice, "Well it's too hot to cook; thought you'd appreciate something that goes down cool."

Andy laughed as she poured milk into her cereal bowl, "Ha, you just say that because it was your turn to cook! Tomorrow you'll want your eggs and hash browns." She didn't really mind and the cold breakfast did taste good.

They ate companionably then Gramps got up and went into the living room, coming back with the carton in hand. He sat the box on the floor between his chair and Andy's. He saw her surprise and expression of dismay.

"Andy, we've got to do it sooner or later and it might as well be now. Let's get this over with. I don't like doing it any more than you."

He slowly pried up the cardboard flaps and opened the box wide. Reaching inside, he drew out the book that Jason had wedged on top of the pile and sat it on the table surface. Next came a man's leather wallet; Andy recognized it as one that she had given her father for Christmas two years ago. The driver's license and credit cards along with bits of papers Brian had tucked into it were surprisingly intact. A woman's gold watch and a small enamel pin had been placed in a white envelope. Gramps kept stacking the small items on the table as he worked to empty the box.

Andy fingered her mother's purse and its jumble of contents: the face powder compact had a cracked mirror and a red lipstick was melted down from the heat of the fire, a twisted comb, a key ring filled with blackened keys, an empty change purse. A pocket notebook that her father usually carried with him had the cover burnt and the edges of the pages curled brown. Little trinkets and objects lay together, symbolizing the people who had left them behind.

Andy's hand shook as she picked up a single earring, its mate lost, her mother's favorite pair. Another envelope contained some loose coins and money paper-clipped together; a post-it note was stuck on the top bill with the total jotted down. Sam lifted the last item from the box – Brian's flight log, a leather bound square book that he had carried ever since he first earned his wings. A ribbon-like cord tied the book closed together like a portfolio and Andy opened it slowly.

She turned the pages, reverently caressing the paper with her father's handwriting in neat and precise lettering. Every destination, date and time was recorded. How much fuel he took on and preflight notes, maintenance records were all noted there. He had always been so meticulous in his record keeping. Andy raised questioning eyes to her grandfather. He was silent as he watched her closely. Giving her a nod to continue, she flipped to the back of the book and read the last entry.

"'Torrington, Wyoming, July 20th - arrive 1:00 PM. Depart 4:00 PM. Flight plan filed, south by southeast to Cheyenne. Land Cheyenne Airport - 5:20 p.m., overnight stay, parking available Lane Aviation hangars. Cheyenne, Wyoming, July 21st - depart 10:30 AM. Flight plan filed, north by northwest to Laramie airport. Stopover in Laramie, then northeast to Platte County airport.'"

"They never made it past Laramie. Why were Mom and Dad traveling to Torrington and Cheyenne both? Was it ranch business?" Andy questioned with a catch in her voice. Closing the cover, she gently laid the logbook on top of the pile of belongings.

"I don't know, Honey. All your father said to me the day he left was that there was something he had to check out and that he would be gone for a couple of days. I assumed it had to do with the ranch, what else was there?"

"Not much here, is there? What do you want to do with this? I don't think I could bear to throw anything away. Mother's things, her jewelry, I'd like to save because they were hers. I could never wear them, but they belonged to her and she touched them and well..."

Slowly, Gramps and Andy began to repack the various items back into the small carton. They had cleared away most of the pile when Gramps picked up the old journal.

"What's this? This book was with your father the day of the crash?" Gramps turned it over in his hands, examining the musty cover and parchment like pages. He opened the cover to reveal the pages of handwritten script and his eyes widened as he saw the dates of the entries.

"Jason and I found it in the top of the box, just like you see it. It looks like an old diary, but I haven't any idea why Dad would have been carrying it with them. Maybe he found it in a flea market or auction while they were visiting Torrington. You know how he and mother used to haunt those places." Andrea watched her grandfather inspect the antique journal.

Samuel Dunlap silently read the beginning entries of the diary then gently laid the book down, afraid it might disintegrate. He looked over to Andy with wonder on his face.

"I believe this is my grandmother's journal. The names mentioned here are my grandparents. See this date? That's when they first arrived in this country over a hundred years ago. I don't know where your father would've found this book, but more puzzling is why he had it with him!"

Andy was even more perplexed upon hearing the identity of the journal's author. She stared at the book in amazement as if it were a living thing. Instead of finding answers to her parent's accident, she was confronted with more questions.

Jason voted early in the morning then spent two hours walking up and down the main street of Deer Springs greeting people or shaking hands. He chatted with friends and laughed with the old timers as they retold the stories of long ago sheriffs when Deer Springs was a boomtown and the West was wild. He stopped back at the office and picked up his messages, checked in with Mac then went down to the diner for a light lunch.

As usual The Eatery was busy with its noon day crowd and Jason had to take an empty stool at the counter, all the comfortable booths were full. Clarisse and Maybelle were bustling, moving in two directions at once and doing at least four different things. Jason leaned over the counter and grabbed a clean coffee cup from where Maybelle kept them stacked on a shelf and poured his own coffee. Maybelle grinned and mouthed "thanks" as she served up two sandwich platters and carried two more plates of food to a couple waiting in a back booth. Her order pad and pencil in one hand, she grabbed a pot of coffee and hurried back behind the counter.

"Hi J. C., now what can I get you? Special today is open faced roast beef sandwich with mashed potatoes on the side. See you need a refill on that coffee already. Here you go."

"Just want something light today Maybelle. How about a Caesar salad with some extra dressing?" he said as he stirred his coffee. "Been down to vote yet?"

"Yes I have; voted early before I opened up this morning," Maybelle told him as she prepared the salad and sprinkled on a handful of croutons. Setting the bowl in front of him, she asked, "How's the election going? Got a good turn out today?"

"Turn out seems to be a little better than average I think. Of course it's too early to tell about the outcome. Have you seen Leonard Wood in here today? Mac was telling me that he's been driving around with a bull horn shouting 'a vote for Wood is a vote for law and order!' That's pretty funny when you consider how many brawls he was always in the center of when he was younger."

"Guess people were surprised when Sheriff Miller decided to retire suddenly and Woody was the only person who volunteered to run against you. I do think the opposing party could have come up with a better candidate, but we all know there isn't a better man for the job than you, J.C." Maybelle laughed and winked at him as she moved off to serve another customer.

"Thanks for the compliment madam." Jason tipped his hat to her. He had wanted to ask her about that sedan parked in front of the diner yesterday, but she was too busy now. He'd have to check with her later.

Andrea put all thought of the journal to the back of her mind as she went about the rest of her chores. She rode out to one of the pastures to speak with Frank about Thursday's drive then back to the barn to check the tack room and the supplies gathered there. Normally a chuck wagon was packed for cattle drives, but since she was traveling with only three hands they would use pack mules to carry the needed supplies. Bill and Frank had been busy filling plastic jugs with water and burlap bags with foodstuffs and cooking utensils. They would bring enough to see them through the days on the trail and provide for the two men who would stay behind with the line camp until it was time to move the herd again.

It was late afternoon when Andy entered the house again and decided that she would make herself useful by at least going over the books. She knew how much Gramps hated doing paperwork, maybe this was one chore she could take off his hands. Andy poured a large glass of lemonade and carried it to her father's desk. She cleared away some papers so she could find a spot to set the wet glass and stared at the mess before her. Invoices and statements were mixed with unopened letters and cards of condolence. Beginning to regret her decision, Andy took a deep breath, rolled up her shirtsleeves, swallowed some lemonade and dug in. She started by organizing stacks of mail, personal correspondence in one corner and ranch bills in the other. It was evident that the ranch bills were piling up higher than the other tower of papers.

Dragging out the adding machine, Andy began totaling the outstanding invoices and cross-referencing them with the check book register. She was shocked at the amount of debt mounting before her. It was worse than she had thought. Unless they got a very good price for their cattle and soon, the Circle-D wouldn't make it through the next winter.

CHAPTER 6

Andy tugged on the straps of the ice blue sun dress, pulling the bodice into place then turned from side to side in front of the cheval mirror, straining to reach the back zipper tab and glide it upwards. Uttering a groan at the difficulties of dressing alone and what a nuisance it was trying to get dressed up anyway, Andy fidgeted with the waistline of the slim sheath. The knee length dress was inexpensive and only a polished cotton fabric, yet stylish in its simplicity. A short bolero jacket fashioned from the same blue cloth hung on a hanger on the closet doorknob. Andy reached for it and put it on, admiring the charcoal gray soutache braid that her mother had sewn along the front edges. She stood in front of the mirror again; the image of a cool, sophisticated woman reflected back. It was a false image, Andy knew. She wasn't the woman in the pale sheath with the high heels. She was underneath somewhere, with an old shirt and jeans over muddy boots. That felt more natural. But it seemed important to look her best for Jason tonight, because tonight was important to him.

Running a brush through her hair, Andy parted it on the side then let the mass hang loose to her shoulders. Applying a light mauve lipstick was all the makeup Andy decided she could stand. She tossed the lipstick into her clutch bag and dropped in her house keys. Turning out the bedroom light, she went downstairs to wait for Jason.

As she entered the living room, she heard male voices in conversation. Jason quickly stood as she approached; his face lit with appreciation as he took in every detail of her ensemble. Gramps smiled and his eyes twinkled with affection as he too admired the graceful woman before him.

"Andrea, you look as lovely as your mother when she was a young girl." Gramps kissed her lightly on the cheek. "Now go have a good time and forget about the ranch for at least one night."

"The way you look, makes me wish we were going someplace fancy tonight. I hope you don't mind Andy, but my folks are putting on a big spread and want us to come back to Cedarhill. It's a celebration party for me. Oh, I almost forgot to tell you— I won the election." Jason beamed proudly.

"Was there ever any doubt Sheriff Hartman? I'd love to join you and your parents," Andy replied sincerely. She inwardly relaxed, relieved to be on familiar grounds. Making small talk in a strange restaurant surrounded by a room full of strange people made Andy nervous.

The drive to Cedarhill was short; the Hartman's southern ranch borders intersected with the Dunlaps' northern boundary. As they entered the driveway near the sprawling stone and cedar log ranch house, Andy was dismayed to see numerous vehicles parked about the grounds. Her surprise must have shown as Jason turned to her.

"I'm sorry, I should have warned you. Mom and Pop invited a few friends over. If you'd rather go somewhere else, we can leave. I did say, anywhere you'd like to go."

"No, don't be silly. They're expecting you. I had thought that I'd have a chance to visit with your mother again, that's all. I haven't seen Ingrid in a long while." She started to open the door of the Explorer as she glanced back at him. "Come on, they're waiting."

Jason reluctantly stepped down from the truck and hastened to Andy's side. Now he regretted not making better plans. He would rather be alone with Andy and her disappointment was obvious. He cursed himself for being so stupid.

The noise of a party in full swing hit them as soon as they opened the front door. Chords of music floated across the shrill laughter and boisterous voices of guests milling about the great room. Crepe paper banners proclaiming "Hartman for Sheriff" were draped across doorways and colorful streamers hung from the wagon wheel light fixture above the long dining table. Huge stoneware platters were piled high with delicious smelling foods and a large sheet cake decorated with "congratulations" in a gooey butter cream frosting took center stage. Andy stood at Jason's side, amazed at the sights and sounds before them. It looked like the entire county's population was squeezed into the Cedarhill great room.

Brent Logan moved throughout the crowd like a politician, greeting townspeople and advancing his business interests with neighboring ranchers. You would have thought he was the host of the party instead of his friend Jarrod. He beamed proudly when he spotted his daughter Veronica among the guests but raised an eyebrow as he spied his host's son with that trashy Dunlap gal.

Ingrid, her Nordic blonde hair piled high giving her an even taller height, moved among the throngs of people straight toward Jason with that radar device that is only known to mothers. She smiled warmly and held out both of her hands in greeting to Andrea, then linked her arm in Jason's, pulling him into the center of the room.

"Look everyone! Our new Sheriff is here!" Ingrid proudly clapped her hands as the applause built, the sound echoing off the high ceilings and walls.

Jason waved and grinned, acknowledging the well-wishers gathered. The applause started to die down as someone in the back of the room yelled out, "Speech, speech!"

"Thank you everyone for coming tonight and most especially for voting today. I'm proud to be Platte County's sheriff and promise to serve you all with the best of my abilities."

Ben Miller approached Jason and shook his hand warmly. He reached into his pocket and withdrew a tin star and a set of keys. Holding the left lapel of Jason's suit jacket, he pinned the sheriff's star to Jason's chest.

"Congratulations J.C., you'll make a fine sheriff and I'm pleased to be leaving the county in such good hands. We were supposed to do this stuff tomorrow in an official ceremony and all, but hell, everyone from town is here now anyways! So wear your star with pride and here are the keys to the official sheriff's wheels; the Jeep is parked outside. Now you don't need to run that fancy rig of yours into the ground." Ben laughed and clapped Jason on the back.

"Thanks Ben, appreciate it. How're you going to get home if I have your Jeep?"

Bending his head closer to Jason's, Miller whispered loudly, "No problem, see that pretty red head standing by the bar?"

"Aha... see what you mean. Well, enjoy."

"Come eat everyone. There's plenty of food, no one leave here hungry!" Ingrid encouraged her guests to fill a plate as she ladled some roast beef and gravy onto a crusty roll of bread and dished out mounds of German potato salad.

Jason greeted some neighboring ranchers and thanked two more well-wishers as he made his way back across the room to Andy. She was standing talking quietly with Maybelle and another woman as Jason approached. Her eyes shone with pride as she watched Jason walk toward her. *"He's so good-looking"*, Andrea thought; his broad shoulders needed no padding in the dark blue suit coat. The smooth-shaven tan skin accentuated a strong jaw line, giving him a classic profile. Andy smiled and blushed slightly at being caught admiring the new sheriff; her affection was written across her face for all to see. Catching her look, Jason grinned broadly.

A buxom blonde wearing a tight red cocktail dress observed the couple from where she sat. Her crossed legs rocked in a quicker tempo as her agitation rose. She was seething with jealously as she watched Jason's arm go around Andrea Dunlap. Her venomous thoughts were well hidden though behind a composed mask. She turned toward the gentleman near her, smiling sweetly with lips painted a deep crimson. With a manicured hand, she casually flicked her heavy blond locks off her shoulder.

"My, Mr. Hartman, you do cut a dashing figure tonight! If you weren't my Daddy's dearest friend, I'd have designs on you. I'm sure you've turned more than one pretty head here tonight." She turned sultry brown eyes to him in a smoldering look.

Jarrod Hartman coughed embarrassedly and looked around quickly to see if they had been overheard. He was flattered by the attention of the spoiled beauty, but my goodness, he had known her since she was a child. She still was a child to him. Besides, Ingrid would pull the girl's hair out by its peroxide roots if she had witnessed this conversation.

Taking the girl by her elbow, Jarrod escorted her to the dining area. "Let's go say hello to Jason, shall we?"

Jason was surprised to see his father with the cloying blonde but hid his expression behind the glass of beer that he was sipping. Andrea wasn't as successful to hide her dislike for the woman; she well remembered the antagonism built between them since grade school. Gray feline eyes narrowed dangerously as Andy watched the other woman slither toward them.

"Hello Ronnie, enjoying yourself?" Jason asked.

Bristling at the nickname, she spoke through gritted teeth, "My name is Veronica. I don't like being called a boy's name, unlike some people." Running her hands down her slinky dress, drawing attention to her curvaceous body, she silently dared Andy with hooded eyes. "That's a cute little dress you're wearing, Andy,"

Veronica sneered and pointedly stared at Andrea's lesser endowments.

Caught off guard by the complimentary words, Andy replied quietly, "thank you, my mother made it for me."

"Hmm, yes, I could tell." Veronica shook her blonde mane lightly, causing the mass to fall about her bare shoulders, returning all of her attention to Jason.

Both women stood glaring at one another. Andy eyed Veronica's manicured nails skimming Jason's sleeve;Ronnie itched to scratch out some gray eyes. Andy speculated on how it would feel to pull out that blonde hair by its roots.

Jarrod Hartman read the blonde's intention and thinking to ward off a cat fight; he faced Andy and offered his arm. "Have you fixed yourself a platter yet, Andrea? Ingrid's been cooking all day and would be very disappointed if you didn't eat something."

Grateful for the diversion, Andy smiled sincerely at Jason's father then raised a quizzical eyebrow in Jason's direction. She wondered how Jason was going to pry himself away from Veronica's vise-like grip as that woman clung to Jason's arm and suggestively rubbed her pampered body against him. Jason caught Andy's look and its meaning then raised his eyes upward as if asking heaven for help. He knew he was going to have difficulty extricating himself from this situation.

"Thanks for the rescue, but I think Jason is in worse danger," Andrea joked to her host as they selected from the banquet table. Her plate brimming with delectable choices, she decided to head for the brick patio with its empty tables and chairs. Lanterns lit earlier adorned the gardens and adjoining pool area; their soft glow beckoned her. Andy drank in the soft fragrance of the potted blooms – the tiny white petals of the Alpine penny grass and wild hollyhock glowed almost iridescent against the dark Red Indian paintbrush.

"I think I'll let my son stew for a few more minutes before I lend him my aid again. I'll send him out to join you. Go ahead and eat your dinner while it's warm."

Andy watched Jarrod join the party again, talking and laughing with various guests. He was a handsome man dressed in his black western cut suit and string necktie adorning a crisp white shirt. Andy smiled as she silently compared Jason's father with an old favorite television character—he rather looked like Maverick in that outfit. She could just imagine him gambling at a high stakes poker table.

She liked Jarrod and Ingrid Hartman and as a child spent many hours visiting in their home. They were good neighbors and she always thought both families got along well. She and Jason with his sister Jessica used to play for hours on end. Andrea always thought it was natural when both she and Jason started thinking of each other as more than just friends. At least she did until her father had told her otherwise.

Andy picked at her plate and stared into the night sky as her thoughts replayed an ugly scene she had with her father shortly before his death. She closed her eyes and could still picture it so well, like a bad movie; it ran over and over again in her mind. He had been so angry, pacing the floor of the living room back and forth, his face flushed and his voice shouting. Andrea cried softly as she faced her father, her hand on his arm, her eyes pleading. "Why?" she had demanded. But her father only insisted that she end her relationship with Jason.

She was so lost in her memories that she did not hear Jason approach and jumped guiltily when he set his plate down on the patio table. "A penny for your thoughts," he offered.

Andrea shuttered her memories and tried to concentrate on her date. "It's nothing really, I was just thinking of my father."

"Did you have a chance to look through that box of things we brought back from Laramie?" Jason questioned her quietly.

"Hmm? Oh, yes, Gramps and I went through it," she answered him distractedly, her mind still wrestling with the past.

Jason ate some of his supper and allowed Andrea some time with her thoughts. She would tell him when she was ready. He had learned long ago that a person could not push Andy into doing more than she wanted, especially when it meant letting another person get close.

Andrea sensed that Jason was watching her and waiting, he was patient that way. She sighed and sat listening to the strains of music floating outside through the patio doors. Leaning back in her chair, she attempted to imitate a relaxed position.

She wasn't fooling Jason. "Would you rather not talk about it?" he prompted.

"It's all right. There really wasn't much of interest, just things. You know… wallets and keys, jewelry, personal stuff. My dad's flight log and that old diary were the only items of any real value."

"I'd like to read that log book, if it's okay with you. If you're still serious about fighting that NTSB report, I'd like to help. It would be best if we could reconstruct your father's route from the time he left Deer Springs. I could work on that for you."

"I don't know. I don't want to take you away from your duties, Jason. Are you sure you can spare the time? I don't care if you read the log; I just don't see where it will be of much use to you."

"Why don't you let me be the judge of that?" Jason rose with his glass in hand. "I'm going to get a second drink. Want another Coke?"

"Thanks, just half a glass." Andy replied as she handed him her mug.

Moonlight reflected off the surface of the still pool. Crickets chirped in the summer night. The sweet fragrance of columbine rose from the lush flowerbeds along the patio. Andrea relaxed against the soft patio chair cushion, drinking in the sights and sounds of the peaceful evening, she tried to absorb some of its calm and soothe her worried mind.

Footsteps clip-clopped as high heel shoes rapped against the brick patio surface. Andy looked to the source of the noise as Veronica stepped into the diffused lantern light.

"Well, if it isn't poor little Andy out here all by her lonesome! Where's J.C.? I thought you had him chained to your side. When are you going to realize that this pity act will wear thin?" Veronica sneered, not bothering to hide her hatred and jealousy.

Andy's hackles rose at the other woman's tone. Her peaceful mood shattered, she decided to come out fighting. "What's wrong with you Ronnie? Don't you have enough men panting after you or can't you believe that Jason has good taste when it comes to women?"

Veronica's fingers curled as she thought of clawing the ivory skin before her. "At least I don't have to be ashamed of my family. A pity your father was such a coward that he had to commit suicide."

Andy jumped to her feet, "What do you mean? How dare you!"

"Grow up Andy. Everybody in town knows your family is broke. You probably ran to the bank to cash in the insurance checks. Too bad your mother had to die just because your father couldn't face his debts."

Veronica's cruel words hit Andy like a slap across the face. Shock and hurt mixed with anger. Her delicate jaw set in a stubborn line as she faced the other woman, eyes sparking furiously. Acting on pure animal instinct, Andy drew back her arm, hand balled into a tight fist and let fly with a well-aimed punch. The force of the blow made Veronica stumble backwards and she cried out in alarm as she tumbled into the cold pool water.

Andy smiled in satisfaction as she rubbed her knuckles while crowds of people ran outside to investigate the source of the screaming and thrashing coming from the pool. The blond vixen resembled a drowned rat now; her hair was plastered flat against her head and streaks of black mascara ran down her face. She spluttered and gasped as two men each grabbed an arm and hauled her out of the water like a sack of potatoes while other guests stood gaping and laughing. Surrounded by onlookers, Veronica stood dripping water, puddles forming at her feet. She had lost one shoe, still at the bottom of the pool, and her dress had shrunken enough to be indecent even by her standards. Women on seeing the outrageous display tugged on their men's arms, leading them back into the house and out of temptation.

Jason pushed his way through the crowd in time to witness Andy's smug expression and Veronica's scowl. Ingrid hurried forward with an armload of towels, wrapping several around Veronica. Jason looked from one woman to the other, uncertain who was the victim.

"Jason, I think I'd like to go home now," Andy informed him then walked over to Ingrid. "Thank you for a lovely evening, Mrs. Hartman. I can't remember when I've had a better time." She smiled sweetly and nodded her head in Veronica's direction.

Veronica's eyes were shooting daggers as she gently touched a finger to a cut lip. "You bitch! I'll get you for this! Wait until my Daddy hears about this."

Jason chuckled as Veronica yanked a towel tighter around her shoulders. "Better be careful who you threaten Ronnie, you don't seem to come out on top."

Taking Andy by the arm, he escorted her into the house, nodding to a few people as they stared dumbstruck then hustled her out the front door. Now that they were out of sight of the party Jason turned to Andy for answers.

"You mind telling me what that was all about?"

"God that felt good! I can't believe the way I feel." Andy started giggling and couldn't stop. Every time she tried to stop, she pictured Ronnie dripping on that patio with her breasts partly exposed and her skirt clinging to the top of her thighs. She didn't look very elegant now!

Jason recognized the release of pent up grief and tension. Maybe Andy needed tonight more than she realized. They were halfway to the Circle-D before she was able to calm her laughter.

"I'm sorry, Jason, for ruining your party. Ronnie said some terrible things and I just lost my temper."

"That's an understatement if ever I heard one. But don't worry about ruining the party, it will be the talk of the town for weeks, I'm sure. I won't even ask what Ronnie said, probably isn't worth repeating anyway."

"Were you serious about wanting to help with investigating my parent's accident? I think I really need some answers." Her voice was solemn now. She waited for his reply as they came to a halt.

"Yeah, I'm serious. Maybe I can turn up more information, anything to give you a clearer picture of what happened."

"Okay, I want you to try. See what you can find. I'd like that."

Jason took Andy's hand as she started to step up onto the front porch. She halted and turned to him as his hand lightly stroked her cheek, fingers caressing her jaw then sliding under her hair to the nape of her neck. He drew her toward him as his lips lowered to hers. The kiss was gentle and tender. Jason waited for her response, a signal to continue. Andy ached with longing but withdrew, shaking her head negatively and ending the kiss in sweet poignancy.

How could she let herself love this man knowing that she was guilty of betraying her father's wishes? How could she even begin to explain to Jason when she did not understand herself? Her heart told her yes, but her mind kept repeating no.

Jason's eyes silently questioned; his arms dropped to his sides as he watched her enter the house. Would she always hold herself from him? How much time will go by before Andrea Dunlap admits that she loves him? Even a patient man had his limits, Jason thought as he drove home silently.

Dim lights cast shadows across the expansive desk and mahogany bookcases lining the walls of the quiet library. Smoke spiraled upward from the glowing cigar embers as Brent Logan paced the floor. He thumped his fist on the desktop as he turned once more to scowl at his daughter.

"How could you let that Dunlap trash get the better of you? You were a laughing stock! No daughter of mine is going to be treated that way," Logan's voice roared, breaking the silence of the room.

Veronica stood wringing her hands behind her; fearing she would anger her father further. She had changed from her wet clothes into a silk nightgown and robe and now tried to look sweet and innocent in hopes of winning her father's sympathy instead of his wrath.

"I'm sorry Daddy. I don't know why that bitch Andy hit me. We were just talking and suddenly she went crazy. I think she must be unhinged. I would never do anything to embarrass you, Daddy," her voice whined.

Logan's face melted at the sight of his little girl; memories of her crawling up onto his lap and reading bedtime stories came flooding back. Of course, it wasn't her fault, how could he doubt her? It was that Dunlap family again; chalk up one more wrong to be righted.

"It's all right honey. Don't you worry; I'll take care of everything. You know I'd never let anyone hurt you. You go ahead and go to bed sweetheart."

Veronica kissed her father on his cheek and hugged him tightly, pleased with herself for once again being able to manipulate him. She'll deal with that bitch in her own way but for now she did not need her father directing his anger towards her.

CHAPTER 7

Dawn brightened the eastern sky as Andy moved about the bedroom. She had lain awake for most of last night then decided to take action. Any action was better than this vacuum that she had allowed to grow. Dressing in her jeans and denim shirt, she added a pair of leather chaps and a clean cotton bandanna around her neck. She brushed her hair and tied it back with a rubber band into a ponytail that would help to keep the luxurious mass out of her face. Andy rolled up two more changes of clean clothes that would be carried in her bedroll. She glanced around her room to see if there was anything else that she needed and decided she was set. The weather forecast promised to be another scorching day and Andy wasn't looking forward to spending it on horseback in the sweltering heat but at least it would cool down some as they neared the mountains and gained elevation.

In the kitchen, she filled her two canteens with cold water from the sink and tossed a couple of apples and granola bars into a plastic bag. She'd tuck them into her saddlebag for munching along the trail. As she poured two mugs of coffee, Frank entered the kitchen with Bill and Danny at his heels. They would be making the drive with her; Charlie would stay at the ranch to help Sam take care of the other stock.

"Mornin' Andy", greeted Bill as he quickly removed his hat in her presence. Andy had to smile at his polite gesture; Bill was definitely of the old school.But she couldn't complain, most men treated her gentlemanly and she did not worry about being a lone woman on a long trip with three men. These men especially were more than cow hands to her, they were family.

"Everything ready to go? We'll pick up the herd in the north pasture and start heading them up toward the Saratoga Valley," Andy asked.

"Good morning everyone," Sam addressed the group assembled in the kitchen. "Up earlier than usual aren't we?"

Andy handed him a mug of coffee as she took a sip of hers. "You fella's want some?" she nodded toward the coffee maker on the counter. "We're going to start moving the herd today, Gramps. I didn't see any reason to wait until tomorrow and Frank's got all the supplies ready. So as soon as we all finish breakfast, we're heading out."

Sam tried to read Andy's face but today it was a clean slate; what he always thought of as her business face - no emotion allowed. He had seen it before when she had to deal in a man's world doing a man's job. He caught Frank and Bill's eye and nodded his head slightly toward the door; giving each a signal to take the hint and take young Danny with them.

As soon as they were alone, Gramps turned to Andrea. "I didn't hear you when you came in last night. Have a good time?"

"The party was very entertaining. I'm sure you'll hear all about it the next time you visit Maybelle." Andy tried not to meet her grandfather's probing eyes.

"Now what's that supposed to mean? Something happen last night? Is that why you decided to leave today?"

"Veronica Logan was there; we didn't exactly get along. In fact you could say that at one point sparks were flying so bad, I had to help put them out." Andy grinned, relishing the memory.

"Andrea Dunlap, what did you do? I see mischief on that face of yours."

"Nothing that she didn't deserve. All I did was push her into the pool."

"You what? How, may I ask and why?"

"With my fist in her face. She called Dad a coward and said he deliberately crashed."

A wealth of emotions crossed Sam's face as he heard Andy's explanation - first pride at defending herself so well, that's what comes from being a lone girl raised on a ranch full of men; and then shock and sadness upon learning that a vicious rumor was being spread about his son. Sam ran a callused hand through his thick gray hair and sat down weakly.

Andy hated telling him that awful slander because she knew in her heart that that was all it was. There was no truth in it. Now she had all the more reason to dig out the truth about what happened.

"Jason wants to read Dad's flight log. He said he would nose around a little and see if he can find any more information about Mom and Dad's trip. I said he could. Is that all right with you?" Andy laid her hand on his shoulder. Gramps reached up and patted it absently.

"Yeah, fine. It was kind of Jason to offer; the Hartmans are good people."

"Well, I always used to think so," sadness tinged her voice.

Samuel scrutinized his granddaughter. "Does that mean you don't now?"

"I don't know what to think! I'm so confused Gramps. I like the Hartmans, but I feel so guilty every time I see Jason and especially last night after visiting his family."

"Why should you feel guilty? I think I'm missing something here. You better explain yourself gal."

"I forgot. You weren't home the day Dad and I had a big argument and he told me to break up with Jason. He was furious and actually forbid me to see any of them again. I close my eyes and I still see him ranting and pacing back and forth, waving some book in the air then practically pushing it in my face."

Andy stopped and stared at Gramps, bewilderment written on her face. She had been playing that scene in her mind over and over but until now she had forgotten all the details. Now she clearly pictured an image of her father holding a book in his left hand while he shook his right. A plain covered book that reminded her of the diary they had just found.

"Gramps, I think that journal has something to do with this. Dad had it then; I'm positive it was the book he was waving about like a Bible. He was reading it when I came into the house; I'd been out riding with Jason. He was so angry; I don't ever recall seeing him like that."

"Your father was a stubborn man on the best of days and just plain pig-headed most of the others. If he had gotten an idea into his head, no one was going to change his mind. I can say that because I loved him, and it was the truth."

"But he was so mad; he kept saying 'stay away from their kind.'"

"And you're too darn stubborn for your own good, just like your father. You don't up and change your opinion overnight about a family that you've known for twenty years. Give me some credit, will you gal? I'm not the complete doddering old fool you seem to take me for."

"Oh Gramps I never said anything of the kind!"

"Well, don't fret over the Hartmans, no matter what your father said. We'll get to the bottom of this when you get back. Maybe that old diary holds some answers for us. It was important enough for your father to keep it with him; reckon we better read it."

"All right Gramps, and thanks. I think I'll take the book with me, read a bit when we make camp at night." Andy hugged her grandfather and adjusted her Stetson then picked up the diary from the box still sitting in the corner of the kitchen. She tucked it into the plastic bag holding her snacks. "See you in about three weeks."

"You be careful out there. Let one of the boys ride point."

"I will. Promise," Andy called back over her shoulder as she walked toward the corral and her waiting palomino. She double-checked the cinch and stirrup on the saddle then mounted up, signaling to the men to be on their way.

They rode relaxed in the saddle, an easy pace that would not tire the horses, as the foursome entered the north pasture where the cattle were grazing on the last remnants of prairie grass. Frank would ride point and lead the herd. Bill and Andy would each ride alongside for swing and flank while Danny was elected to ride drag. The trained cutting horses went to work; twisting and turning the animals into the correct direction until the herd was set into motion moving toward the high valley. Andy waved her hat or slapped it against her chap encased leg to encourage the cows to keep moving as the dusty, hot drive began.

It was almost noon when Sam heard the sound of a vehicle entering the yard. He walked to the screen door and looked out as Jason climbed out of a Jeep. Walking onto the porch, he met the younger man as he started up the steps.

Jason extended his hand to Sam in a friendly handshake as he glanced about for signs of Andy. "Howdy, Sam. Thought I'd swing by to pick up that flight log of Brian's, if you don't mind? Andy around?"

"Come on in, I'll get it for you. Andy mentioned it this morning before she left."

"Left? Where she'd go?" Jason stood casually slapping his hat against his leg as he waited on Sam to return with the book.

"She and the boys are driving those steers up to our pastures in the Saratoga. Guess she decided to get a head start by leaving today."

"What makes her so damn stubborn that she thinks she has to do it all herself?"

Sam chuckled listening to the exasperation in Jason's voice. "Funny, I told her almost the same thing myself just this morning. But don't be too hard on her Jason, she can't help it, she inherited it."

"Well.... I just wish she wouldn't try to carry all the worries of the world on her shoulders. She could ask for help, it wouldn't kill her, you know."

"She means that much to you?" Sam asked as he watched Jason closely.

Jason looked Sam squarely in the eye, no hesitation, as he said quietly, "she means the world to me. I love her. I just hope that someday she will let me tell her so."

"She's got a lot on her mind right now Jason. Give her some time. There're some problems that got to be worked out first, family stuff."

"Yeah, I understand. Maybe I can at least help with some of it." Jason held the flight log, bouncing it lightly in his hand as if to weigh its contents. "Let's hope I can find some answers in here."

"Maybe this will help too." Sam rummaged through the cardboard box, pulling out the tattered pocket notebook. "Brian used to make small notes in this thing, always carried it with him. Some of the pages got burnt, but you should be able to read most of it."

"OK, Sam. I'll let you know if I uncover anything."

"Thanks J.C. Sorry you missed Andy." The two men shook hands again as Jason took his leave.

Jason drove back into town and decided he would start to read the log at the office and maybe make a few phone calls. Mac was on duty later and so the office was empty when Jason parked the Jeep out front and went into the single-story brick building.

He opened the flight log on the desk, spreading its pages before him. The neat script annotated the details of countless trips flown by Brian Dunlap. Jason browsed through several pages, studying the type of information recorded and the precise details concerning each flight. He flipped to the back of the book and more recent dates, noting the dates and locations of some of the trips leading up to the last one. Searching for a pattern or any repetitive locations, Jason read carefully. He brought out a pad of paper from his desk drawer and began making notes, turning pages of the log back and forth as he cross-referenced different entries. Finally, he studied the last dates and places starting with the Torrington flight and ending with the Laramie crash.

"Hmm, what did you find so interesting in Torrington, my friend?" Jason spoke to the author of the log lying in front of him. He reached for his telephone directory and finding the number he needed, quickly punched in the numbers on the phone's keypad. After a few short rings, a voice answered.

"Hello Gordon, how're things in Goshen County?"

"Hey J.C., congratulations, Sheriff. Things are fine here. Abigail says to say hi. What can I do for you?"

"Thought I'd drive up to Torrington tomorrow. Just wanted to stop in, professional courtesy and all that, let you know I'm in your neck of the woods."

"Great, looking forward to seeing you again. On a case?"

"Just running down some loose ends for a friend, may be something more, too soon to tell yet. I'll tell you about it when I see you."

"Sure, stop by the jail when you get to town. See you tomorrow."

"Thanks Gordo. Bye."

Jason drew out the small notebook that Andy's father had carried. He read several pages, hastily scribbling his own notes about the comments he saw.

"Now all I have to do is figure out what you were doing for three hours in Torrington and why it was important enough for you to underline it twice on this page." Jason thought to himself as he studied Brian Dunlap's cryptic message.

Andy spread her bedroll out on the hard ground and tried to get comfortable. Her muscles ached from riding all day but she knew her body would adjust to the strenuous exercise in the days to come. Bill prepared supper for the crew over a carefully banked campfire. The countryside was as dry as tinder; a stray spark could easily set off a dangerous wildfire. Frank had eaten and was bedded down on the far side of the campfire, trying to get a few hours of sleep before it was his turn to take the night watch. Danny was riding night guard now; moving about the cattle, watching for strays and singing a soft, calming tune.

The horses stood hobbled within a rough remuda. The pair of pack mules tied to the string. Andy drew out the worn journal and decided to try reading some of it before the last of the early evening light faded away. Opening the musty cover, she read the beginning pages written over a hundred years ago by her great-great grandmother.

CHAPTER 8

Journal of Margaret Doherty-Dunlap

June 1, 1884

Two months by ship then overland coach and river boat to Independence, Missouri - the jumping off place. We have spent most of our savings to bring us this far. Tomorrow we join the Hogan wagon train and will follow the Fremont Trail westward. Our wagon is packed to the brim with large barrels containing a hundred pounds each of flour, lard, and beans. It seems a vast amount of food to me, but not nearly as much as some of the other settlers. We were told to supply enough coffee beans and salt along with any dried fruit to last us for the months on the trail. I've even sewn tiny pockets into the hemlines of my skirts and added pieces of lead buckshot to keep my skirts from blowing in the wind. James and I can hardly sleep for the excitement; we've worked so hard preparing for the long trek. Our expectations are so high.

August 4, 1884

More delays. First, we had to wait to cross the Missouri River because of the flooding caused by the late spring rains, and now the Army cavalry troop that is supposed to escort us through the Sioux Territory is late arriving. I fear we will not cross the mountain passes in time.

September 15, 1884

Weeks walking and riding across the wide prairie; my limbs feel numb to the exhaustion. Three of our oxen are dead from exhaustion and the wagon has a broken axle. The wagon train has continued on without us. James says we are stranded here and must make the best of it. Our dreams of reaching Oregon are dead.

This country is so rugged; the mountains rise fiercely from the sea of grass stretching across the Great Plains. Our Scottish Highland is tame compared to this land; it frightens me. I watch James stare at the ridge of towering peaks on the horizon as if he is trying to see over them and foretell our future.

The locals warn winter will be upon us soon, already the great clouds are gathering above the mountain tops threatening snow. We are desperately trying to build some meager shelter.

October 20, 1884

Our misfortune may turn out to be fortunate after all. James has filed for a homestead of one hundred and sixty acres… we never dreamt of owning so much land. The law allows a man to claim some of this vast land if he promises to settle and work it.

We met a young family from Ireland, the Canavan's, who are seeking their fame and fortune in the New World too. They helped us clear a small parcel of land and cut timber for the house. We women worked to mix the adobe mortar then packed it between the log chinks to fill the gaps. Still the air whistles through the openings we missed. The packed dirt floor will have to do until we can lay some wooden planks. At least our cabin looks better than the sod houses we passed along the trail. The log cabin we built is primitive but sturdy enough with a large stone fireplace and should get us through the winter. The house helps to reinforce our claim upon this land.

Deer Springs is bustling and growing day by day as more men move into the area searching for gold and silver. The land is richer beyond all our dreams. James wants to try his hand at panning. I think it is a foolish notion, our wealth is in the land itself and he should well know it. I fear he has caught the gold fever.

October 30, 1884

Our first snow fall in this wondrous land, thank God it is light. We have been steadily collecting more food and dry goods to see us through the winter. The cabin is becoming more like a home to me; the wood floor planks have helped to ease the dampness and warm the room. James and Michael Canavan have left today for hunting. The men hope to bring back enough venison to provide for both families. Rose Canavan has become a dear friend; I don't know what I'd do without her at times. She's much more learned than I in the way of life here and seems so worldly, you would think that she is the older woman, instead of four years my junior. Today she is teaching me how to tan hides; an old Indian squaw showed her. It's a disgusting process, but Rose assures me I'll appreciate the warm leather clothing we'll fashion from it, come winter.

Next to Rose, this journal has become my only companion. It helps to fill my time during the lonely days. James doesn't understand the comfort it holds for me by filling the pages with 'senseless scratchings', as he calls it. Since he never learned to read or write, he cannot see the reasoning in it. Sometimes at night I read to him parts of my journal, but mostly I feel the need to keep it private. I cannot explain why.

November 14, 1884

James and Michael have returned carrying a man who looks more dead than alive. He has clearly been shot in the chest and has been left to die in the freezing snow. I fear for his life. There is little we can do 'cept make him comfortable and warm. I directed James to spread a soft pallet down on the floor before the fire and our visitor lies there sleeping even now.

I watch his face for signs of movement as I try to gently wash him. My face flames at being so familiar with a strange man, yet I am a married woman and am not unfamiliar with a man's body. I keep reminding myself that the act of nursing makes it proper. He could be a handsome man if the thick black beard was removed and along with it some of the grime.

November 16, 1884

The wounded man awoke yesterday. He began to thrash about, and I had to call James for assistance to help hold him down. His body is raging with a high fever and all I can do is pack handfuls of snow about him to try to cool him. The bullet wound in his right shoulder is bound tightly and no longer bleeds. He will surely tear it open with these violent movements.

The fever broke during the night and this morning I felt a pair of eyes studying me as I sat writing this journal. It's a queer sensation; his eyes follow me about the room with my every action. A woman would die to have eyes the color of this man's - a deep, deep blue and with thick lashes.

A rich baritone voice seemed to fill the small confines of the log cabin as he spoke for the first time, "Good morning."

I abruptly put down my sewing and knelt by his side, my hand testing his brow for signs of more fever. "Lie still sir. You've been injured and near death's door I'm afraid."

"If that be true, dear lady, then it must be your gentle hands that have pulled me back. Might I know the name of my savior?"

Feeling a blush rise to the roots of my hair, I replied, "Margaret Dunlap. My husband James brought you here almost three days ago."

"And where is here, Maggie? I'm sorry, I'm forgetting my manners, you have introduced yourself and I haven't even told you my name. Cody Jarvis, ma'am, and most grateful."

"You're in my home Mr. Jarvis, just outside of Deer Springs. I would appreciate it, though, if you would use my married name when addressing me. I'm not in the habit of being on a first name basis with strangers."

"Perhaps in time then you won't feel we are such strangers. Where's your husband now, Maggie? Err, I mean Mrs. Dunlap."

Suddenly, I felt afraid to tell this man that James was gone and that we were very much alone. Perhaps it was his watchful eyes, like a hawk, they followed my every move. I can't explain why I hesitated, but he saw it and must have read the reason. I saw him smile slightly as he lay back against the pillows, relaxed now, so that I had not even realized that he'd been holding himself tense before.

"Do you feel strong enough to eat some solid food? You must be hungry. I've got some stew simmering."

He rubbed a hand against his face; the bristles of his beard grating against his fingernails. Cody winced as he sat more upright, the floor pallet unyielding to his tender shoulder. He adjusted the heavy quilt that was draped over him and propped a pillow behind his back against the solid cabin wall. Balancing the bowl of food on his lap, he slowly ate the hot stew while the steam rose into the air.

I tried to occupy myself with small chores as he took his meal. But within the confines of the small room, I could hardly ignore his presence. The sound of his cough seemed to echo in the cabin and I glanced his way, worried about his wound with such unaccustomed movement.

"You haven't asked me yet how I got shot. Either your manners are too good, or your sense of curiosity is lousy." His short laugh ended in a barking cough and I could see that the exertion of sitting up and eating was beginning to take its toll.

Andrea rubbed her eyes, grown tired by reading in the faint light. She closed the diary and slipped it back into her saddlebag. Stretching out, she rested her head upon her crossed arms and lay staring at the star- studded night sky. She could pick out the Big Dipper easily and searched the black velvet sky for other constellations. She thought of her ancestors and the hardships they had overcome as they carved a home out of the wilderness under a night sky that must have looked just like this one, a hundred years earlier. The mountains would have looked the same too, towering into the horizon, only their outline would have been sharper without the hazy pollution that modern man has added.

Andrea listened to the comforting sounds of the still night. The cattle murmured quietly, and she could just make out the tenor voice of Dan as he sang a wrangler's lullaby. The summer wind blew gently across the tree tops, making the branches sway slowly in a soft rhythm. Andrea closed her eyes and was lulled into a dreamless sleep for the first time in weeks.

CHAPTER 9

Jason tucked the flight log under one arm and carried a thermos of coffee in the other as he left the sheriff's office in the early morning and fired up the county Jeep. He checked the map and decided which road he would use before angling his way over to Interstate 25 north to Torrington. It would be a long ride. At least the temperature had dropped slightly overnight; he wouldn't feel like he was completely baked by the time he got to Torrington.

He was looking forward to seeing his friend Gordon again. It must be close to six months since they'd gone elk hunting in the Medicine Bow. Jason allowed his mind to reminisce about the carefree weekend the two men had shared as the Jeep began gobbling up the miles. Once he turned onto the highway, Jason directed his mind to methodically reviewing his notes and the facts concerning Brian Dunlap's trip. He intended to visit Gordon's office first, enlist his help if necessary, then swing by the airport and check with the flight office.

Steel oil derricks dotted the landscape around the city of Torrington. Jason watched the metal monsters as they pumped up and down devouring the deep earth, oil spurting upwards like blood. The city itself sprawled at the base of the Buffalo Mountain near the North Platte River but the scenic beauty was over shadowed by the hundreds of oil refineries located on its perimeters.

Jason drove towards the city square where the county jail, courthouse and city office buildings were located. The city had a decided western style with its rough stucco exteriors and exposed wood beams. Hitching posts stood alongside the curb lane in front of the county building, parking for horses and cars alike. Jason maneuvered the Jeep into an open space between a cruiser and a pickup truck, and then walked toward the jailhouse.

Sheriff Gordon Brand searched through the tall file cabinets then exclaimed loudly as he triumphantly pulled out a manila folder. "I knew this had to be in here. You boys just don't appreciate my unique filing system."

His two deputies shook their heads in amazement. They both turned in unison at the sound of the door opening and closing. "Howdy Sheriff, can I help you?"

Gordon sprinted across the narrow space and extended his hand for a bone crunching handshake as he welcomed his friend. "J.C., come on in! Welcome to Torrington."

"Hey Gordo, good to see you again." Jason had to laugh at his giant friend with his carrot top hair and its pair of cowlicks that resembled devil's horns. At just over six and a half feet tall, Gordon had to stoop to pass through most door frames and his clothes were always ill fitting. He looked more at home riding a Brahma bull in a rodeo than a desk chair in an office.

Gordon swung open the small gate that separated the vestibule from the rear office space and motioned Jason toward a desk in the corner. Gordon's desk resembled the man behind it, oversized and cluttered. Several framed commendations hung on the wall next to a faded map of the state with Goshen County outlined in red marker.

Gordon poured himself a refill of coffee and offered a steaming cup to his friend as he sat back and propped his feet atop the piles of paperwork.

"So J.C., what's the big mystery? What brings you to Torrington? You weren't very talkative on the phone."

Jason reached into his upper shirt pocket and withdrew the pocket notebook. A tattered black and white photograph poked out from the edge of the notebook. He withdrew it carefully and slid it across the desktop. "Ever see these people around town? They're my reason for being here."

"No, can't say as I ever have. But then again, I don't see everyone who wanders into town. Torrington is a fair size. What'd they do?" Gordon asked as he studied the picture of Sarah and Brian Dunlap.

"They died. Remember hearing about a plane crash outside of Laramie about a month ago?"

"Yeah, I saw it on the news."

"Well, I promised their daughter that I'd follow up on a few details. They were supposed to be here in Torrington the day before the crash; I'm trying to reconstruct their schedule."

"It was an accident, wasn't it?"

"According to the NTSB it was. Trouble is, Andy doesn't believe that, and I've begun to have some doubts myself. You know that lawman's twitch you feel when something bothers you, and you can't quite put your finger on it? Well I feel it now with this case.

I'm not sure yet what there is, but I plan on digging until I'm satisfied."

"Got anything to go on? How do you know they were in Torrington?"

"Dunlap kept a detailed flight log; it puts him in Torrington on the afternoon of July 20th. According to the log, they were here for about three hours, I just don't know where."

Gordon's feet hit the floor as he slid his chair backwards. Grabbing his hat, he gestured to Jason, "Come on, let's drive over to the airport. Reckon you need to start there."

The Goshen County airport was divided into three sections: air freight, commercial aircraft, and small private planes. Sheriff Brand turned the cruiser toward the terminal building that serviced the freight and private aircraft. The parking ramps were full of various models of Piper Cubs, Cessna and Lears. The two men strode through the double glass doors and headed straight for the flight scheduler's desk.

The clerk watched the pair of lawmen approach and recognized Sheriff Brand in his olive-colored uniform, but the other man in the light tan uniform was a stranger. As he stepped closer, the clerk could identify the Platte County insignia and wondered what brought the sheriff over one hundred and fifty miles. He didn't have to wonder long as the sheriff came right to the point.

"I'd like to verify some information, please. Would you check your logbook for the date of July 20th, this year, and tell me if you show the arrival of a red and white Cessna Skyhawk, call number GLW994, piloted by a Brian Dunlap?" Jason read from his notes.

The man turned to a large flat book, resembling a hotel register, lying open on the counter and flipped through several pages until he turned to the July day in question. He ran his finger down the row of entries then stopped.

"Here it is; arrival time was 13:04, and departure was recorded as 16:10 - military time, saves confusion you know."

"Fine. Could you tell me if there are any car rental offices here or which taxi lines service the airport?"

"The only car rental counters are in the main airport terminal. Most folks who fly in here either have their own vehicle parked in the lot or take a cab. Both the Yellow Cab and Metro come out to the airport."

"Thanks, you've been a big help. One more thing, do you remember seeing these people that day?" Jason handed the clerk the photograph of Brian and Sarah.

The man looked at it thoughtfully then handed it back to Jason. He seemed to stare out the window a minute, snapped his fingers as he looked back at the waiting sheriff. "Yeah, I think I remember them. The woman was laughing and the man had his arm around her shoulder, like they were sharing some private joke or something. You could tell that they enjoyed being together."

Jason listened to the man's description as his mind's eye remembered Andy's parents in a hundred different settings. He slipped the photograph back into his pocket as he looked back at the clerk.

"Sounds like them. They were people who cherished life and each other. Thanks again."

Jason and Gordon left the terminal and decided to try the cab companies first, instead of any car rental agency. Gordon drove to the Yellow Cab garage that was located about a mile from the airport terminal. He parked outside the large, flat roofed, cinder block building. A sign above the door identified the taxi company. A radio dispatcher stood behind a tall counter enclosed by a filmy sliding window. The dispatcher spoke into a microphone and was providing a driver instruction as the two men approached the window.

"Hi. I need you to check your trip log and see if any of your drivers picked up a fare from the airport cargo terminal on July 20th." Gordon spoke to the dispatcher as Jason stood to one side. This was Gordon's town so Jason decided it would be best to let him handle the inquiry.

"Give me a minute; I've got to pull out last month's records." He thumbed through a bound book of green bar computer paper, the pages detailing the daily dispatches of passengers.

"What date did you need? Oh yeah, the 20th, right? We had some pickups that day, what are you looking for?"

"Do you list any pickup for around one o'clock or one-thirty, man and woman?"

"No, we've got a ten o'clock, another at noon, then the next one at three-thirty. That's it."

"Okay, thanks for checking."

"Sure, any time sheriff. Always glad to oblige." The man turned back to the radio as a voice squawked over the speaker.

Jason and Gordon walked back outside and climbed back into the cruiser. "Now we try Metro. How far is their garage?" Jason asked.

"They've got two locations, but their main office is closer to downtown. Let's try there, maybe we'll get lucky."

A few minutes later the Metro garage came into view. This building was more modern than the other had been. A two-story frame structure with the exterior painted a bright white, the green lettering spelling the name Metro stood out vividly. Three bays were open and drivers waited near their cars. The adjacent parking lot had a row of five more taxicabs. A few of the drivers looked up in curiosity at the two lawmen entering the terminal.

A glass enclosed office filled one corner and a woman sat at a desk surrounded by two-way radios and computer terminal screens. She smiled politely and waved them in as Gordon rapped lightly on the office door. She spun her swivel desk chair to face them as both men snatched off their hats.

"Good afternoon gentlemen. What can I do for you?"

"Howdy Ma'am. Would you mind checking your records for us for last month?"

"What date, Officer, and do you know the location of origin?" She typed in some search data into the computer; her fingers moving rapidly over the keyboard.

"July 20th, about one or one-thirty pick up time from the Torrington airport cargo terminal."

"Thank you, it helps to have a little more information to work with. We had two fares that day from the airport location. One was a woman picked up at 1:05 and the other was a couple picked up at 1:14. Could either of these be who you're looking for?"

Jason stepped closer to her desk to study the computer screen. The cursor was blinking next to the last line with the time of 1:14 highlighted. "Can you tell us which driver picked up the couple? I'd like to speak with him if I can."

"Yes sir; that would be Bobby Williams. He's on duty now. You should be able to find him still in the garage."

Jason smiled broadly as he thanked the woman for her help. He and Gordon strode across the concrete flooring with its various oil stains toward the group of men lounging by the door.

"Bobby Williams?" Gordon asked of the group, noting the young man who jumped up as his name was called.

"That's me, but I haven't done anything. What do you want?"

"Easy boy, you aren't in any trouble. I just want to ask you some questions about a fare you had last month." Gordon watched the boy relax and sit back down. His freckled face was returning to its natural color, the sudden hot blush fading. Gordon knew he was probably hiding something, his face read guilty, but he wasn't going to hassle the boy. He needed his cooperation now. He exchanged looks with Jason and received a slight nod from his friend to continue. J.C. had also read the kid's body language.

"According to your office, you got a call to pick up a man and woman from the airport on July 20th at 1:14 in the afternoon. What I want from you is to look at a photograph and maybe review your car's log and tell me their destination."

"Okay, I guess I can do that. Let me see the picture." He nervously looked back and forth between the two sheriffs. The tall red head seemed to be doing all the talking but he noticed that the other guy didn't miss a trick. He just stood quietly, his eyes scanning the room and coming back to bore into each man seated in the lounge. Bobby shivered as if the guy could really read his mind. God, he hoped they didn't find the nickel bag of marijuana he had stashed under his spare tire!

The three of them walked outside to the row of taxis; the cabby reached across the driver's seat of the number twelve car and pulled out a notebook. He laid the book on top of the hood, hoping it was as far away from the trunk and its spare tire as he could get without being too obvious. Opening the book, he flipped through pages, stopping on the July records.

His hand trembled as he asked, "What day did you say I picked up those people?"

"July 20th." Jason handed the driver the Dunlap snapshot and studied his reactions as he looked at the photo.

"I meet a lot of people every day. I can't say if I remember these two or not."

"Well check your log, where did you take your 1:14 fare?" Gordon asked brusquely, he was losing his patience with the boy.

"Let me see, here it is. Corner of Center and Yellowstone, said they had to go to the county courthouse."

"Thought you didn't remember them? How can you recall that someone 'said they had to go to the courthouse'?" Gordon interrogated.

"Um, I didn't mean that I remembered, what I meant was ...um, I made a note next to my entry. See what I wrote in the margin?"

Jason and Gordon both inspected the log book; the pencil notation was dirty and smudged but it clearly stated the word 'courthouse'.

"Did you wait on them or return to pick them up later?" Gordon continued his questions.

"No. I left, got a call from the dispatcher with another trip. I don't know anything else."

"All right, thanks for your help."

Bobby closed the log book and tossed it back onto his front seat when Gordon's voice made his blood freeze.

"If I find out you're carrying drugs of any kind boy, my next visit won't be so friendly. I'd hate to come back here and roust you; do I make myself clear?"

"Yes sir!"

Jason laughed as he and Gordon drove off. "Gordo, I believe you made that young man wet his pants! You were right though. I'd bet a week's wages that he was hiding drugs."

"Yeah, he sure was fidgeting." He joined in his friend's laughter. "Let's go back to my office and then we can walk over to the courthouse."

As they pulled up in front of the jailhouse, Gordon pointed to a green station wagon parked out front. "Looks like Abby's here."

An attractive, tall woman with curly auburn hair stood pouring herself a mug of coffee and smiled affectionately as Jason and Gordon entered the room. She kissed her husband quickly, and then embraced Jason in a warm hug.

"Hello J.C., it's been too long. How've you been? Is this a social call or business? Gordon, were you planning on bringing J.C. over to the house later?"

Gordon and Jason both laughed. "Kind of takes your breath away, doesn't it? You have no idea how difficult it is keeping up with this woman!" Gordon threw his arm around his wife.

"Fine, some business, and I can't, but thanks for the invitation." Jason answered her in the order of her questions, winking to his friend.

"So where have the two of you been off to, or can't I ask?"

"Oh, out to the airport and around town some, just running down some information. No bad criminals to catch today." Jason replied.

"Well, I only stopped in for a minute, Gordon. I've got to meet the Bradfords in twenty minutes; I'm showing them some properties today in the new Melrose development."

Jason sat at Gordon's desk and pulled out the small notebook. He wanted to check some of Brian's notes and add a few of his own from their earlier interviews. As he turned to a blank page, the photograph slid onto the desk top. Abby reached for the worn photo and studied the happy looking couple with curiosity.

"Who's this, J.C.? Are they from around here?"

"That's Brian and Sarah Dunlap. They used to live in Deer Springs. I'm investigating their death as a favor to their daughter."

"Oh." Abby's voice was hushed as she looked at the vibrant couple again and heard the sadness in her friend's answer.

Jason went back to reading his notes, turning to Brian's last entries. He stared at the cryptic numbers and letters and wished he knew what they meant. Thinking it might be a code, he tried rearranging the digits, writing down the combinations on a scratch pad.

Gordon and Abby both watched his notations with interest. Abby brushed Jason's hand aside to get a better look. Jason had written **T2N R3E 105 42.5**.

"I recognize that! Those are coordinates on a plat map. You know; ranges and township lines." Abby grinned proudly as the two lawmen stared at her in surprise.

CHAPTER 10

They were climbing into the higher elevations now and the cattle were grazing on sage and golden balsam roots. Their progress was slow due to the cattle wanting to stop and feed on the sweet grasses. Frank was riding point and laying a salt trail to entice the cattle to follow.

It was the third day out before Andy had a chance to read more of the journal. Bill had relieved Danny with the herd, moving slowly among the contented animals, watching for stragglers and keeping the herd in a tight group. Andy had prepared the supper tonight; the tin coffee pot still simmered among the campfire coals as Frank reached for one of the remaining sour dough biscuits. He smiled tiredly at Andy as he stretched his weary bones and found a comfortable spot.

Andy braced her bedroll against the saddle apron, leaned back and propped the book against her knees. She sat for a few minutes enjoying the evening solitude and watched the streaks of heat lightning flash across the sky. No rain in sight yet, just the ever-present heat. Andy tilted her head back, relishing the caress of the cooler night breezes against her face and throat. Enough light shone from the bright moon overhead to illuminate the pages of the antique book as Andy turned to the last page she had read. Once more she felt herself become absorbed in the lives and events of a hundred years earlier.

He slept through the night, only stirring once towards dawn. I kept watching for signs of movement from him, fearful to let myself fall into a deep sleep. The sound of the door opening and closing jarred me into immediate alertness. I started up, then relaxed and laid back down as I recognized James in the faint fire light. I felt such a feeling of relief and joy at seeing my husband. My nerves are on edge having this stranger in the house.

James crawled into bed and I rolled to his side, laying my head upon his shoulder. His arms instinctively encircled me, drawing me closer. There was so much that I wanted to ask him and tell him, but the sound of his heavy breathing told me that it would have to wait. He had fallen into an exhausted sleep. Warm and contented, I stayed in the shelter of his arms until the morning began to lighten.

Chores that could not be neglected filled my morning. I labored to carry in fresh water from the nearby stream, and bread dough had to be kneaded and left to rise for the day's baking. There was always so much to do and now with the winter weather pressing down upon us, our daily labor meant another day of survival in this rugged land. James had risen and carried in an armload of firewood. He stacked the split wood neatly as I began cooking a breakfast for us all. Our visitor lay awake watching our toil; I could not read his thoughts behind the blank expression that he wore.

"Good to see you awake, lad. How are you feeling?" James inquired of our guest.

"Better. I reckon I owe you and your missus my life. We haven't been properly introduced yet, but I take it you must be James Dunlap? I'm Cody Jarvis." He leaned forward and stretched out his hand to James in a firm shake that must have pulled on his injured shoulder, although I didn't see him wince with the pain. His words were friendly and a smile touched his face, but I noticed it didn't extend to his eyes; they were still distant and icy.

Where I was reluctant to question our guest, James had no compunction. He poured himself a cup of coffee then offered one to Mr. Jarvis as he turned his chair to directly face the man.

"How did you come to be shot and left all alone, Mr. Jarvis? Were you jumped by bandits or Injuns? What line of work are you in? Did you say you live around these parts? The wife and I just settled here about three months ago, ourselves. We don't know too many people yet." James paused to let the man start explaining.

I watched Cody choke on his swallow of coffee as James began his list of questions and he tried to cover the sound with a short laugh. I couldn't help staring at him, waiting for his answer. He seemed to be thinking of a plausible story.

"I was on my way back to Deer Springs from a cattle-buying trip to Denver; I had hoped to build my own spread a few miles from here. At nightfall I decided to make camp and was just hunkered down by the campfire when these four cowboys came riding into the light. I reached for my rifle, but I guess I must've been too slow, 'cause the next thing I felt was the bullet hitting my chest. They took my bankroll and lit out. Reckon you know the rest."

"So you know cattle then?" James eagerly jumped on the one fact of Mr. Jarvis' explanation that interested him. "I'm thinking to get us some cattle and turn this into a ranch instead of farming, course we don't have much money to spend right now." James scratched his scalp as he let the idea sink in and began to relish the prospect. I could see the excitement in his eyes; James is always dreaming of a more prosperous life and a quick way to achieve it.

I know Cody studied James and recognized the gleam in his eyes and saw the abrupt decision for what it was. "You don't need a lot of money to start a good herd if you round up the mavericks in the spring. Then you only need to buy a good breeding bull."

James leaned forward in his chair, the back legs rising off the floor in his excitement. "Just what are these mavericks you're talking about?"

"Unbranded cattle, strays. Come spring there are plenty of cows that roam the prairie and their calves are unbranded until claimed by some cattleman. I'm just saying that the early bird gets the worm if you know what I mean? Why shouldn't you be the one to pick up a few calves here and there? The mothers will probably wear a brand and it's considered cattle rustling if you try to include them in your herd, but the young calves are easily separated."

"Oh, I see what you mean. So tell me, Mr. Jarvis, have you a home you were heading to? If you've nowhere to go, you're more than welcome to spend the winter with us."

He glanced up, his eyes meeting mine. I prayed he couldn't read my dismay, or was it fear, at James's suggestion? He nodded his head ever so slightly then smiled graciously as if we had just offered him some wonderful prize.

"That's a very kind offer Mr. Dunlap. The winters in Wyoming can be fierce and I'd just as soon not be out in them. And as soon as the weather warms a bit, I'll be glad to help you round up some of those mavericks."

James looked very pleased with himself. It was written all over his face that he thought he had maneuvered Mr. Jarvis into staying and helping with a spring round-up. I nodded to him as he turned a jubilant face to me, but it was the intense stare from the blue eyes across the room that held my attention.

November 20, 1884

Cody, as he prefers to be called, is recovering very quickly. He washed and shaved off the thick beard yesterday, displaying quite a handsome face, as I had suspected. He has offered to help with some of the lighter chores and is getting stronger daily. It is almost disconcerting to turn around and find the man standing close or not hear him when he walks up behind me. I swear the man moves like a cat.

James and Cody act like long lost friends; I think James spends as much time with him as he does me. The two men talk for hours on end about all their big plans, spinning dreams. But I can't help but think that it is James who does most of the talking and Cody who sits silently listening and watching. James intends to go out again tomorrow hunting, but he says he will be back before nightfall. I pray he will; what can he be thinking to leave me alone with a strange man? I'm so nervous and I cannot put my finger on exactly what there is about Cody that makes me feel this way.

Dawn is already breaking; the meager sunlight is shining through the cabin window. James is dressed and packing some rations to carry with him for the day's hunt. Cody lies still on his pallet, whether asleep or not, I cannot tell. I grabbed a shawl and wrapped it around my shoulders as I walked outside with James. He stuffed the food into his saddlebags and slung the rifle across the saddle.

James turned to kiss me good-bye and I wrapped my arms around him, trying to hug him closer through the thick layers of his wool coat. He kissed me a second time then laughed at my desperate expression.

"I'll be home before dark, Margaret. Now stop your worrying. Cody is here to protect you, you'll be fine."

"Oh James, you thick clot. It's Cody that scares me. I don't like being alone with him."

"Now don't act like a silly woman. The man won't harm you. He's our friend and I'll be glad of his help with the ranch. Go inside before you catch a chill. Keep the fire stoked good and hot and we will roast some elk when I get home."

I could see that nothing I said would matter to him. He had made up his mind about Cody Jarvis and it would be up to me to be on my guard; James had only one thought in his mind... cattle and the wealth it would bring.

The terrain continued to climb, and the ground became rougher as Andy and the men moved the cattle onward early the next morning. Andy let the herd move at a relaxed pace since the purpose was to try and fatten the animals, not run them in this heat. It was slow going but with no pressing schedule to be met, both riders and cattle journeyed north.

Despite the higher elevation, the heat throughout the day seemed to intensify. Andy wiped her face for the tenth time and looked longingly at the shade offered by a grove of aspen trees just ahead. She reined in and turned her mount until she was riding abreast with Bill and pointed to the canyon ahead and the grove of aspens.

"Let's stop and cool 'em down for a while. We deserve a shady spot for lunch too."

"I've been keeping an eye on the sky, Andy. I don't like the looks of those clouds blowing in; think we're in for a storm later." Bill gestured to the bank of ominous looking clouds building above the western horizon. As if to prove his words, streaks of heat lightning flashed jaggedly across the sky.

CHAPTER 11

Jason closed the book of surveyor's plat maps and slid a large volume listing the county grantor and grantee deed recordings across the wide counter. Opening the dusty cover of the yellowed pages, he scanned the dates and property descriptions. Motioning to the clerk with a wave of his hand, he looked up briefly from the page full of entries.

"I can't find this property. Can you help me? This is the range and township designation and according to that plat map, it covers these southeast acres of Goshen County, stretching across Converse into the northern most sector of Platte County."

The clerk studied the information and the state wall map hanging up before coming back to the counter with a current tax register in hand. Flipping through pages quickly until he found what he needed, the clerk placed the register on the counter and turned it toward Jason, pointing at one of the entry pages.

"Here's your land and the taxes are being paid by Brent Logan. He's listed as the owner according to our tax rolls. Now if you go to the grantor book and work from the current date backwards, you can trace the ownership of the property. That is, if it has been sold over the years. Some land ownership has title because of a grant given before Wyoming was a state. Territorial records are kept in Cheyenne."

"Interesting. Thank you for your help. Oh, by the way, how far back do your records go? What's your oldest date?"

"I'd say that our records start about 1899; yes, anything earlier than that, if it was recorded at all, would be in Cheyenne."

"Hmm, thanks again." Jason spent another hour going through the deed registers but found no mention of the property with any other name except the Logan family. He studied the plat map again and the overlay of the state map with the county lines and roads drawn in. The one interesting point he found appeared to be the Dunlap property lines running adjacent to the parcel owned by the Logans. Was that what had interested Brian Dunlap?

The drive to Cheyenne was long and uneventful. Jason missed the comfort of his own truck as the Jeep bounced over the tedious miles. He arrived too late in the afternoon to catch the state administrative offices open, so he checked into a local motel located off the interstate. After dining in the small restaurant adjacent to the motel, Jason stretched out across the bed and snapped on the television as he pulled out his notebook and reviewed the day's findings. He read again the cryptic notes written among the pages of Brian Dunlap's notebook and compared them to the names and dates that he had jotted down from the courthouse records. There had to be a connection here, but what was it? All of the records appeared to be legal, everything registered and notarized. Still, a nagging doubt gnawed at Jason. If it had been anyone else but Brent Logan's family, Jason would consider the matter closed. Logan was just too slick to be trusted.

Jason picked up the telephone and got an outside line as he dialed the number to Cedarhill. "Hi Pop, I'm down in Cheyenne and will be staying over. Just wanted to let you and Mom know I'm out of town on business." Jason cradled the telephone receiver against his shoulder as he reached across the bed for the TV's remote control. "No, nothing like that. Just tracking down some old records. Fine ... see you tomorrow."

Jason laughed at himself as he hung up the phone. He was probably the only sheriff who still checked in with his parents; some tough guy image he projected! It wasn't as if he had to; but living under their roof made Jason feel obligated to keep them posted. Anyway, his dad would worry needlessly and with the memory of his father's heart attack last spring still fresh in his mind, it was enough to convince Jason to extend a few courtesies. Once he finished building his own home and got his ranch operational it would be different. Maybe by then he would have someone to share it with too, he mused.

The next morning found Jason striding up the stone steps of the courthouse to greet the clerk as she unlocked the recorder's office door. Her warm smile masked her surprise as she greeted the handsome sheriff.

"Good morning Sheriff. My goodness, aren't you an eager one?"

"Can I help hold those files for you ma'am?" Jason asked her as she juggled several heavy folders and reached for light switches. Obviously, her morning routine was not used to intrusions.

"Thank you, I can manage. I'll be with you in just a minute."

Jason politely waited with his hat in hand and studied the various portraits of past governors and paintings depicting early Wyoming that decorated the plastered walls.

"Why do all federal and state office buildings always use either that bland celery green or boring gray putty paint?" Jason thought, as he continued to scan the room. One building looked like another.

Finally, Mrs. Hughes indicated that she was ready to assist the lawman. "Now, what can I do for you?"

"I need to see some records concerning any land grants for this parcel that may be dated prior to 1899." Jason handed her the sheet of paper with the plat map coordinates as well as the legal description of the Logan property.

He watched as the clerk read the information and then walked over to several rows of bookcases filled with heavy bound ledgers. She glanced at the paper again then moved slowly along one row, reading the spines of the ledgers until she found the one she wanted. Pulling out the heavy tome, she motioned for Jason.

He quickly took the book from her and set it down on a long conference table positioned along the side of the room. Jason made himself comfortable as he began to leaf through the huge book and started reading the many transactions that formed the history of his state.

"Can I get you a cup of coffee? You're probably going to be awhile unless you're one of those speed readers."

"Thanks, coffee sounds good. Black is fine ma'am." Jason did not look up as he studied the information before him.

Mrs. Hughes quietly set a mug of coffee on the table then returned to her desk in the rear of the office. She listened cautiously for a moment, then reassured that the sheriff was occupied, carefully picked up the telephone and dialed the number written on the corner of her desk blotter. The number rang three times before a servant answered and then another voice came on the line.

"Hello, this is Mrs. Hughes at the courthouse. Yes, that's right. You told me to call if anyone else came around inquiring about a certain property... well there's a young man here. No, I don't know his name. What? ...Oh, blond hair, tall and he's wearing a sheriff's uniform. Does that help?"

She listened for a few minutes as the voice gave her instructions then started to nod yes, catching herself and remembered to speak her affirmative. "Thank you, that would be most generous of you sir." Pleased with herself and already planning what she would do with an extra hundred dollars, Mrs. Hughes silently hung up the telephone.

Jason made some final notes then closed the ledger; checking his watch, he realized that over two hours had gone by before he knew it. Sliding the book back onto its shelf, he returned to the front counter.

"I'll be leaving now. Here's your coffee cup. Thanks again."

"That's quite all right. Have a good day." She nodded her head in a thoroughly satisfied manner.

Outside, Jason was descending the courthouse steps when he recognized an obese, burly man squeezing out of the rear door of a black Cadillac. Brent Logan was easy to recognize anywhere, his sheer size alone made him a memorable character, add to that heavy jowls and a jagged scar running along the left cheek, it was not a face you forgot. Jason watched with hidden amusement the effort it took for the man to simply exit an automobile.

Standing to one side, holding the door open was one of Logan's associates, henchman would be more accurate. The man looked very familiar for some reason as Jason gave him the once over. As the driver's door opened and another man came around to the passenger side, Jason knew where he had seen them. Logan's associates were the same two men that Jason had spied in Laramie and followed him back to Deer Springs. If he had any doubts before, their appearance today confirmed them.

Reaching the sidewalk, Jason touched two fingers to the brim of his hat, tipping it in acknowledgment to the man. "Brent, you're a little far from home, aren't you?"

"It's Mr. Logan to you, sonny, and where my business takes me is none of your business."

Jason's friendly demeanor changed, and his voice took on a steely edge, "It's Sheriff Hartman to you, Logan. Why my father sees fit to include you among his circle of friends is a mystery to me. In my book, you're just two steps on the right side of the law but if I ever see evidence you've crossed that line, I'll nail you."

Logan's temper flared as he growled, "You impudent little pup! Are you threatening me? Don't let that shiny star go to your head."

"No threat Logan— promise!" Jason turned and strode away. Behind him Logan's two goons stood speechless as Logan shook a fist at Jason's back.

Jason drove over to the municipal airport and verified the departure time of the Dunlap plane the day it crashed. Comparing it to Brian's flight log, he noted the times agreed then left the airport for the drive back to Deer Springs. He had a clear picture now of what Brian and Sarah Dunlap were doing in Cheyenne and Torrington, but not why. Despite the appearance of Brent Logan outside the courthouse, there was no evidence of any wrongdoing. The Cheyenne records showed a land grant dated 1887 to Zachary Logan in the territory of Wyoming and there didn't appear to be any transfers of the land other than to the Logan descendants. It was a clear-cut land grant, almost too clear. And that's what bothered Jason.

An hour outside Cheyenne the interstate began twisting and turning as it climbed Iron Mountain and wound its way north again. The mountain range cutting the state in two along the continental divide spread out its fingers of hills and mountains and created deep valleys between. Jason's thoughts were on Andrea, wondering where she was this morning and how the cattle drive was moving, as he descended the higher elevations of Iron Mountain. The highway signs warned of a steep 5% grade ahead as another sign posted a dangerous S curve. Jason tapped his brakes lightly, then began to pump the pedal as the Jeep continued to pick up speed on the downward slope. The brakes weren't reacting and the pedal sunk to the floorboard as Jason tried pumping them once more. Tires screeched and the Jeep rocked precariously as Jason took each curve, hurling downhill like a runaway train.

The speedometer read seventy miles per hour as Jason reached for the gear shift lever and down shifted to third gear. The transmission whined in the lower gear, slowing the Jeep slightly but still sped recklessly around the hairpin curves. Jason fought to control the steering as he shifted again into the lower second gear and prayed the transmission did not blow from the strain. Ahead, along the side of the road, Jason spied a trucker's runaway ramp. He steered toward the gravel ramp, pulled up on the emergency brake and downshifted into the first gear. The engine sound was deafening as the transmission screamed this last abuse and the Jeep climbed the hillside ramp, plowing into the deep bank of sand at its end. The vehicle shuddered as the engine shut down and came to a halt. Jason unlatched his seat belt and climbed out. Steam and smoke spilled from under the hood as Jason knelt down and peered under the Jeep. Fluid still leaked from the broken brake lines.

Jason stood next to the crashed vehicle and gazed out across the interstate highway. He removed his hat and ran shaky fingers through his thick sandy hair then took a deep cleansing breath.

"Now that was an interesting way to start a day. Wonder what I can do for an encore?"

Reaching back into the Jeep, Jason picked up the microphone of his police radio and switched on the transmitter. Hopefully the mountains wouldn't block the radio waves and he could call for some help. It would be a mighty long walk if he had to start hoofing it.

The radio crackled with static as Jason tried the emergency frequency. "This is Platte County Sheriff Hartman, over, do you copy?"

A voice came over the speakers, breaking up and fading, "Go ahead Sheriff. This is the Laramie post of the state highway patrol, over."

"Signal 7A on Interstate 25 north bound, about mile marker 118, I'm code six and request tow vehicle. No injuries, over."

"Roger, Sheriff. We'll notify the county road service and dispatch your location, ETA twenty-five minutes, over."

"Roger, ETA twenty-five minutes. Thanks Laramie. Hartman out."

With nothing more to do but wait, Jason sought a shady spot under some aspen trees growing out of the hillside where he could watch for his rescuers. He leaned back against the tree trunk and stretched his legs out before him.

It was late afternoon before Jason walked into his office at Deer Springs. He was carrying his brief case and had a small duffel bag slung over one shoulder. Mac looked up as he entered the room.

"What happened to the Jeep? Your telephone message was kinda sketchy. Did you say you left it in Laramie?"

"Brake line blew coming down I-25 from Cheyenne. I had to plow the Jeep into a sand bank on one of those trucker ramps. For awhile there, I didn't think I'd get the damn thing stopped. Anyway,

I got a tow into Laramie since it was closer, then I hitched a ride on an eighteen-wheeler coming northbound."

"Whew, that's hairy. Did you find what you were looking for up in Torrington? What were you doing in Cheyenne?"

"I followed Dunlap's movements in Torrington and that's what led me to Cheyenne. Guess who I ran into outside the state building in Cheyenne?"

"Who?"

"Brent Logan and a pair of his flunkies. He didn't look like he appreciated my being in Cheyenne either. Tell the boys over at S&G's garage to give that Jeep a thorough inspection when it comes in. I want to know exactly what caused those brakes to go out."

"You think they were tinkered with?"

"Maybe. Let's just say I'll sleep better if I know for sure. How about giving me a lift to Cedarhill? I need to change clothes and get my truck."

"Sure thing, J.C. Let me grab my keys."

An hour later Jason pulled into the Circle-D yard, parking the Explorer near the barn. He rapped on the screen door and impatiently slapped his hat against his thigh waiting on Sam to answer. He turned quickly as he heard the sound of a hammer hitting an anvil in the barn and hurriedly strode off in that direction.

"Sam, you in here?" Jason called loudly. The interior of the barn was dark and shadowy, but he spied Sam working near the tack room.

"Howdy J.C. I didn't hear you drive up. What's on your mind?"

"I'd like to have a look at that old journal if you don't mind. I think it must tie in somehow with Brian's research. I've been thinking and thinking and it's the only link this puzzle seems to have. Brian was searching through old land grants and the only thing we have that is dated just as old is the journal."

"Hmm, well I don't have the book or I'd be glad to show it to you. Andy took it with her to read while she's on the trail."

"Andy has it?! Where did you say she was headed to?"

"Why? What's wrong J.C.?"

"If she has that book with her, it may be inviting danger. I'll explain later. I'm going to go find her."

"They're traveling north into the Saratoga Valley. Don't let anything happen to her, she's all I've got left."

"I'll find her Sam, don't worry." Jason shouted over his shoulder as he ran back to his truck. He drove quickly to Cedarhill and rushed into the stable to saddle up Blazing Star. He'd go on horseback since there were no good roads leading into that valley and ride all night and day to make up the time Andy had already spent on the trail. Jason tossed some provisions into one saddlebag and grabbed his slicker, extra ammunition and a rifle to sling across the other. He strapped on a bedroll and with a quick final check of his gear, rode out of Cedarhill, heading toward the Circle-D's northern pasture and the path leading into the Saratoga.

CHAPTER 12

Dark clouds shrouded the mountain peaks and crept down into the valley as rolling thunder echoed. Flashes of lightning created a brilliant light show against the stormy purple sky while gusts of wind blew stronger across the land. Andy pushed her Stetson lower on her head and tied her cotton bandanna to shield her nose and mouth from the swirling dirt. She saw Frank wave his lariat overhead and shout to Bill instructions to bunch up the herd, but his words were carried away by the howling wind.

"Keep 'em out of that box canyon, if they spook they'll trample each other,"Andy shouted to Frank as they tried to control the nervous cows and lead them into a more open space.

Suddenly a bolt of lightning streaked across the sky above them and crashed into the nearby grove of aspens, splintering one of the trees with an explosive fireball. Cattle panicked and turned, stampeding away from the flames and smoke. The four riders grasped their reins tightly and rode in the direction of the stampeding herd, their only choice. The constant risk was getting thrown from a horse directly into the crushing path of the terrorized animals.

Hard pellets of rain struck Andy's face like shards of glass as the heavens opened up and the downpour began. They had been praying for rain and an end to the drought for so long, but not like this. In a matter of minutes her jeans and denim shirt were soaked through with the cold water. Andy cursed under her bandanna as she rode low against Buttercup's neck and fought to get ahead of the herd to try and turn them. She searched for Frank, riding on her right flank, and could just make out his outline through the pouring rain. She couldn't see Bill or Danny and hoped they were still behind them.

A narrow gully, cut into the parched ground, snaked its way down the hillside and crossed their path directly ahead. Some of the cattle were jumping the narrow opening and others were bolting into the depression before climbing up the other side. Above the noise of the thundering hooves a new sound could be heard. A torrent of rushing water rumbled down the gully; a flash flood racing toward them. The first waves of water hit the bawling animals as they struggled to swim against the swift tide and scramble up the far side of the gully.

She screamed to Frank as the wall of water and debris swept her along, "Stay with the herd no matter what!"

Andy clung desperately to her saddle as Buttercup valiantly fought to keep her head above the water. A landslide of earth and rocks mixed with broken tree limbs churned within the rushing current and threatened to crush horse and rider. A large log tumbling in the rapids slammed into her leg, causing Andy to cry out.

Churned up earth and crushed prairie grasses gave evidence of the Dunlap herd's passing as Jason sought their trail. Andy had kept to the more open areas as the cattle pushed northward. Jason chose to cut the distance in half by riding closer to the tree line and climbing the mountainous terrain. He rode relaxed in the saddle as he steered Blazing Star in and out of the clusters of junipers and cottonwoods. Jason was careful not to tire the stallion as he kept up a steady but fast pace, devouring mile after mile of ground. He rode throughout the night, eating dried beef jerky and biscuits then washing it down with a canteen of water, while maintaining the grueling pace. He stopped once near dawn to sleep for an hour and rest the horse then roused and climbed back into the saddle.

A burnt-out campfire site encircled by stones reassured him that Andy and the men had been there the night before, encouraging Jason to push on. Jason studied the sky as storm clouds gathered above. He had just thrown on his slicker when the afternoon rain began. He turned up the stiff collar and settled his hat tighter as the rain water trickled down the brim.

Jason reined back Blazing Star and continued cautiously when lightning cracked ahead. A narrow ravine had turned into a raging river as the storm created a flash flood that moved with a deadly current. A scream pierced the air and penetrated above the noise of the storm. Jason focused all of his attention on the direction of that cry for help; his senses strained to catch any sight or sound. Another burst of lightning illuminated the sky above him like a bright flare and suddenly the pale yellow color of a horse and rider contrasted with the murky water.

Jason recognized the palomino that Andrea usually favored and kicked his mount into action as he galloped toward the water's edge. Uncoiling his lariat, Jason rode along the bank, trying to get within throwing distance.

"Andy!" Jason shouted and was relieved to see the rider raise her head and look toward the direction of his voice. "Grab the rope!"

He twirled the rope in a tight circle above his head then thrust it forward; the rope falling short into the swift current. The lariat caught on broken branches bobbing in the murky water. Jason swore frustrated, tugging sharply to free the snag. Precious minutes were wasted as Jason feared Andrea would be swept out of reach. Quickly pulling the rope back in, Jason concentrated on his target as he calculated the force of the wind and current, then made a second attempt. This time the rope found its mark, falling into waiting hands that clutched it tightly. Jason watched as Andy quickly looped the rope around her saddle horn, anchoring it as she pulled with all her strength on the life line and urged the horse toward the bank as Jason began to tow her in.

As soon as the palomino felt firmer soil under its hooves, the horse began to scramble up the slope to dry ground. It stood panting and exhausted from the ordeal as Andy slid out of the saddle and collapsed onto the ground. Blood ran from a gash in Andrea's thigh. She hovered on unconsciousness from the pain throbbing in her leg and fought to keep her mind clear.

Jason dismounted and ran to her side, gathering her trembling body into his arms. He scooped her up like a wet rag doll and carried her toward a stand of dense junipers. He laid her down gently under the tree's thick branches, providing some shelter from the pouring rain, then he ran back to lead both horses into the wooded area and secured their reins.

Andrea sat under the shelter of the heavy branches and watched in a detached way. She couldn't seem to focus as her glazed eyes stared ahead yet saw nothing and everything at the same time. The rain droplets fascinated her as they clung to the branch tips before falling gently to the earth. The wet evergreen smelled pungent, almost tangy. Andy inhaled deeply then began to shiver in her wet clothes that were molded to her body. The cool rainwater against her skin should have been a welcome relief, since earlier in the day it had been so hot. So why did she feel so odd?

Andy's slender shoulders shook again, from the cold or fright, she wasn't certain. Jason returned to the bower and instantly recognized Andrea's symptoms of shock. He quickly peeled off his rain slicker and put it around her shoulders. The coat still held the heat of his body, enveloping her in its warmth. Then he drew her to him, holding Andy in a crushing embrace, determined to fuse his body's greater strength and heat with hers.

She raised her head, her eyes locking with Jason's, and suddenly his mouth lowered to hers. The kiss was sweet, yet fiery and warmed her as no mere campfire could. His strong arms held her even tighter as he pressed another kiss against her forehead and tucked her head under his chin. Jason struggled with the urge to either kiss her again or shake her soundly to knock some sense into her. He sat holding her secure for the moments it took to calm his own heartbeat and gain some control of his ragged emotions.

"Oh Andy, you just scared ten years off my life! What would I do if I lost you, gal? Are you all right?"

Reluctantly releasing his hold on her, Jason kneeled in front of her. He ran his hands down her arms and legs checking for signs of broken bones, grimacing when he saw the jagged gash on her thigh.

Her teeth chattering, she could only nod. A thousand questions marched through her mind. What was he doing here; how did he find her? But for now, she was just thankful that he had.

"I'll get a fire started for us as soon as this rain lets up. First, we better put a bandage on that leg. I've got some things in my gear. Lay still, I'll be right back."

Jason crawled out from beneath their evergreen roof and hurried over to the horses. He rummaged through one of his saddlebags, finding the first aid kit he always carried. Slipping both rifles out of their sleeves, he tucked them under his arm and returned to the makeshift shelter.

Andy's shivering had stopped as she sat huddled in the folds of Jason's coat. He squatted down next to her and began peeling back the torn edges of her jeans to expose the cut flesh. Cleaning the cut with a gauze pad soaked in antiseptic; Jason wiped away the blood and applied a sterile bandage. Satisfied that it wasn't too deep and that he had done everything he could, he breathed a sigh of relief.

"Well, that ought to hold you. Better check it tomorrow and maybe put on another clean bandage."

"You should have been a doctor instead of a sheriff. Such tender care, and you do have a wonderful bedside manner!" Andy smiled with a mischievous look.

"Hmm, I'll just have to be around every time you get hurt, but of course I'd rather not see you ever hurt again." His voice turned serious when he cupped her face gently in his hands as he watched her eyes. "I'd spend my life protecting you, if you'd let me."

The gray eyes that looked back at him were not stormy with anger as he had witnessed in the past, but now shone iridescent like pale pearls. Tears glistened in Andy's eyes as her heart heard the tender words filled with love and promise. She wanted this man to love her and she wanted to love him in return. It was difficult to remember her father's warnings when Jason looked at her so endearingly. She reached out to caress his lean face, her hand stroking the strong jawbone. Her fingers moved naturally to the lock of sandy hair lying on his forehead. Andy smiled and Jason read the invitation as his lips claimed hers once more. She lay enfolded in his strong embrace again, enjoying the nearness of him, and the safe haven his arms offered.

No words were needed as they both drank in the sweetness of the shared moment. Jason was the first to move as he got to his feet and picked up one of the rifles.

"I better fire off a round or two to let Frank and the others know that you're safe. They ought to be able to hear the shots now that the storm is ending."

He stepped into a clearing and pointed the rifle skyward as he fired one round then waited for an answer. The report echoed off the surrounding hills then faded before a different shot was heard a few seconds later from one of the Circle-D wranglers. Jason returned their answer with another volley then sheathed the rifles.

He stood silently as he patted Blazing Star and his mind replayed the scene from minutes before. He had actually proposed. Andy must have known what his words were saying, but he did not hear an affirmative answer. In fact, Andy didn't reply at all. She didn't tell him that she loved him. He felt her love, he was sure of it. He couldn't be that wrong in reading her emotions and the physical attraction between them. But he knew she was holding back. Why?

Jason gathered wood and brush to start the promised fire, but his actions were automated as his mind dwelled on the woman reclining on the ground nearby.

Tiny flames began to lick at the tinder and firewood within the carefully dug pit. Jason placed several stones around the circle to contain the small fire and prevent it from leaping out of control. Despite the sudden downpour of rain, the terrain was still dangerously dry from the weeks of drought. A forest fire was not something that anyone needed now.

Andy crawled out of her leafy shelter and sat near the fire in hopes of drying her clothes. Jason watched her as she kept turning from side to side.

"Why don't you just take off those wet things and put on something else? Have anything in your saddlebags that I can get you?"

"I've got some clean jeans and a shirt but I don't know how dry they'll be. Buttercup and I were pretty well submerged back there."

She grimaced at the memory and realized just how lucky she was to be sitting here now.

Andy looked up at Jason; she had him to thank for being safe. She quite literally owed him her life. That was a sobering thought. Andy turned and stared hard at the horizon, her emotions churning.

Jason walked over to where Andy sat absorbed in her thoughts and handed her the sodden saddlebag and bedroll. She was right; the leather bag and bedroll were soaked, including their contents. Realizing that those clothes wouldn't be much use, Jason rummaged through his own bags and found an extra shirt that he had rolled up and that had been under the plastic bag holding his foodstuffs. The plastic had helped to keep it dry. He silently offered it to Andy.

Well, it wasn't the first time that she had to undress outdoors. If you ride the range, you learn to do without the niceties.

"Um, if you don't mind…?" Andy inclined her head and waved a hand to Jason that he took as a hint to at least turn his back.

Andy decided the evergreen offered the only hope of privacy and so she crawled back to its drooping haven and began to peel off the sodden shirt and pants. Her bare skin actually felt warmer as soon as the wet things were off. She left on her panties for modesty and donned the large shirt, buttoning it clear up to the neck. The long shirttails hung to mid-thigh on her, covering her body but not what anyone would call modestly.

Andy shook out her wet shirt and jeans and tried draping them on some branches near the fire. Her movements were followed every inch of the way by Jason's devouring eyes. She was quite a sight in his shirt. His hot eyes were making Andy feel very self-conscious and she was suddenly aware of their isolation.

"This is silly," she chided herself. She'd been alone with Jason before. She was acting as nervous as a schoolgirl on her first date. She was safe. Nothing was going to happen. Nothing. Her thoughts continued until she stopped pacing by the fire and her eyes found Jason's.

He stood with his arms crossed in front of his chest. Jason waited silently while his eyes stalked Andrea as she nervously fidgeted and wrung her hands. Each time she crossed in front of the fire, Jason thought it would be his undoing. The fire light shone through the cotton shirt until it appeared to be only a thin film against the delectable body boldly outlined. He always knew that Andrea had a good figure and was a beautiful woman, but the sight before him now strained the tenuous control he held on his raging desires.

The casual, easy-going man that Andy was familiar with had been replaced with a sensual stranger that both excited and frightened her. Why hadn't she ever noticed before the span of his chest or the bulging muscles rippling in his arms and shoulders? He appeared as a virile lion ready to pounce. Andy anxiously looked up to find him studying her movements with blue eyes that smoldered to a dark midnight hue.

His eyes were intense— speaking volumes, silently questioning, as he slowly approached Andy and reached for her hand. "I want you," he whispered.

He picked her up in his arms and cradled her body against his chest. Andy could feel the throb of his heartbeat against her racing heart. She clasped her arms around his neck and looked into the face of her childhood friend that would be no more, if she said yes to him now. They would be more, so very much more. Did she dare? Her mind shut out all the familiar worries and voices and only listened to her heart.

Andrea closed her eyes and opened her soul to the man who clasped her to him and waited for her decision during the split second that seemed like an eternity. She kissed his cheek then slid her lips to his demanding ones. Jason drank in her sweet answer as he carried her back to the shelter of the juniper and their waiting bedrolls.

He kissed her deeply and longingly; the nearness of her releasing a flood of passion that he had held in check for too long. He had always been the complete gentleman around her, never overstepping those invisible boundaries that Andy had erected. Feelings magnified and exploded as the sight and smell of her filled his senses. He touched her damp skin and inhaled her sweet fragrance as his lips pressed a fiery trail across her cheek, her neck, across a smooth shoulder and returned to capture her waiting mouth again.

"Andy, Andy! I love you so much. I've waited so long to hold you like this."

Andrea's world tilted crazily. Her head spun; she felt lightheaded and breathless. Jason's words penetrated her foggy mind as she pulled him closer and stroked his back and neck. He was life and real.

He was the sweet haven of today and the promise of tomorrow. Nothing mattered right now but Jason and being in his arms. Her body ached with the need for him. He awakened a cauldron of passion that had been simmering beneath the surface of the usually reserved woman.

His hands caressed her, worshipping her body. Andrea's skin tingled wherever he touched, leaving her warm and glowing, wanting more. He whispered words of love in her ear as he deftly unbuttoned the last button on the large shirt, parting it with one hand. Jason's work callused hands glided across the velvet skin and his lips followed, pressing kisses and nibbling the tender flesh. Andy moaned softly and arched her back, pressing closer, wanting to touch every inch of her body to his. She vaguely heard her name being called again.

"Andy!"

Her passion-drugged mind slowly began to surface as she heard her named called out once more and realized it was not Jason's voice.

This time Jason heard the distant shout as well. He rolled off of Andy, sitting upright with one knee bent. Jason took a deep breath and swore as he dragged his fingers through his hair, pushing it from his forehead.

"Damn, that sounds like Frank's voice. I could strangle that man!"

Andrea was still confused and struggled to sit up.

"Frank? Oh my God, Frank!" Now she was awake and taking in her appearance. Trying not to panic, she franticly began to grab clothes and cover her nakedness.

Jason was also quickly restoring some normalcy to his attire. Outwardly he may have looked calm, but inwardly he was experiencing a frustration that could only have been worse if he had progressed a few minutes longer. Yes, he would definitely like to strangle the worried cowhand riding toward their campfire.

Jason pulled Andy's jeans and blouse off the makeshift clothesline and tossed them into her.

"Better get dressed again in these. Wouldn't want to give old Frank any wrong ideas."

Andy glared at Jason as she grabbed her clothes and the waves of shame and embarrassment washed over her. What was the matter with her? Look what she had almost done! She had broken her promise to her father and let her emotions carry her away. She knew better than that. Where was her control? Andrea's face flamed as she fought for calm before she had to face Jason and her wrangler. The guilt would be written all over her face for anyone to read.

"Andy! J.C.? That you?" Frank rode into the clearing and dismounted. "You fire those shots?" He glanced around, taking in the secluded scene.

"Hey, Frank. Glad you found us. I pulled Andy out of that flash flood, but she's hurt her leg; had to take shelter under those trees 'til the rain let up."

Andrea emerged from under the heavy boughs as if on cue and played her part by limping across to the campfire. She tried not to over act and prayed Frank wouldn't ask too many questions that would force her to lie. She never could tell a lie convincingly and Frank would surely put two and two together.

"You sure had us worried gal. You really okay? We had our hands full with the herd and the storm. I wanted to follow you, but…" Frank's voice wavered and he coughed to hide the raw emotion that was choking his throat. His eyes met Andy's and his relief was evident.

Andy hugged the older man. "I know, Frank, I know. It's alright."

"What're you doin' out here, J.C.?" Now that Frank had his gruff cowboy face back in place, his normal curiosity rose to the surface.

Andy waited to hear Jason's answer too. She stole a quick look at Jason and then at Frank, hoping neither man would realize that she hadn't even thought to ask that same question. She had been too swept away with passion to care about such logical things.

"I was searching for Andy. I just didn't expect to find her shooting the rapids!"

"Why were you trying to find for me? Is anything wrong? Is Gramps okay?"

"Don't jump to any false conclusions, Andy. Everything is fine on the Circle-D. Your grandfather told me you were driving the herd into the Saratoga. I wanted to tell you about your dad's log."

Her fears calmed and her brief embarrassment forgotten, Andy jumped on the one statement of interest that Jason had made. "What about my dad's log? Did you find something?"

Jason's eyes darted to Frank, uncertain how much he should say in front of the wrangler. He looked back to Andy for a sign to continue. She understood his silent question and nodded.

"Well, I drove up to Torrington and then Cheyenne following your dad's schedule. I found out where he went, but now I have a whole lot more questions. What I'd really like to do is have a look at that journal."

"That the book I seen you reading? Whatcha' say it was, some kind of diary?" Frank questioned as he scratched his beard and waited with interest.

"Something like that. Gramps said it was written by his grandmother when the family was building the ranch."

"What's that got to do with Brian and Sarah? What's going on that I don't know about?" Frank asked suspiciously.

"It's a long story Frank. I'll tell you later. How far ahead did you leave the herd?" Andy asked over her shoulder as she tied her bedroll onto her saddle again and checked the cinch straps. Stepping up into the stirrups, her leg stopped in mid-air at Frank's acute observation.

"Humph, bet it ain't half as interesting a story as the one that explains why you're wearing that shirt inside out, Andy. Better go fix it; Bill and Danny ain't as polite as me," Frank said as he chuckled when Andy jumped down from Buttercup and stared down at her chest. She ran behind the shelter of the thick evergreens, stripping off the blouse and carefully dressed again.

Laughter rang in the air as both men rode ahead; Jason grinning at Frank's smug, know-all expression. Andy, mortified with a face three shades of scarlet, rode silently behind the pair glaring at the men's backs.

CHAPTER 13

The cattle had scattered in the storm and it had taken the better part of the next day and a half to round them all up. Andy was grateful for Jason's help but still furious with him for embarrassing her in front of Frank. Every time she looked at the man, she felt her face color red. It was a foreign feeling that Andy did not like one bit. She didn't care to admit that Jason had aroused strange desires in her and that she had wanted him to make love to her.

Only now, with the stars shining above and the peaceful quiet of the night enveloping her, did Andy let her thoughts wander and return to those moments of passion. Andy relaxed as she stretched out on a bed of soft grass; a smile curving her lips. She closed her eyes and rested her head against the apron of her saddle. Once again, she felt the heat of Jason's kisses and the warmth of his embrace. Her thoughts floated, her young body starting to respond to the desires of the mind. The sound of loud male voices brought her abruptly back to reality. Andy sat upright, startled from her reverie; her desires doused as if a bucket of cold water had hit her.

Jason strolled over to the campfire, squatting down to reach for the coffee pot simmering atop the coals. He looked over at Andy, nodding to her with a knowing smile on his face.

Andy turned her back to him. *The man must be a psychic ...he sees into every corner of my mind!*" her thoughts screamed.

Nervous, Andy jumped up and slapped her hat against her leg and strode purposefully toward the remuda. Buttercup snorted as

Andy grabbed a handful of mane and mounted the horse bareback. Thumping her heels against the horse's flanks, Andy galloped away from the camp and Jason's prying eyes.

Bill finished his shift with the herd and entered the campsite. "What's gotten into her?" he asked Frank and Jason after witnessing Andy's hurried departure.

Frank studied Jason's face for a minute then poured a cup of coffee, taking his time before he answered the cowpoke, "Oh, she's all right. Just needs some time alone, I guess. Imagine she's still torn up about her folks and all. Keeps too much bottled up and it makes her a bit touchy. I wouldn't want to see anyone hurt her or take advantage of her right now."

Jason understood the last comments were meant for him. He had always respected the older man and spoke sincerely as he said, "I wouldn't hurt her for the world and would fight anyone else that tried. That's partly why I'm here."

Frank nodded to Jason then said, "Maybe you better explain what you mean by that before she comes back."

The three men hunkered by the fire; the Circle-D riders listened carefully as Jason quietly told them of his truck accident and suspicions.

"First, Andy and I were watched and followed the day we were at the airport then, someone tried to get me out of the way just for asking questions in Cheyenne. What would happen to Andy, all isolated out here, if somebody thought she knew something or had some kind of evidence?"

"I still don't get it. What could an old book have to do with all this? Are you saying that the crash wasn't an accident?" Frank and Bill exchanged worried looks.

"Tell you the truth, I don't know. Too many things just don't add up. I need to see that journal and put more pieces of the puzzle together." Jason dragged his fingers through his hair and paced the small area of the campsite. He stopped and looked up sharply, peering into the inky darkness surrounding the camp.

Andrea stepped into the firelight, walking silently as she led Buttercup back to the remuda. She tied her securely then slowly returned to the waiting men.

"How long have you been standing there?" Jason questioned Andy as she sat down.

Andy took off her hat and shook out her hair. She rubbed a trembling hand across her face.

"Long enough." Her voice was barely a whisper as she raised frightened eyes to Jason's anxious face, "Why would anyone want to harm my parents? Why?"

Jason gathered her into his arms, offering her the only comfort he knew how. He felt so powerless. Nothing he could ever do would change the past or take away the grief. Anger simmered deep within him for the person who would cause such pain to the woman he loved. He sat holding her tightly, not finding the words to answer her plea.

Andrea pushed away his arms and pulled herself erect. She gathered her pride about herself like armor and gained control of her shaky emotions. She glanced at the expectant faces watching her, waiting for her reaction.

"Okay. You think the journal is important, let's look at it. I've been reading it. There isn't anything in it so far except my family's account of the wagon train west and settling here. I don't see what's so mysterious."

"There has to be something in it. Remember, your father had it with him and thought it was important enough to keep by his side. I'm not sure what we're looking for, but the answers have got to be in that book," Jason spoke with certainty.

"All right, so maybe I need to read some more. But it can wait until tomorrow because I'm not up to digging through the past tonight."

"Tomorrow we should be at the line camp, Andy. You'll have more time to read it then. We can handle the herd; get them bedded down in a good pasture," Frank offered.

Andy smiled gratefully at her good friends. Her nerves were jangled; she felt like she'd been on an emotional roller coaster all day. Stretching out once more on her bedroll, she pulled the blanket around her shoulders and tried to find some much-needed sleep.

The line camp consisted of a small bunkhouse and corral surrounded by cool, sweet pastures. The Saratoga Valley was a welcome sight to the riders as they steered their cattle into the tall grass lands. Andy unsaddled Buttercup and gave the mare a thorough rub down before freeing her to romp unfettered in the wide corral. She deserved the freedom to relax; the old gal had performed well.

Carrying her saddlebags and gear, Andy headed for the line shack. She started the routine of unpacking supplies and brewed some coffee then put on a pot of chili for lunch. Everyone would be hungry and would drift in whenever their chores permitted. Deriving a small satisfaction from completing the mundane tasks, Andy dragged the journal from her gear and went back outside. She stood scanning the area until her eyes fell upon a shady spot under the spreading branches of a tall aspen. It looked very inviting, the perfect spot for relaxing and reading. Andy strolled toward the thick, grassy carpet as Jason hurried to meet her.

They both leaned back against the tree trunk and Andy opened the diary in her lap. She leafed through the pages then began reading out loud the next entry.

November 27, 1884

James has not returned, and I am growing more and more worried. The air has a taste of snow in it. Where could that man be? If he lies hurt somewhere and cannot get help, I would never forgive myself.

Cody spent the morning chopping wood and stacking it by the hearth. He knows I am anxious over James; I look out the window every few minutes and run to the door at every sound, only to find it is the wind or the cabin creaking. He seemed to come to a decision as he reached for his gun belt and strapped it around his waist. Cody checked his Colt, spinning the revolver then slid it into the leather holster. Shrugging into his heavy sheepskin coat, he stood next to the door, one hand on the latch.

Cody turned to me and I had to strain to hear him over the wind. "I'll find him for you, Maggie. I owe you and I always repay my debts."

I ran to the door to beg him to be careful and to bring James home, but he had already left, galloping off into the swirling snowflakes. Bolting the door securely, I threw another log onto the fire then began the long wait. Mending sat on my lap as my mind conjured scenes of first one or the other man in danger. My mind betrayed me as I worried for Cody's safety as much as James'. I feel guilty for allowing concern for the stranger to even enter my thoughts.

It was past dusk when the pounding on the cabin door brought me out of my seat. I rushed to open the sturdy portal as James and Cody stumbled forward. The two were so snow encrusted that I could hardly tell them apart. Cody's hands shook from the cold as he unbuttoned James' wool coat, then discarded it. He carried him, unconscious now, to our sleeping alcove and dropped him onto the bed. I was relieved to see no signs of blood.

"What happened? Is James hurt? Are you? You better get out of those wet things too."

"I'm all right, just need to get ww…warm. Think his horse threw him. May have broken his right leg, not sure. I need some of that hot coffee. My teeth are chch…chattering so hard, I can hardly talk."

Cody wrapped his hands around a mug of the strong brew then collapsed into a chair near the hearth. The heat from the fire brought the color back into a face blue with cold.

I bent my full attention to James as I ran my hands along his body, feeling for injuries. The right leg lay oddly twisted, clearly broken below the knee. It would need to be straightened and splinted. It was a blessing that James lay unconscious, oblivious to the pain.

"Cody, I need you. I can't set this leg by myself. I'm afraid I don't have the strength to hold him or pull it into place." Worry and fear were mirrored in eyes that beseeched his help.

"Get an old blanket; we'll need some wood for splints and let's see…" Cody scanned the room until he spotted the freshly tanned hides. He unsheathed his sharp hunting knife and cut four long strips from the hides. Seeing my puzzled expression, he quickly explained as he dipped the hides into a pot of boiling water that hung over the fire. "These will hold the splints in place; the wet leather will dry and tighten like bands."

Grateful for his calm and commanding manner, I followed his instructions and assembled the necessary items. We found two small logs. Cody hurriedly split them with the axe and shaved the bark, smoothing them as best he could. I swallowed hard and nodded for him to begin.

I gently removed James' boot and Cody slit the length of James' pant leg along the seam with his knife blade. Cody held James' foot and ankle firmly while I pressed down on his shoulders. A quick pull and the leg straightened but not without a bellow of pain from my poor husband. He writhed and twisted in my grip as Cody labored to tie the blanket-padded splints. Steam rose from the leather bindings and I worried James might be scalded as the strips were tied in place.

Cody stepped back to survey his work as I gently stroked James' forehead and murmured soothing words. I kissed his cheek and patted his shoulder, covering him with a warm quilt. He seemed to slip into a more normal sleep and that reassured me. I looked up to find Cody watching me with a rather wistful expression.

I smiled as I reached for his hands, clasping them warmly between my own. "Thank you. I don't know what I would have done without you. James would still be lying in the wilderness, as good as dead, I'm sure."

He smiled at me; the melancholy demeanor vanished, making me wonder if I had imagined it. He visibly relaxed as we both returned to the warmer sitting area and his face took on a boyish appearance.

"I'm glad I was here for you, Maggie. James would have done as much for me - has in fact."

It didn't occur to me until later that he had fallen into the habit of addressing me as 'Maggie', and that I had accepted it. But then, many of my fears and misgivings about Cody Jarvis were beginning to dissolve.

James began to sleep fitfully, thrashing about throughout the night. Twice I had to awaken Cody to help me hold him still. The leg is paining him badly and I am at a loss as to what else to do.

Cody has suggested that we give James a good stiff drink of whiskey. I held the cup to his lips as he coughed and sipped the burning liquid. As much as I hated it, the whiskey did seem to put James to sleep and for that I was grateful. At least he is lying quiet now and not moving the leg. I had to repeat the dose twice more during the long dark hours.

The whiskey fumes are now so thick within the room that I feel like swooning. Wrapping James' heavy wool coat about me, I stepped outside into the crisp morning air. The sunlight pierced my eyes, so accustomed to the dim cabin interior. The cold air made my breath appear in tiny vapors, floating upwards. I stood enjoying the peaceful serenity of the clear blue sky and the sparkling snow glistening over the land. It was a beautiful scene and I felt calm for the first time in days. I belonged in this land.

The cabin door eased shut as Cody moved forward until he touched my shoulder. He stood studying me; seeming to be drawn to me in a way that couldn't be explained. My scent lingered in the cold air, blending with the smells of the farm and the woods and he appeared to drink it in.

His nearness engulfed me, but I felt no fear or desire to move. Secure, safe. Cody made me feel safe. Why did I suddenly feel this change, when before I only felt distrust and suspicion?

I turned to face him, startled to find his eyes burning with such intensity. "Thank you for all you've done for James. I know I've said this before, but words don't seem to be enough." Swallowing hard and feeling my face flush, I admitted, "I owe you an apology."

His look became quizzical and he started to speak, but I pressed my finger to his lips to stop him.

"No, let me finish. I haven't behaved very nice to you. You frighten me sometimes and I'm ashamed to say that I still don't think you've always been truthful with James and me."

His expression closed to that blank mask that I had seen him wear before and it suddenly saddened me to see him revert to it. He stepped back, putting a tangible distance between us; that to me, seemed to stretch into a chasm. Whatever softening I had sensed, had vanished. Taking a last deep breath, I returned to the cabin and my husband.

December 12, 1884

James' disposition has only grown worse. He is cranky and restless at being confined to bed. The winter has taken a strangle hold upon the land and will not let go. Cody ventures out in search of fresh meat for us and for that I am glad to have his assistance. He and James still sit and talk of plans for the spring, but James does not seem to be as enthusiastic now. I try to tell him that his leg will mend, it was a clean break. He must learn to be patient.

Preparations must be made for our Christmas celebration. I long for the glorious holiday parties that were so abundant back home. It seems a lifetime ago now when I twirled around the great ballrooms waltzing with my former beau, magnificent candelabras flickering. Our humble log cabin looks shabby and poor in deed. Oh well, I'm determined to make this a joyous holiday.

December 20, 1884

A loud knocking interrupted my writing, and I looked anxiously toward James and Cody, uncertain whether it was safe to answer the door. Cody waved his hand, motioning me to stay back then slowly moved to the entry. My eyes met James' worried expression then fell to the pistol held behind Cody's back.

Rose and Michael Canavan's voices called out to us as Cody cracked open the door and I sensed their surprise at being greeted by a stranger. Jumping up, I pushed Cody aside as I threw the portal wider and welcomed our friends.

"What are you doing out in this bad weather? How have you been? Come in; come in out of the cold!" I hugged my dear friend.

Cody went to sit quietly near the hearth, his eyes missing nothing.

Rose hugged me again and I realized how much I had missed seeing her. She glanced nervously toward Cody then her eyes fell on James' splinted leg. "Whatever happened to you?" she exclaimed as she hurried to his bedside.

Michael was at her heels as they both began asking questions at once and I heard James laugh out loud for the first time since the accident. I couldn't help smiling at the commotion their sudden arrival created. It might as well have been a storm that had blown into our small cabin.

"I'm fine, be up and about soon. Damn horse threw me; that's all. Cody here hauled my butt home."

Michael looked over at where Cody still sat quietly, studying him rather quizzically.

"Cody, is it?" Extending his hand, he made his own introductions, "Michael Canavan, sir, and my dear wife, Rose. I didn't catch the last name…"

I watched Cody as he shook the other man's hand briefly and appeared to hesitate before I finally heard him reply.

"Jarvis, Cody Jarvis."

He offered no other explanation or personal history. It seemed odd. I rushed to fill the void, feeling I owed my friends some explanation. "Cody is the man you helped rescue, don't you remember? He's been staying with us ever since he recovered from his wound and has offered to help James this spring with the ranch."

My voice dwindled as I realized that I was rambling on and none of the men were listening. I looked inquiring at James and Michael then back to Cody. Cody shrugged his shoulders and leaned back against the hearth. James was as puzzled as I.

Michael's demeanor visibly changed and his voice stiffened. "I've heard that name in Deer Springs. Jarvis, a gunslinger and low-down murderer, as I recall." He faced Cody and I held my breath waiting for his reaction to such an insult.

Cody's eyes met mine across the crowded space. I couldn't read his expression; couldn't read what he was thinking as he arose slowly, the chair legs scraping the wooden floor as it slid. Michael took a step backwards, nervous and uncertain now. Tension in the room was thick.

"Maggie, I'm going to go outside and see about that firewood we need for tonight."

"Thank you, Cody." My voice was barely a whisper, and I knew without a doubt that my 'thank you' was meant for more than firewood.

As soon as the door closed behind Cody, Rose turned to her husband, "Michael! Are you crazy? Are you trying to make me a widow?" She threw up her hands then flounced onto the edge of the bed, jiggling the mattress. James groaned loudly at the sudden movement, causing Rose to jump up guiltily. "Oh, I'm sorry James."

"Michael, are you sure you know Cody Jarvis?" James finally asked. "What makes you think he is this gunfighter?"

His answer greatly interested me too as I turned my full attention to the normally jovial man; although, it would explain some of my own niggling suspicions.

"The name's well known in town. Fella hangs around that rough bunch from the Diamond Bar Ranch, especially Zachary Logan. You folks havena' been here very long and don't know the trouble we've had in Deer Springs."

James shook his head in disbelief. "Have you seen Cody with this Logan man? What kind of problems are you talking about?"

I saw him glance between Michael and I, torn between his feelings of loyalty to his two new friends. I reached across the bed and patted his shoulder, trying to comfort him and convey my understanding. My own feelings careened crazily.

"Well, no, I havena' seen the two exactly together, but there's been talk. Logan's a bad sort. I heard he killed a man to get that big ranch of his, of course no one can prove it. His riders are all outlaws outside of the territory. Decent men willna' work for him."

"But that's no proof that Cody is mixed up with those criminals. Just because a man carries a gun does not make him a killer." I couldn't stop myself from defending him. Rose looked up sharply at my outburst.

"How much do you know about the man? Has he told you anything about himself? I don't like the idea of you two being alone with him. Do you think it's safe? And James laid up like he is, too."

Rose fretted and began to wring her hands; her eyes beseeched her husband to do something to help protect her friends.

"I suppose I could ride over once or twice a month; see how you're getting along. We only came today to wish you both a Merry Christmas. What with the heavy snow, didn't think we would have a chance to visit with you again for some time."

Michael suggested a plan he hoped his wife would approve. Although I had my own doubts as to whether such trips would be possible when the winter snows deepened, and the temperatures dropped even lower. Michael's danger would be far greater. I tried to remind him and Rose of the risk Michael would be taking and reassure them that we would be fine. They hastened to push my concerns aside and insisted that Michael would be able to do this. The argument continued for a few minutes more and I could see it was of no use. Michael would come or not; only the weather could prevent it.

Serving our guests hot tea and sweet rolls that I had baked special for the coming holiday, we talked of trivial matters and tried to forget the serious worries of the past hour. The time sped by in Rose's company; she was truly more a sister to me than a friend. Afternoon light began to dwindle as the Canavan family prepared to depart. We hugged each other fiercely and bade farewell; Michael repeating that he would return in two or three weeks.

As I watched them ride away, my thoughts returned guiltily to Cody. Was he the man that Michael spoke about? Was he a killer? Surely a ruthless gunfighter would not allow himself to be so insulted and then walk away from such a challenge. Did he do it for me? Where was he now? Should we trust him? My heart constricted and my head pounded.

CHAPTER 14

"I don't know, Jason, I'm more confused now than ever." Andy walked slowly back toward the line shack. She dragged her feet as her mind lingered on the words of her great-great-grandmother. She turned at the sound of Jason following close behind.

"No, I think we're getting somewhere. We just need to keep digging. After what you've already read, I'm certain the answers are in that book."

Andy looked at the eager expression on his face, surprised by his enthusiasm. Shaking her head in wonder, she stopped before the door and asked, "Why would you say that? I still only see a woman telling her tale of woe."

"Didn't one of the names sound familiar to you? Think. Remember the Canavans speaking of Zachary Logan?"

"Well …yes. Do you think he was related to Brent Logan?"

"I know for a fact that it is one and the same family. That's what I've been trying to tell you about. I saw the land records for the Diamond Bar. The deed references go back to Zachary Logan and about the same date as Margaret Dunlap's journal."

"Alright. So? There are a lot of people whose families put down roots a hundred years ago. Besides, isn't Brent Logan a close friend of your father's? I don't understand why you're trying to make a connection here. Am I being dense?"

"Call it a lawman's hunch. Call it anything you want. Something stinks and I smell trouble whenever Brent Logan is involved. He's been too interested in my affairs lately for me *not* to be suspicious. There's got to be a connection; I just haven't figured it out yet."

"All right, Sheriff. Boy, nobody better cross your path when you're in this kind of mood!" Andy laughed as she reached for Jason's hand and pulled him into the cabin.

"I think we better be riding back tomorrow. The boys can stay with the herd, can't they? I'll be impeached or something if I don't get back to town soon."

"Sure. I wasn't planning on remaining long after we set up the camp. Bill and Danny will stay and Frank can return with us."

"Good. I want you to promise me something. Don't travel alone. Make certain one of the guys is with you all the time. I just want you to be on your guard. Okay?"

Andy saw Jason's worried expression and his concern deeply touched her, making her forget that she was supposed to be angry with him. She reached out to brush that errant lock of hair from his forehead. Her fingers lingered to smooth the creases of a frown. Jason captured her hand in his own and drew it to his lips for a soft caress. He continued to hold her hand as his eyes imprisoned hers with a look of such heat and longing that Andy blushed. Time stood still as their eyes continued to speak volumes; the air around them crackled with sparks of hungry desire.

A loud cough broke the spell and Andrea hastened to pull her hand from Jason's grasp, moving backwards as Frank entered the cabin. Frank studied the young couple, their discomfort evident and laughed aloud.

Jason cringed at the thought of what the older man had witnessed. He would have liked to spare Andy more embarrassment. He knew she was angry with him for the other incident on the trail.

"We'll be heading back home tomorrow, Frank. Tell Bill and Danny that we can come back up in probably two weeks to drive 'em back down. That should give Gramps enough time to arrange a buyer for some of the head."

Andy tried to sound all business-like and not let the older man know that he had interrupted a very intimate moment. As she glanced from Jason to Frank, she realized that she had not fooled anyone.

"Fine Andy. I'll tell the boys. Think it's a good idea that we start heading home," Frank agreed as he walked back outside.

"Now what did he mean by that?" Andy asked exasperated, as Jason began to laugh again. "I don't see what's so funny!"

"You are, Andy my girl. You are." And with that Jason strolled outside too.

Ben Miller waited for his former deputy to hang up the phone. Dark circles shadowed his eyes and his hands shook nervously; he appeared to have aged twenty years in the past three weeks. He stared out the front window, not really watching anything, absorbed in his thoughts and jumped at the sound of Mac's voice speaking to him.

"So how've you been, Ben?"

"Huh? Listen, what I came in for today, I saw my old Jeep over at the S&G Garage. Looked pretty banged up. What happened?"

"Yeah, J.C. had a runaway coming off Iron Mountain."

"Where is J.C.? I haven't seen him around town in over a week." Ben paced the small office, wringing his hands. Beads of sweat glistened on his neck.

Mac took note of the retired sheriff's behavior and tried to reassure the older man. "J.C.? He's up in the hills. Hey, if you're worried about him, don't be. He's okay. You know J.C. rolls with the punches."

"That Jeep was in good condition when I gave it to him. He can't blame that accident on me." Ben grabbed his hat and hastened out of the jail.

"Hey, no one thinks that. Where're you going?" Mac called after his former boss, but he was already climbing into the cab of his pickup and hurrying off.

Ben Miller drove directly to his home and rushed to his telephone. Quickly rummaging through his desk drawer, he pushed papers aside until he found the memo pad that he needed. Tearing off the top sheet, he read the digits on it and crumpled the offending paper, tossing the scrap aside. He had to dial the number twice as his shaking hands pressed the wrong digits. Finally, the ringing stopped and a voice came on the line as he held the receiver with both hands.

"Is he there? I don't care what your orders are. I need to speak with him." He pulled a wadded handkerchief from his pant pocket and wiped his face while he waited. Eventually, he heard the sound of footsteps and the receiver being picked up.

"I don't like this one bit," Ben informed the other end of the line. "I want out. Yes, you heard me; I want no part of this. It was bad enough before, but I won't be a party to murder. What do you mean, I already am? You're crazy. I didn't have anything to do with that! It was an accident."

Ben sat down slowly as he listened in horror, shaking his head from side to side in disbelief at what he'd been told. "You can't make me help you anymore. I'm done. No, I mean it."

He slowly hung up the telephone and walked dejectedly into the kitchen. A half-empty bottle of Jim Beam sat on the table where he had left it from the night before. He grabbed the whiskey and picked up a filmy glass, studied the water spots on its side, then hurled it against the kitchen wall. The glass shattered into a hundred pieces. Ben took a long pull on the whiskey bottle, the fiery liquid burning a path down his throat, numbing him to the shame and guilt he felt. His life was as shattered as the broken tumbler strewn across the floor.

He sat drinking in the dark house. The black of night descended and enveloped him. He was alone. In a moment of crystal clarity, he realized what he needed to do. His service revolver lay on the table; he had cleaned it just yesterday. Picking up the gun, he spun the chambers, cocked the trigger and pressed it to his temple.

It was still early morning when Jason left Cedarhill and drove past the Deer Springs cemetery on his way into town. He slowed his truck as he watched the hearse and funeral procession turning into the lane. Jason raised his hand to shield his eyes from the morning sun as he peered at the line of cars. Wonder who had died? Have to get into town and get caught up on events after being gone over a week.

Local traffic was light as he passed the Eatery and noted the closed sign on the front window. He hastened toward the sheriff's office and found it empty as well. Mac had left him a note and other messages were piled on his desktop. Jason picked up Mac's note first, scanned it quickly then read it again; it explained his whereabouts. He sat down slowly, the paper held loosely between his fingers. He couldn't believe it… Ben Miller had committed suicide. Why?

The question echoed in his head over and over as he mechanically sorted through the other paperwork. Jason spied a group of newspapers piled in the corner and hurriedly sorted through the stack, tossing aside the older dates until he found what he was looking for. The headlines of the Deer Springs Gazette announced the sudden death of the town and county's former law officer, Ben Miller. Jason's eyes flew over the article as he absorbed the details of his old friend's death. 'Three days ago, apparent suicide, shot in the head, body found in his home' the report outlined. Cold facts but no reasons only led to more questions for Jason.

He sat mulling over the sad news, a coffee mug clutched in his hands as he leaned forward, elbows resting on the desktop. So lost in thought, he didn't even hear Mac as he entered the room. Jason kept staring at the wall, seeing Ben in his mind's eye, remembering the man who had been both his friend and employer.

"Glad you're back, J.C. Guess you've already heard the news and saw my note."

"Yeah, guess that was his funeral I passed on the way in; looked like half the town turned out. I just can't believe it." Jason ran his fingers through his hair, agitated and angry with himself. He got up to pace the room once more.

Mac watched in silence as his friend adjusted to the sad news. "Did you find Andrea Dunlap and get everything worked out, or whatever it was you had to do?"

"I should have been here, Mac; should have seen some sign or warning of Ben's state of mind. Do we have any more details? Did you seal off the area like a crime scene? What did the coroner's report state?"

"You can't blame yourself. I don't think there was anything either of us could have done. Fact is, he stopped in here just the day before he died and asked about you."

Jason's head jerked up and he abruptly quit pacing. "What did you say? He was in this office and asked about me. Why? What did he say exactly?"

"Well… he saw the wrecked Jeep and wanted to know what happened. I told him you had a runaway but weren't hurt. Then he said something odd, told me you couldn't blame him because the Jeep was running okay when he gave it to you."

"Now why would I have wanted to blame him? I never even thought about it."

"Maybe old Ben was getting paranoid." Mac told Jason as he pulled a folder from the file cabinet. The label on its edge read 'Miller, Benjamin'.

"Ben Miller might have been overly cautious at times, but paranoid? No, he worried a lot and maybe he retired too early, let it get on his nerves. Still…let me see that file. I want to look over all of the evidence. Who found the body and how long had he been dead?" Jason's mind started clicking, methodically arranging bits of information, as he tried to make sense of this latest puzzle.

"Ben's daughter Julie found him on Tuesday morning. Coroner said he'd been dead about twelve hours, rigor mortis had set in. Julie usually cleans his house once a week; poor girl got a hell of a shock finding him in a pool of blood. We found an empty bottle of Jim Beam on the table and some broken glass all over the kitchen floor," Mac relayed.

"Think I'll drive over and have a look around. Maybe try to make some sense out of all of this," Jason decided as he tucked the file under his arm and grabbed his Stetson.

As he drove the short distance to the Miller house, Jason tried to imagine what would drive a man to kill himself. Were there financial worries or a health problem that Ben had kept secret? The cold factual details of the coroner's report and a thousand questions replayed in Jason's mind like a broken record.

The weather-beaten frame house came into view as Jason turned the corner of Maple Avenue. Yards of yellow police tape marked a perimeter fence around the end of the house. Jason spied Julie's car parked next to the side door and pulled to a halt. The screen door cracked open, Julie peeked outside, drawn by the noise of the approaching vehicle.

"Oh, hello J.C. I was afraid it might be another one of those reporters. Come on in." Julie stepped back into the house and let Jason follow her.

She sat on one of the kitchen chairs; the floor at her feet still stained with her father's blood. Just this morning the coroner had permitted some neighbors to try and clean away the horrid reminder, but the red ooze had left its mark. Jason watched her make an effort to keep her eyes raised and not be drawn to the gory pattern.

"I'm sorry I wasn't here for your dad's funeral. I just got back into town this morning and hadn't heard the news. Is there anything that I can do for you? You know how I felt about Ben; he was a good man." Jason slowly tapped his hat against his leg. He felt so awkward and helpless. What do you say to a woman whose father just ended his life?

"Find out what happened, Jason. You owe Ben that much. And don't tell me what's been written down on some damn report. I know he shot himself. If you really want to help me, you'll find out why." Julie covered her face with her hands and began to cry.

"All right Julie. I guess I owe both of you that much. But I'm going to need your help. Can you tell me if he had been ill, or what had been bothering him lately? Was he worried about money? Give me some place to start."

"He never shared any problems with me but I think his health was okay. I can't think of anything else now. I'll try to call you later."

Jason patted her lightly on the shoulder, offering his silent condolence. He stood next to her while his eyes scanned the room, taking in minute details, mentally cataloging each item to review in his mind later and compare with the crime photos.

"Do you mind if I look around the rest of the house? I won't disturb anything."

"Go ahead, if you want. There isn't much here. Dad wasn't much for hanging on to things; he was never guilty of being called a pack rat."

"Thanks, Julie. I'll only be a minute then I'll leave you alone. I hate intruding."

Jason slowly walked into the living room, studying the neat but sparse furnishings. Julie was right; Ben definitely had not been a pack rat. A bookcase sat against one wall was filled with a few dime store paperbacks, mostly cheap detective stories. Jason ran his finger down a few book spines, reading the titles then dismissed them. One desk drawer spilled out an assortment of papers. The drawer lay partially closed, crooked on its track. Occupying a place of honor in the center of the small desk sat a framed photograph of Julie and her father. Jason glanced at it as he noted the other desktop articles: two pens and a pencil lay near a scrap of memo pad; the memo pad printed with some pharmaceutical company's logo, like the kind you get as a free sample in the mail. Jason picked up the paper; a slight impression on the paper drew his attention.

Feeling like one of those detectives in Ben's cheap mysteries, Jason rubbed the side of a lead pencil against the impression. Digits of a phone number magically appeared as white lettering on the dark lead coloring.

"Hey! It works." Jason laughed out loud. He tore off the notepaper and folded it carefully. Anything could be a lead.

The wastebasket was empty, no clues in the trash. The bathroom proved to be just as empty - no prescription drug bottles, nothing out of the ordinary. Jason returned to the desk and opened its three drawers, rummaged through a group of clipped papers and receipts, looking for anything or something that might catch his eye. Nothing did. Blank, empty… just a household checkbook, various bills, papers and some paid repair receipts. Jason took the checkbook; he'd inquire about the bank balance and look for any odd transactions, standard operating procedure. Who knows?

"Julie, I've got a few items from your Dad's desk. I'm going to check out a couple of things and I'll return these to you in a day or two. Okay? You call me if you think of anything, anything at all."

He paused briefly next to her chair, touched her shoulder again lightly, then courteously tipped the brim of his hat, and left the house.

Jason tossed the few items into an empty envelope, slipping it into the Miller file folder lying on the front seat of the Explorer.

He headed back to the office to make some calls.

CHAPTER 15

Andy shook out her rawhide lariat then checked its honda, adjusting the loop, and began twirling the lasso above her head. She roped the hitching rail on the corral fence a few times; stretching the muscles in her arms, practicing her throw. Sam stood to one side of the corral gate as he watched his granddaughter.

"You thinking of entering the roping contest this year at the rodeo?"

"Thought I might. We could sure use the prize money. How else are we going to pay that stack of bills?" Andy said as she swirled the braided rope once more and let it fly. Satisfied that she hadn't lost her touch, she slowly coiled the lasso as she strode toward the cattle pen. Andy settled her Stetson firmer in place, tugged on her leather gloves and mounted Buttercup. Leaning across the horse's neck to unlatch the pen's gate, she swung it open, a determined look on her face. She led the quarter horse into the pen among the few calves. The animals shied away from this new threat, bawling and moving to the opposite side of the corral. Andy did not need to coax Buttercup as the trained horse sensed her purpose and began to pursue one of the calves, cutting back and forth as the animal ran. Andy pressed her knees against the horse's flanks as she held the lariat with her right hand, spinning a tight circle above her head then letting it fly forward. The loop fell gracefully around the calves' neck and Andy drew it tight, quickly looping the rope around her saddle horn. The taut rope yanked the animal to a halt as Andy leaped down from her saddle and ran to the calf. In a few seconds she had tied three feet together and the calf lay helpless.

Andy looked toward the elder Dunlap. "Gramps, how much time?" She knew she would have to practice in order to keep her total elapsed time short enough for competition. Some of the best cowboys in the county would be at the annual Frontier Days fair and rodeo.

Sam studied his watch then shook his head negatively, "Pretty slow gal. Your aim's fine, but too slow yanking that calf down. Gonna take a lot of practicing before you're ready."

"Then I guess that's what I'll have to do. I'm just warming up," Andy informed him, as she untied the calf and it quickly sprang to its feet. She gathered up her lasso and ties and climbed into the saddle for another try. Andy gave her grandfather a look that said she would practice until she dropped. She had to do something to bring in some extra money for the ranch.

"Get ready and I'll signal go," Sam told her, shaking his head at her stubbornness and watching the second hand of his timepiece.

Andy and Buttercup went into motion again, cutting out a calf from the group and roping the animal in a few seconds. Andy worked for the better part of three hours before she felt her time was improving. She raised her arms and stretched tired muscles, bending from side to side then flexed her hand and cramped fingers.

"Guess I forgot what hard work this can be. Think I'll rest Buttercup for a few minutes while I get some cold water to drink."

Sam laughed as he watched her walk slowly toward the house. "You do that!"

A tow truck sat parked out front and both garage bay doors stood open in the afternoon heat. A late model Chevy station wagon sat perched atop one of the hydraulic lifts. Gaskets and belts of varying sizes decorated the walls while cans of motor oil and transmission fluid filled three steel shelving units along the west wall. Smitty wiped the grease from his hands and began picking up his socket wrenches. He looked up from his chore as Jason entered the garage.

"Hey J.C., you here to pick up the Jeep? Me and George tried to fix her up the best we could; front end's got some damage from where you smacked into that sand bank. We also had to completely replace the brake line."

"Could you tell whether or not the line had been cut or if it just broke?"

"Oh no doubt about it, cut cleaner than a whistle; no ripping or snags on the hose."

"If it had been cut all the way through, why would I have had any brakes at all? I didn't make any stops on the road after I left Cheyenne, no one could have tampered with the Jeep, and my brakes were rock hard before then. It would have to have been during the time I was in town. Are you sure you didn't overlook something?"

"Hey, we went over that Jeep with a fine- tooth comb, just like you asked. Did find one thing odd … some kind of sticky goo on the brake line where it had been cut." Smitty snapped his fingers and a grin lit his face like a hundred-watt light bulb. "Yeah, maybe that stuff kept the brake fluid from pouring out; would only leak slow, until finally it'd be all gone, and you'd be left with a brake pedal on the floor."

"All right Smitty, that's all I needed to know. If the Jeep's drivable, Mac can come back and get it later. I've got some other stops to make right now." Jason stood next to the dented Jeep, rubbing his chin, deep in thought as he mentally filed the mechanics conjecture for future use. "By the way, Smitty, did you save any of the goo you found? I'd like to have a look at that."

"Well, here's the line we took off, you can still see the junk," the mechanic replied as he handed J.C. a length of rubber encased hose.

Jason touched the sticky substance, rolling some it between his fingers. "Hmm, okay, thanks for all your hard work. Hey Smitty, think this stuff could be used on other kinds of engine lines?"

"Dunno, maybe. Whatcha' driving at?"

"Hmm, just a thought. I may stop back in. Oh, before I forget, make up an invoice and drop it off; the county will pay your bill." Jason spoke over his shoulder as he walked toward his car.

"Right. See you later, Sheriff."

Andrea winced as her fingers touched a tender spot on her right shoulder where she had body slammed a large calf on her last yank. The bruise would be a lovely blue color by morning. She closed her eyes and savored the soothing hot water as she sank lower into the bubble filled tub. Her head throbbed as much as her shoulder; the intense heat of the day combined with the unusual exertion and stress were taking their toll. Andy dipped a cloth into the steamy water then laid it gently across her forehead, relaxing under the warm compress. Sighing contentedly, she decided to lie there until her knees wrinkled. Nothing could entice her to move. She'd indulge herself in this purely feminine luxury. Sometimes, recalling that you really were a girl had some advantages. Andy reached out and blew on a handful of frothy bubbles.

Her mind drifted, lulled by the soothing warm water with its light jasmine scent. Andy's thoughts turned to Jason, his face swimming before her closed eyes. A smile curled her lips as she remembered the feel of his arms around her and the fiery kiss they shared before they had parted. She missed him. She hadn't seen him in the last couple of days; she'd been so busy on the ranch. Even with the main body of the herd up-country, there were always plenty of chores to be done and they were shorthanded until Bill and Danny returned.

"Andy! You ever gonna get out of that tub, gal? Other people in this house might like to use the bathroom, you know," Sam's voice called up to her from the foot of the stairs.

"All right, give me a few more minutes," she shouted through the oaken door. Andy reluctantly stepped out from the now tepid water and reached for a fluffy bath towel. She started rubbing her arms and legs dry while her mind wandered, settling once more on the topic of Jason Hartman. He was beginning to consume more and more of her mind these days. "I think I'll go into town tomorrow," Andy told her reflection in the mirror. She smiled mischievously at the image before her, her headache gone, replaced with the anticipation of seeing Jason.

It was close to noon when Andy finished her chores and ran upstairs to change. She gave her hair a quick brushing and surveyed her appearance in the dresser mirror. She liked what she saw – the white eyelet embroidered blouse felt cool on yet looked crisp and clean over the pair of black twill shorts. She donned a pair of black leather sandals, pleased that they helped to flatter her tanned legs. A picture of health and happiness showed on her face; an expression that had not been there in a long time.

Andy skipped gaily down the stairs, calling to Sam as she passed through the house, "I'm on my way into town, Gramps. I might do a little shopping or something. See you later for dinner. Need anything?"

"No, you go ahead and have a good time. Don't worry about me for supper if you want to stay." He watched her move with a spring in her step and a glow on her face. *"She's in love. I wonder if she even knows it,"* Sam spoke to the door post as the old pickup rumbled down the gravel drive. He slapped his thigh and chuckled as he went back to his work.

Andrea pulled to a halt in front of the sheriff's office, telling herself that it was the only open parking space along the street. She closed the truck door and glanced nervously around, not wanting her destination to be obvious to any casual observer. Strolling along the sidewalk Andy stopped to peek into the windows of three different shops, browsing the merchandise displayed there, before turning back and pausing by the entrance of the jail. Taking a deep breath, she pushed open the door and scanned the vestibule before her eyes fell on Mac.

"Hello. Is Sheriff Hartman here?"

"Hi Andy. J.C. is having lunch at the Eatery. Did he know you were coming to town today?"

"No, I'm just doing a little shopping. Nothing important. Really, I just wanted to say hello. Maybe I'll see him at Maybelle's." Embarrassed that Mac might recognize her true intentions, Andy gave a quick smile and waved goodbye, practically stumbling as she backed out the door. She wasn't certain as she slid onto the truck's seat and turned the key, but she thought she heard Mac laughing.

Andy's cheeks were just beginning to cool down as she parked by the Eatery. Jason's Explorer was in the lot. She swallowed and took a deep breath; she'd just order lunch and casually ask how things were going. OK, that was a good plan. Confident again, Andy strode toward the entrance.

The Eatery was filled with the customary lunch time crowd. Maybelle had her regulars and a few new faces sat among the group. Veronica Logan sat sipping her cup of coffee, watching Jason closely. She wasn't one of Maybelle's usual customers but had entered the diner when she spied J.C.'s truck in the lot. Now her impatience was rising because he had yet to greet her or come to her table. She had just decided to rise and approach him when her attention turned to a new attraction. She stood waiting, a smug smile pasted on her face.

"Hey Andy, been busy? Haven't seen you in here in weeks," Maybelle greeted her warmly as she watched the girl scan the seated diners then stop in mid-stride.

Jason sat in the rear booth, his back to the door. Pretty Julie Miller sat in front of him. They were speaking quietly, heads lowered, and Jason's hands reached across the tabletop to clasp both of Julie's in his stronger ones. Andy stood frozen, watching the intimate scene. Pain pierced her chest and the ugly barbs of jealousy wrapped around her heart.

Julie raised her eyes and recognized Andrea Dunlap standing in the center of the aisle. Andy's wounded expression made Julie pause in mid-sentence as she was thanking Jason for all of his help following her father's death. Her behavior caused Jason to turn in his seat, curious as to the reason for the distraction. His eyes instantly fell upon Andy.

"Andy!"

Seeing him move broke Andy's hypnotic stare and spurred her to action. She spun on her heel and ran for the door as she heard

Jason call her name. Her heart pounded in her ears and her face felt on fire. She had to get away from here, as far away as possible. Tears of humiliation rolled down her cheeks. It hurt that Jason could so openly display his affection for another woman when he had declared his love to her. And she like a fool had believed him and was ready to admit her love to him. Thank God she had been spared that last shame. He would never have that satisfaction.

Jason jumped up and hurried after Andrea, pushing aside another woman standing in the aisle. He muttered "sorry" without even glancing back as he ran for the parking lot.

Veronica swore viciously as Jason bumped her shoulder in his haste to rush after Andy. She lost her balance and plopped abruptly onto the seat of the booth, seething at the laughter ringing in her ears. Maybelle nodded her silent approval and two men in adjoining booths snickered.

"That bitch Andy! This is her fault. I'll pay her back; I swear I will."

Andy's foot pushed the accelerator to the floor as the old truck roared down the dirt and gravel road, skidding dangerously in the turns with the break-neck pace. Gravel spewed under her tires. Steam poured out of the radiator and Andy could barely see to steer. She drove the familiar road home by memory, slamming on the brakes as she entered the Circle-D gates. She knew Jason would be catching up with her in a matter of seconds; he had run out of the Eatery as she had raced down the street ahead of him. His newer, more powerful truck would quickly overtake her older one.

Police lights flashed, the siren blared, but to no affect. Andy did not stop or even slow until she had reached the Circle-D. Jason cursed as their speeds reached 80mph on the winding gravel road. He worried that Andy's rickety jalopy wouldn't be able to stand up to such torture. Damn her, why won't she stop?!

Andy's truck door stood ajar and steam hissed from under the hood as Jason screeched to a halt. jumped out of his Explorer; the red and blue jelly-bean lights still flashed as he ran for the front porch of the Dunlap house. Pounding his fist on the door, he planned to confront Andy about her reckless driving.

Sam stood calmly facing the angry young man; sounds of Andrea's sobbing drifted down from her upstairs bedroom. He wasn't certain what had happened, but it had to be serious. Andrea was not the type to throw a feminine fit and Jason was usually always in control. Life had turned upside down for these two young people. Sam crossed his arms against his chest and waited patiently for Jason to begin.

"I want to speak to Andy."

"She's not available at the moment."

"I am an officer of the law and when I signal her to pull over, she damn well better do it. Those are flashing police lights and she disobeyed every traffic law in the book! I demand to see her."

Jason's temper was still riding high as he began to pace the length of the porch. He ran his hand through his hair, then letting his hand fall back to his side, returned to stand in front of Sam.

"Look Sam, will you just tell her that I need to talk with her. She doesn't understand."

"She's upset right now Jason. It would be better if you both wait until later. I don't know what's wrong between the two of you, but I don't think this is a good time."

"Maybe you're right. She's wrong in what she thinks she saw. You tell her I said that."

Jason angrily strode to his truck, flipped a switch to shut down the flashers and drove off.

From her upstairs window, Andrea watched the colorful lights go dark and the cloud of road dust floated upwards as the sound of Jason's engine faded into the distance. She'd never felt so lonely. "Dad was right, you can't trust the Hartmans. I should have listened."

CHAPTER 16

January 3, 1885

The New Year arrived in a flurry of more snow. The wind rattled the roof planks, knocking one loose and dumping a pile of the wet, cold stuff right in the middle of James' bed. He, of course, bellowed loud enough to wake the dead, scaring me to death. Cody calmly picked up his coat and wrapped my heavy woolen scarf about his head and neck and prepared to go out into the storm.

"Do you have a hammer? I'll do what I can."

What tools we owned were collected in a canvas sack that hung on a hook near our food stuffs. I reached for the bag and handed it to him, my hand lingering on his.

"Be careful up there. Don't you go falling off and giving me another invalid to care for."

A brief smile touched his lips and his eyes narrowed as he studied me for a long minute before he patted the top of my hand in reassurance. "Don't worry Maggie. I'll be all right."

Aware that James was listening intently to our conversation, I moved hastily away and began to prepare a meal for us all. I could hear Cody grunt with the exertion of climbing onto the roof while his cautious moving about caused more snow to fall through the cracks. James attempted to get out of bed, standing on one leg, so I propped my shoulder under his to lend support while he hobbled over to the chair by the hearth. The bed covers were quickly becoming soaked, and I struggled to pull them off the heavy feather tick.

Cody swept away the piles of snow to expose the warped shingles then hammered the loose nails, pushing the slats closer together. I watched his efforts as the amount of daylight shining through the rooftop diminished. The chilly whistling of the wind seemed to lessen too, thanks to his attentions; one more thing for which I would have to thank this man. Truly he was a blessing at times. I stopped stirring the porridge as I realized just how much I was relying on him. Of course, that would all change as soon as James was well again. That's all it was.

Cody came stomping back into the cabin, his cheeks and nose bright red from the cold. I started to laugh when I saw him.

"You look like Saint Nicholas! Look at that red face."

"Well, that's a fine way to thank a man for risking his life to keep you warm and dry."

I looked at him shame-faced, but I could see the laughter in his own eyes now and I relaxed. Our jovial mood was in sharp contrast to James' sullenness. Suddenly I felt guilty for forgetting my husband, left to wait uncomfortably in a chair. I used to be able to joke with James like that; but now he was forever in such a sour mood. Sometimes I think that fall broke more than his leg; it broke his spirit too. I turned my mind back to the chore at hand and shaking out the heavy quilt, tried to restore the bed to a warm, dry condition.

"Cody, can you assist James back to bed while I serve the food?"

"Here James, let me get a shoulder under you. How's that leg feeling today?"

"Oh just dandy… no thanks to the nonsense I have to sit and listen to. A man could starve around here. Where's that bottle of whiskey?"

"Do you really need it, James? I thought the leg was mending?" I had noticed that he had been liberally helping himself to the spirits ever since the night of the accident.

"And I say it hurts. I should know if I need it, not you!"

"All right, here." I reluctantly handed him the bottle and his breakfast tray. I had baked more sweet rolls and added one to his tray along with the bowl of porridge. He never even noticed it and I had only thought to pleasure him with the treat. They used to be his favorite. Nothing I do nowadays seems to please him. I must have made some audible sigh because when I turned, I found Cody watching me.

He lifted the two, steaming bowls of porridge from my hands, carrying them to the small table.

"It's all right Maggie. He'll get over this," Cody's voice held a note of tenderness in it that I had not heard before. Was it genuine concern for us, or pity?

I shrugged and chose not to comment. It would be disloyal to James to speak critically of him and air our marriage problems to another. We had just celebrated Christmas and I would not speak unkindly or be less than Christian. I knew Cody still watched me as

I bent my attention to the plain but nourishing breakfast that was becoming our mainstay.

The silence filled the room as we all ate. Cody cleared his throat and the sound echoed off the timbered walls. It startled me momentarily, making me realize how nervous I had become.

"I'll be going out to hunt again and if the snow's not too deep, maybe go into Deer Springs. We could use some supplies from town. I was thinking of leaving in the morning."

It was the first time that he had suggested going into town. I admit I thought he was avoiding town; I'm not sure why that thought came to mind, just a feeling. Guess I was wrong.

"All right, I'll make a list of what we need the most; bring back whatever you can find. I'll trust your judgment on what's a fair price. There isn't much money."

"Do the best I can, Maggie."

"Don't forget to pick up another bottle of whiskey. It's the only thing that helps kill the taste of this slop my wife feeds me!" James hurled the bowl of half-eaten porridge across the room. The stoneware shattered and the sticky oats plastered the wall and floor. James slumped back upon his bed, clutching the half-empty bottle to his chest.

I bent to pick up the pieces of the broken bowl. Suddenly feeling over whelmed by it all, James with his temper and the wintry isolation, I sat down in the middle of the debris and began to cry. I sobbed so hard, my shoulders shook. I couldn't seem to stop; don't know how long I sat there crying.

Strong arms lifted me then held me against a stalwart chest, stroking my hair and patting my back until the crying lessened. I raised my head from his tear-soaked shoulder and searched Cody's face, trying to find an answer to the questions and feelings swimming in my mind.

His eyes searched mine, reading my soul, then his lips lowered to mine as he kissed me once, ever so gently. Cody held my face in his callused palms as he kissed the tears from my closed eyelids, my cheeks, and the tip of my nose then returned to my waiting mouth. God help me, but I returned his kiss with a yearning that shocked both of us. Breathing heavily, I pulled away from his embrace as shame washed over me. I quickly looked to where James lay, snoring loudly, fearful that he had witnessed my sin.

"I think you better see if you can stay in town when you get to Deer Springs. Please try to understand, Cody. It'll be better."

"Who is going to take care of you if I'm not here, that drunk? Think about what you're saying, Maggie."

"Don't call my husband a drunk. I'll be all right. I need time to think; you're confusing me. Please…"

The small cabin didn't afford any privacy; there was no place to go to be alone with your own thoughts. Cody nodded his acceptance of my decision. He would go. The strain of my warring emotions was etched on my face. How can I face Cody every day, feeling as I do? How can I face every day without seeing him? And tomorrow he leaves.

January 29, 1885

The weather has grown colder if that is possible, but thankfully, no new snow. I chopped and split wood for hours and yet the stockpile was meager. We will burn most of it in one night if the temperatures continue to drop. James blames me for sending Cody away and for making him do without his whiskey. He's become cruel and petty; the fanciful dreamer I married is gone. I don't know if he suspects the real reason Cody left or if he believes the story that I told him. I'm at a point where I don't care anymore what he thinks. Maybe things will be better come spring, maybe we will both begin our life together anew. Isn't that what spring is for, fresh beginnings?

I would surely go mad if not for this journal keeping me company. I swear, at times I think I am hearing things - like now, hoof beats in the distance.

The sound grew louder as I ran to the door to identify the approaching rider. He sat tall in the saddle and even bundled in his thick sheepskin and leather coat, I could tell that he wasn't a heavy man such as Michael Canavan. There was only one other man that would have cause to visit the Dunlap home.

Cody reined his horse to a halt and dismounted quickly when he spied me standing in the open doorway. He tied the stallion in the lean-to and hurried to the cabin. Had I been on his mind as much as he had dwelled in mine? He reached for my hands as I watched his eyes take in my appearance, not missing the tiniest detail.

"May I come in, Maggie?"

"Cody. I didn't think I would see you again."

I watched him scan the dark interior of the cabin. I'd had to conserve our lamp oil and candles, only lighting them in the evening hours. The fire had burned low, only a few logs were stacked within the hearth. James sat in the middle of our bed playing solitaire with a worn deck of cards, his favorite past time now. I saw my home through Cody's eyes as he took in the soiled dishes and the dried food still on the floor from where James had thrown his previous meal. It was the expression on Cody's face when his eyes came to rest on me that was my undoing.

"What happened, Maggie? Did James hit you?" He asked as his fingers gingerly touched my bruised eye and swollen cheek.

I had ceased to care how I looked and now was ashamed at my own filthy clothing and battered appearance. My dirty hair hung down my back in a tangled mess and even my skin was not clean. What had happened indeed?

I shook my head in the negative, not knowing how to begin or even if I should. How do you tell another man that the man you married had changed into a sullen, dark individual? I feel like I am living with a stranger and now the man who entered my life as a stranger means more to me than I am free to say. He reached out to touch me again and I forced myself to take a step backwards, rejecting the touch I so yearned for. It can never be, and I must not let myself dream of something that I cannot have.

Cody always seemed to be able to read my mind and he saw my despair now. He strode purposefully toward James and I watched in a detached way. Cody grabbed James by the arm and pulled him off the bed. James looked startled and I realized that he had not even noticed Cody before that moment.

"James, stand up man! You need some exercise and I'm going to see to it that you get out of that bed and back on your feet. Your wife deserves better and by God you are going to provide it. Get up, I said. Don't even think of sitting back down."

Cody was holding his anger in tight control. He propelled James toward the door by an iron grip on his arm that would not loosen, reaching for James' coat as they left.

The brittle air hit James smack in the face and sobered him like nothing could. He quickly donned his woolen coat and stood stamping some warmth into his feet. "Where the hell have you been? What gives you the right to come back here and drag me out into the cold? Are you crazy?"

"Here, put this to work and it will warm you right up." Cody thrust the wood axe into James' hands and pointed to the dwindling stack of logs that needed splitting. Seeing James adjust his stance to maintain his balance on the still splintered leg, Cody nodded satisfied and walked back to his horse to retrieve several parcels. He had bought supplies and now carried them into the house.

"Maggie, I brought you a few things. You never did make out that list, but I chose a couple of items I thought you could use."

I looked among the packages to discover some new candles, a bar of scented soap, a tin of salted pork, several canning jars of beans, bags of flour, sugar, and oats. Cody handed me one last bundle wrapped in brown paper. I opened it slowly as he watched me closely. A cloth bound book rested atop a folded blue fabric. When I picked up the cloth and shook it out, I realized that Cody had brought me a ready-made, store bought dress. The soft blue cotton was adorned with tiny white flowers, with a lace edged collar and leg-of-mutton sleeves. The wide skirt billowed with yards of fabric that would swirl when I walked. Delight over his gift shone on my face and my hands caressed the dress lovingly.

"Oh Cody, where did you get everything? But I can't accept; the dress is far too lovely."

He knew my protests were feeble as he leaned towards me to speak quietly, "the dress is a late Christmas present. I insist. When I saw it I knew that no one but you could wear it. The book is to help keep you company."

"But Cody…"

"Take it as my way of an apology then, Maggie. To see you like this, I can't forgive myself for letting you come into harm's way. I should never have left you, but I couldn't stay away."

His words warmed my heart and soul. If only it could be so. The sound of wood chopping caught my attention as I shot Cody an inquiring look.

"I put James to work. He needs the fresh air; he will never get better by lying about that bed all the time. Are you going to tell me what happened around here while I was gone?"

"Not now, maybe later, when I find the right words."

"All right Maggie. Can I see you in that dress?"

"I'm afraid I need a good scrubbing before I am fit to touch something so fine."

"Well lady, fill a kettle with water and I'll bring in the firewood to heat it. This cabin isn't much warmer than outside. What were you thinking of to let things get so run down? Never mind, I won't harp on the subject." He reached out to gently caress the side of my face, his hand dropping to linger on my shoulder. "Thank God I returned when I did. It scares the hell out of me to think what I might have found if I had waited until spring."

He turned and went back outside to begin carrying in armloads of firewood. I filled a hip bath with some water and put the kettle on to boil more. Suddenly, the simple idea of a hot bath appealed to my senses and made me feel more alive than I had in weeks.

I draped a long quilt over a clothesline to create a makeshift privacy screen at one end of the cabin and began disrobing as soon as the bath was filled with hot water. The water soothed both my bruised body and tortured mind as I soaked in its liquid heat. A light lavender scent drifted from the rare bar of soap. Memories of formal gardens and moonlit summer nights floated on the sweet fragrance. A happier time remembered - filled with future dreams and promises. It seemed so far away now. Where was the young girl that blushed with her first kiss and vowed to honor a marriage promise agreed between two old families? Did she perish on the trek westward, or did she just mature and face the realities of life?

"Maggie? You didn't drown in that tub, did you? If I don't hear any sound soon, I'm coming in to check on you." Cody's humor was infectious. I splashed the water for an answer.

"She still in that bath? I'm getting hungry. Hurry up Margaret." James hobbled over to sit in a chair by the fireplace and enjoy the hot blaze licking at the fresh supply of wood.

"Here James, have some of this chewing tobacco. I brought this special for you. You know, we ought to take off that splint and let the leg finish mending on its own. You don't need that crutch."

"Since when did you become a doctor? I think I liked you better when you were gone."

"James, how can you say such a thing? After all the help that Cody has been?" My words chastised him through the curtain as I reluctantly left my watery haven and carefully rubbed dry my bruised arm and side. James certainly had regained his strength all right, especially when fueled with liquor. I shuddered slightly at the memory of the ugly fight we had and the cruel beating. Cody must not see these purple marks; his patience with James was dangerously deceptive. I wouldn't know how to control him if he unleashed his anger.

Sliding back the quilt, I stepped from behind my curtain to display my lovely new frock. The dress fit me as if it had been custom made. The high collar accentuated a slender neck and the fitted bodice clung to my round breasts in what appeared indecent without the benefit of a corset. The wide skirt did swirl around my legs making me feel regal with every step.

Cody nodded approvingly, his genuine smile lighting his eyes as well. I stood in the center of the room and slowly turned to model the beautiful gown. For that split second I felt young and alive again, admired by my beau. It was exhilarating.

James snorted in disgust, "Still playing lady of the grand manor? A pity your face spoils the dress." He swung his arm wildly, intent on backhanding me, but stumbled sideways instead.

The joyous smile on my face vanished at the cruelty of his words. My fairy tale had burst. Cody reacted in a lightning swift movement. His recoiled fist connected with James' jaw in a solid impact that sent James sprawling flat. Cody stood with legs spread apart, one hand dangerously fingering the butt of his Colt revolver, as he waited for James to move.

"Touch her again and I'll kill you," he spoke in a deadly calm.

"Cody, no! It doesn't matter; it isn't worth a life."

I watched the silent play in horror. Cody's stark, violent temper frightened me far more than James' abuse. The joy of seeing him again abruptly shattered. This was an ugly side of him that I had never witnessed before.

"Get out. I won't have a gun wielding murderer under my roof. Take back your gifts too." My trembling hands began to unbutton the gown and I slipped it off my body, standing before him in nothing but my chemise and petticoats. I thrust the dress into his arms and pointed toward the door.

"You're making a mistake." His face returned to its cold, chiseled look. No emotion shone behind his eyes; only a small tic in his cheek gave evidence of a clenched jaw. He turned and slowly walked away.

The door shut behind him. I stood in the center of the room staring at the closed door, listening to the sound of my heartbeat drumming in my ears. Cold shivers finally broke my reverie and I dragged my old clothes back on. Now, I must drape the pieces of my life about me like a worn coat, shabby and ill fitting, but serviceable. Any happiness that Cody offered was an illusion. My marriage to James was my harsh reality and it would take some mending.

CHAPTER 17

A clock ticked loudly in the silent room as Jason sat at his desk carefully studying the contents of the file in front of him. He read each document and testimony, scribbled a note here and there in the margins then began reading them again. Searching for the one item that he had overlooked; he knew the answer had to be in there somewhere. Jason stood up to stretch his arms above his head then slowly paced the length of the quiet office.

Mac would be back from traffic detail soon. September and school in session again always required a traffic cop to direct the flow of buses and cars through Deer Springs' only busy intersection. Maybe the Town Council would finally agree to a real traffic signal one day. Move the town right into the twentieth century, wouldn't that be something?!

Jason began to methodically arrange the papers on his desk. Some he placed in one pile with a manila file folder, a second group with Brian's logbook, and others around a county plat map. He stepped back to survey his work then spied a corner of another paper peeking out from under a larger document. He touched the corner and nudged it out from its hiding spot. Jason stared at the scrap with the pencil rubbed telephone number that he had retrieved from Ben Miller's. It had gotten lost in the shuffle.

He dialed the number quickly then waited as the ringing sounded once, twice, a third time and then a click as the receiver was picked up. Jason held his breath as he listened closely.

"Hello?" A woman's voice, vaguely familiar, came across the line. It was velvety smooth, falsely seductive in its tone— Veronica.

Jason began to slowly lower the receiver when his ear caught a belligerent, decidedly male voice in the background and he strained to listen again. "Damn it, I told you to never answer my private line."

"What's all this?" Mac's voice carried across the room as he entered the sheriff's office.

"Quiet!" Jason hissed to his deputy and quickly hung up the receiver; afraid the line was still open.

Veronica stood with the receiver dangling from her hand, the line gone dead. She knew that voice. She'd know it anywhere, soft or loud. That was J.C. Hartman on the other end of that line. Why would he be calling her father? How strange!

"Who was it?" Brent Logan demanded. He grabbed the telephone from her hand then hung it up as the annoying beep wailed.

"Hmm? I don't know. Guess they hung up when they heard a woman's voice. Having an affair, Daddy?" She smiled knowingly.

"My affairs are none of your business or your mother's, so don't think you're going to run and tell tales. What are you doing in here anyway?"

"I need some more money. My allowance is gone and I want to go shopping." She pouted her lips and posed prettily, waiting. Getting her calculated response, she smiled at her father and raised her face to brush a kiss on his cheek as she snatched the stack of bills from his outstretched hand. In two long strides she was through the door and flying out of the house.

Brent Logan stood staring out the window, watching his spoiled daughter. She was the one person he actually cared about and he knew he would never say no to her. All he worked for over the years, all the business deals he achieved were for her, not that haughty bitch he married. He was determined to continue building his empire to make the Logan name respected throughout the state and leave a legacy for the grandchildren he hoped Veronica would give him. His family had lived in Deer Springs for over a hundred years and started their ranch from scratch and nothing or no one would ever stop him or tear down his ancestor's heritage. His thoughts strayed to all that he had done to protect that heritage and knew there was no turning back now.

"I've been trying to make some sense out of all this," Jason waved his hand toward the neat stacks of papers. "Hey, do we still have that extra desk blotter, the one that looks like a big calendar? Last time I saw it was January, I think; stuck between the wall and that file cabinet."

Mac went over to the far wall and crouched down, upon closer inspection he pulled out the object in question. "Is this what you want?"

"Yep. Need your help, Mac. Take this flight log of Dunlap's and jot his name and destination on every date you find that he went out of town during, say, May through July."

"OK. What are we looking for?"

"A pattern… some link. It's here; I just need to dig deeper. I've got an idea." Jason rummaged through his desk and triumphantly produced three different colored magic markers. He spread the plat map open on an adjacent worktable along with a full map of the state.

Mac watched him as he began to draw outlines on each map. J.C. would work a case like a jigsaw puzzle, arranging and rearranging the pieces until he found a match. Mac smiled and shook his head, knowing his boss and friend would be like a determined bulldog, chewing on a problem until he solved it. The deputy glanced down at the dates listed on the singed flight log and got to work on his own project.

Jason stood back and surveyed his artwork, satisfied, then peered over Mac's shoulder to see his results. It looked like there were only three trips made in May by Andy's father, but ten out of town during June and more in July. Wonder why the increased travel?

"That about it? Got all of them recorded, including the day of the crash?"

"Yeah, I think so. Now what?"

"Here's Ben's appointment book and cruiser mileage log. Match any dates and places Ben has with Dunlap's schedule. Use the blue marker and write his on that calendar too. From the looks of the maintenance record on that Jeep, Ben was sure putting on some heavy driving mileage during the past months. The boys down at S&G mentioned they did more oil changes on that thing this summer than the past two years combined."

"I guess I never paid much attention whenever Ben was out of the office. I just assumed he was around town or home. Didn't you?" "Most of the time, Mac, I was too busy with my own duties and juggling chores for the ranch to miss him. Guess that's why I feel so bad now. He was involved with something and getting in over his head; I should have been there to help pull him out."

Both men grew silent as they thought of their dead friend. Mac wrote Ben's name in a square on the July month then paused as he realized that Brian Dunlap's name also occupied that date. Jason and Mac studied the large calendar that now resembled a checkerboard with its color shaded squares. It seemed that Ben and Brian had similar schedules; their paths crossed and met at several locations and always on the same day. Interesting!

Mac rubbed his forehead as he stared at the results and then back at J.C. "What about that? Did you know this?"

"No, my friend, I didn't. But I've been going through Ben's papers and things Julie told me just began to click. It appears Ben had been following Dunlap, but I still don't know why. And if you notice the times, Brian flew to his destinations and Ben would have driven, so how did Ben get there the same time of day? Must have known ahead of time that Brian had intended to go to a particular place; either that or the old Jeep really flies and I haven't found out yet. So who would have known where Brian was going, tell Ben and why? ”

“You’re right. But that’s crazy, Dunlap wasn’t doing anything wrong. Why would he need to be tailed?”

“You’re thinking like a cop. Start thinking like a bad guy.”

White-faced Angus and Herefords moved through the stockyard chutes. Young Thomas Spillman straddled the corral fence railing as he silently counted the bawling animals and scribbled the head count on his clipboard. Charlie Tucker sat astride his horse, watching Frank Costello coax the last of the Circle-D herd into the waiting railroad boxcars. Taking off his Stetson and mopping his sweaty brow with a handkerchief, the foreman looked across the dusty yard to where Sam and Andrea Dunlap waited and watched. The final cow was loaded, and the count agreed upon. Sam signed off on the bill of sale and pocketed Spillman’s cashier’s check.

“We got you the best price per head that we could. Sorry you had to sell out, Sam. Hate to see a ranch belly up.”

“Listen fella, we’re only selling some livestock here. No one said the Circle-D is going under. Don’t you or your Dad be starting a rumor like that; it ain’t so! You hear?” Sam’s face flushed in anger at the younger man’s audacity.

“Yes sir. My mistake.”

Sam walked back to where Andy waited on Buttercup and handed her the check, their eyes met in silent communication. Sam stared at the cloudless sky above and listened to the sound of his cattle crowding into the boxcars. He patted Andy affectionately on her leg and gave her a quick nod.

"It'll be all right. See you later." He mounted his horse in one quick movement and pulled on the reins, swinging the horse around. He would ride back to the Circle-D with Charlie and Frank; Andy headed for downtown.

"I'll see you at home," Andy called after her grandfather. She clucked to Buttercup and thumped her heel lightly on its flank and the mare moved into a smooth canter. Andy rode past the many stockyards toward the business district.

Reining in at the town's lone bank, Andy tied Buttercup to a hitching post that still served the area's ranchers. The mare stood in complete accord between the car and pickup truck parked on each side. Andy patted her nose affectionately and then strode into the bank lobby. She nodded politely to a few people but headed directly to the branch manager's desk in the corner. Swinging the low gate open that enclosed the office cubicle, Andy approached the banker.

"Good afternoon, Andrea. How can I help you?"

"Hello, Mr. Wilson. I'd like to deposit this cashier's check into the Circle-D account and pay the mortgage interest and property taxes that are in arrears," Andy spoke quietly in a business-like manner. Her voice gave no indication of the churning emotions hidden behind her cool demeanor.

"Very well, give me a minute to get your file."

Her back barely touched the chair's backrest, her posture held stiffly erect, as she studied the certificates and photos on the banker's wall. She idly slapped her riding gloves against one leg, the only sign of her nervousness, while she waited. Selling the herd and watching her grandfather give up part of his inheritance, cut a deep fissure into that steel core that the Dunlaps called pride. The hurt tore at her soul.

"Here we are." Mr. Wilson opened the folder and studied the figures on the mortgage statement.

Andy slid the endorsed check across the smooth desktop. She watched the lender rapidly calculate the interest and tax totals and compare the debt with the funds at hand.

"This won't be enough to cover the entire amount, you know. I can pay the property taxes and most of the outstanding interest, but you will need another seven hundred to bring you completely current."

"I realize that. Apply it as needed and the balance will be paid in sixty days. Is that satisfactory?" Her voice took on an edge that could have cut through flint. All she wanted was to get this over with and get out of there.

"Very well, Miss Dunlap. I'll expect you in sixty days." Mr. Wilson accurately read the tone of her voice and dropped the friendly false pretext.

"Good day sir." Andy stood and shook hands briefly then walked swiftly to her waiting mount.

One hand shook as Andy untied the reins; she clutched Buttercup's mane, her face buried in the mare's neck. She stood there for a moment, trying to regain her shattered composure. Fearful of drawing attention, Andy quickly scanned the street, relieved to find it vacant. She didn't want to go home nor did she want to meet anyone in town just now. Not having any particular direction in mind, Andy slowly walked the mare toward the outskirts of town. The *Eatery* beckoned her wandering feet; might as well have something cold to drink before starting the long ride home.

She slowly closed the screen door, not letting it slam as usual, and meandered into the small empty diner. Maybelle smiled as she recognized Andy and waved to her from the end stool.

"Come join me down here. Business is slow and I'm taking a break. How you doing? What can I get you Andy?" Maybelle slid off the high stool and ambled behind the long counter. She filled a tall glass with ice and lemonade and slid it toward Andy.

"That looks good. Can I have a slice of that apple pie too?"

"Sure thing. You look like a gal that's got a lot on her mind. What's wrong honey?"

Andy drank some of the cool lemonade and chewed a bite of the cinnamon laden apples. She needed someone to talk to; she needed her mother, but that wasn't possible. It didn't feel right confiding in a stranger; not that anyone in Deer Springs would ever consider Maybelle a stranger. Her thoughts turned over and over in her mind until the words suddenly came spilling out.

"Oh Maybelle, I'm so miserable. I don't know what to do!"

"You tell me all about it. You got man trouble?"

"I've got every kind of trouble. I wish I knew what to do. Sometimes I feel like the entire world is on my shoulders and I'm scared to death that I'll make the wrong decisions. Gramps tries to help, but I can see he expects me to make the final decision on matters with the ranch. I miss my parents so much; I don't understand why they had to die. Why did God take them from me? Why am I being punished?" She put her face in her hands and cried softly.

Maybelle enfolded the weeping girl in her arms and cradled Andy's head against her ample bosom. She patted the slender back as she heard the agony in her cries. They held each other, as the sound of Andy's crying blended with the swish of the paddle fans in the still room. Finally, Andy straightened and sniffled loudly, ashamed of her sudden outburst.

"I'm sorry. I didn't mean to do that. Don't know what came over me."

"Honey, you needed a good cry. I think you've been keeping it inside for too long."

"Thanks for the shoulder. I don't know…I used to be able to talk to Jason, but I've lost him too."

"What do you mean, 'you've lost him too'? That man loves you. Don't you know that?" Maybelle asked as she pushed a napkin toward her and wiggled a finger at Andy's runny nose.

"What makes you say that, when you know as well as I do, that he was in here with Julie Miller just a few weeks ago? They were sitting in that back booth and holding hands. They were totally engrossed in each other."

Maybelle started laughing so hard she had to hold her side. "Oh sure, Jason was so wrapped up in Julie that he knocked Veronica Logan right off her feet trying to chase after you! Gal, you don't have the good sense God gave you when it comes to dealing with that man. He was only offering Julie comfort because of her Pa. If you had calmed down, instead of dashing off that day, you would have seen that."

"Really? That's all it was? I feel so stupid. But why didn't he tell me that?"

"And when did you give him a chance to do just that? Was he supposed to shout it to your truck bumper? Have you seen him since? Hmm?"

Andy shook her head no. She remembered him angrily arguing with Gramps on the front porch and Gramps giving her his message later that she was wrong in what she thought. She was too hurt and angry to listen and demanded to know how he could read her mind or guess her thoughts. But he did. She raised her eyes to find Maybelle studying her face and nodding.

"I can see your answer written all over your face. Now what're you goin' to do about it?"

"Think I'll try to find Jason before I go home." Glancing into the mirror that hung behind the counter, she self-consciously dragged her fingers through her hair and wiped at tear stained cheeks. "Can I use your restroom to freshen up?"

"Of course, go wash up that pretty face for that man of yours."

"Thanks for everything, Maybelle." Andy hugged the woman and rushed into the back to do as she suggested.

"Right. Thanks for handling things for me, Tom. Any question about the price? Got'em all loaded? I'll have some boys meet you tomorrow. No, not Cedarhill, these are for my own spread. Uh- huh, thanks again." Jason hung up the telephone receiver and turned in his chair as Andrea Dunlap entered the small sheriff's office.

Andy hesitated with one hand on the doorknob as she studied Jason sitting at his desk. Now that she was here, she wasn't at all sure what she wanted to say. Taking a deep breath and exhaling slowly to calm her nerves, she stepped forward.

"Hello Jason. How are you?"

"What brings you to town?" His voice was harsh and abrupt.

Andy was taken aback by Jason's brusque manner but decided to try and start again. "Just sold most of our herd at Spillman's." She waited for some response from him before continuing but he didn't even look up from his paperwork. "Jason, I really came to apologize. I was wrong about you and Julie Miller. I'm sorry I acted so badly."

"Glad you're finally admitting that. By the way, I have something for you," his words were clipped and spoken in a cold voice. He reached into his desk drawer and withdrew a blue carbon papered form. Striding to where she stood in the center of the room, he thrust the traffic ticket into her hand.

"What … you can't be serious?" She looked down at the form in the palm of her hand and then back up to him. Her own anger rising to the surface now, she demanded, "for what?"

"You can read. And the next time, Miss Dunlap, when an officer of the law flashes his lights and orders you to pull over; I suggest you do just that. Now, if you'll excuse me. I have things to do." He sat back down at his desk and deliberately turned his back to her, all of his attention seemingly focused on the report lying open across his desktop.

"Well! It will be a cold day in hell, Jason Hartman, before you'll see me again." She slammed the door behind her with a force that rattled the glass in the front window.

Jason watched her gallop out of town with a satisfied smile on his face. She'd stay at the ranch now because she was good and mad and wouldn't be back in town for a long while, he was certain. That pleased him plenty. She would be safe at the Circle-D and he wouldn't have to worry about her while his investigation took him elsewhere. She would never have stayed there if he had simply asked her; she was too stubborn. He hated treating her this way, but it was for her own good. She'd get over it in time. He hoped.

Someone else watched the angry departure of Andrea Dunlap. Veronica Logan smiled from ear to ear, thoroughly enjoying the heated words and stormy scene that she had witnessed. J.C. was hers now and she planned to keep it that way. Now she just needed to think of how to make that happen.

"That bitch Andy will be sorry she crossed me," Veronica stated to her compact mirror as she applied fresh lipstick. She decided to celebrate with a new dress as she sauntered into Molly's Boutique and fingered the newest arrivals on the rack.

CHAPTER 18

March 20, 1885

I never thought I would be so thrilled to see a bit of green growing again on the earth. This winter has been endless. Spring has finally begun, although I know Rose has warned us this may only be a false start. I keep forgetting how far north we really are. Still, I'd like to think of it as spring and give my spirits a lift.

James and Michael Canavan are off rounding up as many stray calves as they can find. James looks healthier now than he has in months; the fresh air and exercise benefit him. However, I notice he favors his good leg and walks with a slight limp that he tries to hide. He catches me watching him occasionally and turns away. Cody and I did our best to set his broken leg; I'm not a doctor, I did what I could. He blames me for the limp; I see it in his eyes.

Tomorrow we plan to ride into Deer Springs. I feel rather excited about the prospect of going to town; haven't been there since last September. I'm sure that's why I feel as jumpy and nervous as a cat; it's the excitement, not the possibility of encountering Cody Jarvis. If I close my eyes for a moment his face, smiling and gentle, appears before me. But then in a flash my mind's eye recalls the other side of his mask, cruel and violent. I shake my head to clear the vision and calm my breathing once more.

Rose and Michael have arrived; we thought it best if we ride to town together. They say there is safety in numbers. I guess there is some truth to that.

"Rose, I can't thank you enough for all that you and Michael have done for us these past weeks. We would have perished without you, I know it," I told her sincerely as we slowly followed behind our husbands. The horses picked their own pace and we were in no rush.

She reached for my hand and squeezed affectionately, "You make too much of it. We didn't do all that much. I'm just happy we could help, especially now, with you in the family way and all." Her smile spread across her face.

I hastened to admonish her to lower her voice. "I haven't told James yet that I am pregnant. I'll have to tell him soon, but not now."

"All right, Margaret. I don't understand all the secrecy. Won't he be happy about the baby? Michael would be fair to splitting his britches over the proud accomplishment. Men! You'd think we women have nothing to do with it at all," Rose continued in her observations and again I had to remind her to hush.

The weather favored us during our long ride; the breeze blew lightly and the mild temperature prompted me to unbutton my coat and remove my bonnet. The sun on my face felt so good and the air caressed my hair about my neck. It was grand just to be alive and free after the long winter confinement.

As we neared Deer Springs, I was surprised at the changes. The town had doubled its size with new buildings springing up along mud filled streets like weeds in a meadow. We passed the cemetery on the outskirts of town and then slowly rode past the livery stables. The rhythmic pounding of a hammer on an iron anvil rang out as we neared the blacksmith.

Some of the wooden clapboards still showed that bleached look from freshly milled lumber, the older establishments wore weathered or painted fronts. I pointed out the dry goods store next to the barber. A bank had recently been added near the land office where we had first filed our claim for the ranch. The town was definitely prospering, unfortunately that meant the addition of three more saloons, and I noticed a conspicuously tawdry red painted house at the end of the street. Rose and I exchanged looks and giggled, embarrassed at the sight of a brothel.

"You and Michael go ahead, James. Rose and I will meet you outside the mercantile. I need so many things. You men can take care of your business without the pair of us tagging along."

James readily agreed, relieved to be rid of us, I'm sure. He and Michael headed for the first saloon as soon as Rose and I entered the general store. I felt like a child again, thrilled by all the wonderful sights and smells that beckoned and urged me forward. A rainbow of colorful fabric bolts drew me to the back corner and I fingered the lovely materials, remembering the soft blue gown that I had thrown in Cody's face. I chased the image from my mind and turned to search for Rose. She was reaching into a deep barrel, scooping corn seed into burlap sacks. To my left, I spied a wall of shelving laden with mason jars of all sizes and filled with an assortment of vegetables and fruits. Whoever had put up the canned peaches and spiced apple rings did a good job; they looked delicious. I decided not to leave without at least a jar or two. The store bustled with activity as four more women shopped for dry goods and a couple men argued with the clerk over the price of feed. I measured twenty pounds each of flour and sugar, looked longingly at the dress material I knew we couldn't afford then added the jars of the precious fruit to my basket. James had given me two dollars to spend and I was trying to stretch it as far as possible.

He never did tell me where he got the money. I'm afraid he won it playing poker with Michael Canavan. James fancies himself quite a card shark; he spent all winter lying about and playing with that deck of cards. I hate the thought that my friends may be suffering by our hand. Heaven only knows, they can ill afford the loss. He'd only become angry if I question him and I've tried so hard to smooth the relationship between us. With a baby on the way, I must hold my tongue and not rile him.

I nodded politely to an older woman waiting patiently by the cash register. She extended her hand as the clerk painstakingly counted her change into her palm. Her sharp eyes watched his every movement.

"That's right, young man. And you tell Mr. Morgan that if he expects to continue doing business with me, he'll lower his prices. I recognize highway robbery when I see it and so will everyone else if I write an article in the paper about his unscrupulous ways!"

"I'm sorry, Mrs. Fitzhughes. But you really need to talk to Mr. Morgan, gosh, I'm just a clerk."

I watched her gather up her parcels and snap her purse closed. Then she surprised me by giving me a quick wink and a nod before spinning on her heel and walking briskly out the door. I almost laughed but caught myself in time as I realized she preferred to have the clerk think her stern. I was immediately drawn to her sly humor and forthright manner.

"Who was that lady?"

"Mrs. Fitzhughes, she publishes the Gazette. I don't know what she thinks I can do."

"Does Mr. Morgan really gouge his prices?"

"Ah… I really wouldn't know ma'am."

I laid my selections on the counter and watched as the young clerk scratched some figures on a piece of scrap paper, adding the numbers twice and twice coming up with a different total. I bit my lip, anxiously waiting for the outcome, hoping I had enough money. I smiled at him lamely, as he nervously began again.

"Uh, that'll be two dollars and twenty-eight cents."

"Are you sure? Would you consider taking a little less for the peaches?"

"Well, gosh ma'am. I don't know if I can."

"I only have two dollars. Really." He looked up at me and must have taken in my worn apparel and decided that my pleading was genuine because he smiled back and started packing the foodstuff into a large sack.

"Two dollars it is."

"Thank you very much." He would never know how much that moment of kindness meant to me. I gathered up my purchases and went outside to wait upon Rose and the men.

A murmur of voices rode the light wind blowing down the street and I shaded my eyes from the noonday sun as I tried to see the source of the commotion. A group of men were gathered in front of the Silver Spur saloon. Two men stood apart and even from my distance I could make out the figure of Cody Jarvis. I recognized that stoic stance as he waited quietly while the crescendo of angry voices rose around him.

I watched with interest as Cody and another man stepped into the center of the dusty street then slowly backed away from each other until a short distance was measured between them. I had heard descriptions of gunfights before, but until now had never witnessed one. My eyes were transfixed in horror as I realized with certainty that a gunfight was about to commence. Part of my thoughts rebelled in terror at the callous violence, while the center of my being prayed for Cody's safety. I stared at the macabre scene, unable to move, disgusted with myself for watching.

Suddenly the street became deathly silent, even the wind ceased, as a deafening noise split the air and a trail of gray gun smoke spiraled upwards. A man lay crumpled in the dirt while the spurs of the other jangled as he crossed the short distance. Snatches of phrases reached my ears as the grumbling voices began again.

"He deserved it…dirty rotten card cheat. You don't fool with one of Logan's men."

I strained to see, then released my breath slowly as I saw Cody kick the gun away from an outstretched hand lying in the dirt, pivot and stroll back into the saloon. He didn't even bother to check to see if the man might still be alive. My God, was life so cheap here?

My eyes stung from the acrid smoke and unshed tears. Seeing Cody so near yet so far, watching him face danger, tore at my already fragile composure. I didn't even hear James and Michael approach, so engrossed with my thoughts. James' question startled me.

"What?"

"I said, 'who got shot?' What's going on?"

"I don't know James. It just happened."

"Well you were right here watching. You must have seen something."

"I don't know the man and neither do you. It doesn't concern us. Let's go. I'm not feeling well." Only one thought was in my mind now, get home, away from here. I did not want Cody to see us.

"I don't understand what you're so upset about, Margaret. Like you said, we don't know the man. You better get used to things like this; we're in the West now."

"I can't help it, murder distresses me!"

"Come on, James. Can't you see that Margaret really isn't well?" pleaded Rose.

"Oh all right! Did you get everything you wanted in the store? I wanted to spend some time looking around too," James complained but relinquished.

"You can come back on your own another day," I suggested to appease him.

March 25, 1885

James has just returned from town. He is excited about an idea to increase our land holdings. He says we will need more land to build our ranch. I don't know how he thinks we can accomplish this.

I still haven't told him about the baby. I fear it will anger him. I wish I could believe that it has been conceived in love – but my mind recalls too well the night James forced himself on me in a drunken stupor. My punishment for giving my heart to another; it must be God's will.

April 10, 1885

The land blooms in the spring sunshine, renewing life after its winter hibernation. Wildflowers wave their soft white and pastel colored heads in the gentle breeze blowing across the meadow. Rose tells me that the little white flowers I admire are called hollyhocks and pennygrass. I pause in my work, rubbing the small ache in my lower back, and enjoy the sights and sounds surrounding me. Our life has taken on a pleasant routine. I rise early and scratch around in my little vegetable garden then feed the handful of chickens in the nearby pen. James is up and out early, tending to our stock and mending fences. I marvel at what a difference a few months can make. We were so down on our luck at the beginning of winter and now I feel almost prosperous – a house, fenced corral with 2 horses, chickens and cattle on the range. Our ranch is becoming a reality. James has even begun to make improvements on the cabin. He has promised to build on another room; he and Michael plan to repair the roof once and for all.

Maybe now would be a good time to tell him of the baby. I've caught him looking at me with speculating eyes. I try to convince myself that our life together could be happy.

Riders approaching interrupt my musings; two men riding toward the house and one other galloping in from the direction of town. Michael and James slowed as they crossed the western meadow; I shaded my eyes to better spy the identity of the lone rider in the east. Cody Jarvis. I couldn't believe it. Cody reached the yard first, dismounting and walking to my side, still holding the reins of his horse.

"How are you?" His eyes spoke volumes as he studied my appearance, searching for signs of abuse. He remembered too well his last sight of me.

"I'm fine. What are you doing here? I thought I told you to never come back?"

"I keep breaking my word where you're concerned. I worry about you. Don't hate me Maggie."

"I don't, but…" I couldn't continue. James had leaped off the mare and was striding angrily toward us.

"Would you look at the two of you? First time my back is turned, and I catch you playing around. I oughta…" His hand whipped across my face with a stinging slap. I stumbled backwards and fell onto the garden hoe.

"Dunlap, I warned you before what I would do to you if I ever caught you hurting her. You deserve to be shot down like the dog you are." Cody's hand slid to his gun holster.

I crawled the few feet separating Cody and James. My mind was in a whirl. I hesitated between the two. James saw my dilemma and sneered.

"What's the matter Margaret, can't decide between your husband or your lover? You whore! Do you think I don't know what the two of you were doing when I was abed?"

"James, you're wrong! Please, please stop this. I'm going to have a baby!" I blurted out, beseeching both men to be reasonable.

Cody relaxed his hand on his revolver. He smiled at me tenderly, hauntingly, before turning cold watchful eyes to James.

"Am I supposed to believe that's my baby? You lying bitch!" James kicked at me viciously, striking my abdomen and I doubled over in pain. He drew back to plant another kick but halted in motion as an ominous click filled the air.

Cody stood with his gun drawn and pointed menacingly at James. "I warned you; I've given you more chances than any man deserves."

"Cody, please, no. Think of me and the baby," I sobbed. "Please go for my sake."

Cody looked down at me, pity or love on his face I couldn't tell. He slowly lowered the gun's hammer then reached out in a lightning fast move; pistol-whipping James across the side of his head. James crumpled to the ground unconscious. Cody smiled with satisfaction then knelt to me. He lifted me to my feet and carried me lovingly into the house; carefully laying me on the bed. I felt so sore and battered; I gave myself over to his tender ministrations. His hand caressed my face, stroking my cheek and smoothing back my fallen hair.

"Are you all right? Should I get you something?" He was clearly at a loss as to what to do. He held my hand, pressing it between his own.

"Just go. I'll be okay. Can't you see that every time you come back, it makes it that much harder for me to endure? I have to make a life here with James. I have no choice."

He sat on the side of the bed, took me into his strong arms and kissed me with a gentleness that exploded into a fiery passion. I clung to him and kissed him back for all eternity.

"I love you Maggie Dunlap. If you ever need me, I'll come running." He released me back onto the pillows, then stood up and turned to go.

Tears slid down my face as I whispered, "I love you." I'll never know if he heard me or not.

When Cody walked over to his waiting horse, Michael Canavan was tending to his friend. He scowled at Cody, "You better get out of here Jarvis. You've caused enough trouble for one day. Good thing James and me is tolerant, or you'd be the one on the ground!"

"Humph," Cody looked at the pathetic pair. "Maggie could use your wife's help, Canavan."

April 12, 1885

I hemorrhaged during the night. Rose Canavan sat with me, trying to stop the bleeding with packing between my legs. No use. My baby daughter was born and died this morning; poor little thing, conceived in violence and brought into the world by violence. James won't need to worry about the father now. I think I'll call her Anna after my mother. Her tiny form will be buried among the tall elm trees. I don't think I've ever felt so lonely.

CHAPTER 19

Tears slid down her cheeks as Andy slowly closed the battered journal. Her heart went out to the bereft woman that she was learning to know and growing to think more and more of as *Gram*. Her own grief and desperation mirrored her ancestor's and she felt a kinship to this pioneer woman like none other. Love eluded both women as events swirled about them out of control and hurled them toward an emotional abyss. Andy sat quietly staring into the distance, rocking the porch swing ever so slightly, her mind churning, reliving her great-grandmother's story. She thought of herself and Jason and how futile it all seemed, and how much she missed him.

She worried about the ranch and what would happen if she couldn't pay that final mortgage payment in thirty days. The amount seemed so small when compared with what had already been paid – seven hundred dollars, might as well be seven million. The thought that her family ranch might very well ride on her skills and ability to win a rodeo contest shook Andy's resolve. If there was some other way, Andy did not know what it could be. Her mind ticked off a mental checklist of ideas and possibilities. They sold all the cattle that they dared; leaving just enough animals for breeding and starting the herd back up. There wasn't anything else left to sell - no crops or farm equipment. The ranch didn't possess any acreage that could be parceled or mineral rights to speak of. They weren't lucky enough to find oil or gas on their land, like some of the neighboring ranches.

Andy shook her head. Maybe she should try applying for some type of job in town if she doesn't win that roping prize.

Andy stood up and strode toward the stable, determination building in each step. She'll never win that money if she doesn't improve her roping time. Practice and more practice is what she needs and that's just what she planned on doing. Buttercup snorted in surprise as Andy spread the saddle blanket on the mare's back and began to strap on her saddle. She pulled on gloves and grabbed her lariat and tie-down ropes, intending to rope those calves again until she dropped. Satisfied in her performance several hours later, an exhausted Andy slowly entered the house. A hot bath and rest were what she needed now.

A single dim light illuminated the corner of the shabby motel room located off the interstate highway outside of town. Cigar smoke spiraling upward was the only indication that the room was occupied. A man lounged in the over-stuffed chair and waited for his "guest", listening for the quick rap on the door. When the sound came a few minutes later he mumbled, "Come in."

The door opened and closed quietly. Charlie Tucker stood a moment to allow his eyes to adjust to the dim lighting. He spotted the overstuffed chair turned toward the window and the large man reclining within it. Charlie walked toward the chair, deciding to sit on the edge of the single bed.

"What's happening at the Circle-D? My sources tell me a payment was made at the bank. I thought we were ready to see a foreclosure? I need to know what's going on."

Charlie's eyes scanned the room cautiously as he answered, "Sam sold off some cattle and got a good price for them. I don't know who the buyer was; Spillman wouldn't say. Guess the proceeds damn near paid off the note, still have a small outstanding balance that I hear them talk about. Andy is entering as a contestant in the rodeo to try and win the money." He made a snorting sound that doubted her success.

"I don't like it. And now that girl and her boyfriend sheriff are snooping around. I'm disappointed in you Charlie. I thought I could depend on you to see to my interests."

"But Boss, I've done everything you asked! Haven't I kept you informed? What else can I do without tipping my hand to old man Dunlap?"

Charlie watched as the man ground his cigar into the window sill, extinguishing the embers. Nonchalantly, he picked up a pack of matches then flipped the book back onto the table.

"Well obviously it's not been enough. You've been adequately paid, Charlie, and I don't like not getting my money's worth."

The bathroom door stood ajar. There was a quick muzzle flash and a suppressed sound from a 9MM automatic. Poor Charlie never knew what hit him as he was knocked backwards onto the bed. The burly man picked up a match stick and calmly cleaned out a speck of dirt from his thumbnail, flicking the stick and the matchbook onto the body of his dead informant.

"Turn off that lamp and clean up this mess. Make sure no one sees you leave," he directed and quietly walked out to his waiting car and driver.

Jason glanced up as the door to his office opened. He mentally groaned as Veronica strolled toward him. He gave her a quick look up and down from head to toe. If her dress was any tighter it would split at the seams. Does she really think her attire can entice him? Jason's thoughts flew through his mind as he groped for an excuse to get away.

"Hello Ronnie. What brings you to town?"

Veronica bristled at the use of the nickname, but she would never risk angering Jason by complaining about it. She chose to ignore it and smiled instead.

"My goodness Jason, don't you look busy! I swear you put more hours in than Ben Miller ever did as Sheriff. Don't you take any time off to play?"

"I'm sure Ben put in just as many hours. It's a busy job trying to service the entire county. We don't have a big staff and we all work long days. So what can I do for you?"

Realizing the conversation wasn't going the way she had planned, Veronica tried another tack,"Well I just came to invite you to lunch. I've got a lovely picnic basket filled with some wonderful food and a delicious bottle of wine." She smiled and arranged her facial expression in what she hoped was seductive. She had practiced her pose in front of the mirror at home earlier. It always worked on her Daddy.

Jason was beginning to get disgusted with her obvious ploys. "Sorry Veronica, but I really am tied up today. You'll have to get someone else to share your picnic, but thanks for asking. Look, I've got to get going; I have some stops to make and then need to swing by the Circle-D."

Veronica's pride was deflated and then her anger suddenly flared when she heard him say Circle-D. "Oh fine, go ahead and run off to see that bitch Andy! You have time for her, I see."

She spun about and stormed out of the office, slamming the door loudly.

Jason laughed and shook his head, "Whew, that was a close call." Ten minutes later Mac walked into the office, turning to look back down the street.

"I'd issue a speeding ticket to Veronica Logan, but I honestly don't think I could catch that woman. She is some kind of fired up! Did you see her?"

"Yeah, she was in here and I sent her packing. Guess she got a bit angry."

Mac laughed, "Well that's an understatement. Hope I never get her angry at me."

"Well, now that you're here, I'm heading out to the Circle-D and also need to check on a few more facts in Ben Miller's death. I'll be back later," Jason explained.

"No problem Boss. Got anything new on Ben?" Mac asked.

"I think I've found an account with some deposits that could be worth looking at. I'm waiting on a call from the bank in Goshen County. I'll keep you posted."

The early autumn sun began to sink in the afternoon sky. Jason had hoped to arrive at the Circle-D before dusk but got delayed talking with Smitty again at the garage and stopping by Ben Miller's house. Now as he pulled into the side yard he looked toward the log structure and spotted the yellow glow of a lamp turned on upstairs and the brighter fluorescent lighting pouring out two kitchen windows. He glanced at the upper window, Andy's bedroom, as he raised his hand to rap lightly on the rear kitchen door.

He only waited a moment before Sam's lean frame filled the open portal and with one raised eyebrow, questioned silently.

"Evening Sam." Jason tipped his hat further back on his head. "I need to talk with you. Privately."

"Andy's upstairs. We better go out to the barn." Sam quietly closed the door and strode to the darkened structure with Jason following close behind. "Okay, so what's going on?" Sam asked once they were inside. He gestured to a couple of hay bales as makeshift seating.

"I'm worried about Andy. She's been reading that journal and several people know that fact and it may be putting her in danger.

It'd be a good idea if she stays close to the ranch. In fact, with your approval, I'd like to take that journal into protective custody. Too many people have come up dead after being near that thing." Jason dragged his hand through his hair.

Sam studied the worried expression on the young man and came to his own conclusions. "You know something that you're not telling me. About Brian and Sarah? That crash was no accident, was it? My God!"

"I found evidence of a substance that I believe was inserted in a cut hydraulic line of Brian's plane. It may be the cause of the crash, but I don't have enough evidence yet or motive to connect it to anyone," Jason whispered. "No one else knows this. Right now, it's only a theory."

"But you have an idea of who might be behind this, don't you?" Sam leaned forward and looked deep into Jason's eyes.

"Sam, I can't say yet. And you keep this information to yourself, don't even tell Andy."

Sam nodded. "I trust you J.C. I know you'll do what's best for us. I'll get that book to you. I've seen Andy reading it whenever she has spare time. She's been spending hours practicing her roping for the rodeo next month."

"I wish she wasn't entered in that. What the hell is she trying to prove anyway?"

"It isn't that. It's the purse. She's got it into her head that she can win the prize money to help pay the mortgage on the ranch. I don't like confiding this; Dunlaps don't air their dirty laundry in public, but then, you're practically family. The fact is, we need the money."

"All right, Sam. Guess I'll see you in town? And Sam, keep an eye on things. Let me know if anything looks odd or suspicious, no matter how small around here. Be careful."

"Thanks J.C. What are you goin' to do now?"

"I've got a few leads to run down. And hopefully that journal might provide some ideas. I know that book and what's in it are tied to this. I've just got to keep digging."

Both men stood and shook hands; their expressions deadly serious.

Jason climbed into his truck and left the ranch as quietly as he could. His mind mulled over all the bits of facts and ideas of the case as he drove home to Cedarhill.

Two days later Sam Dunlap drove into town, parked near Cooper's feed store and walked the half block to the county sheriff's office. He entered the small office and found Jason sitting at his desk studying a pile of paperwork.

"Your desk looks worse than mine," Sam quipped.

"Howdy Sam. How's it going?" Jason sat back in his chair and propped a booted leg on an open desk drawer. He noted the small brown bag that Sam carried and waited until the older man settled into the opposite chair.

Sam opened the paper bag and withdrew the battered journal, sliding it across the desktop to Jason.

"Andy's pretty upset with me for taking this away from her. She seems to have developed some kind of attachment to my grandmother Maggie. Andy says Maggie is real and sits crying when she reads this darn book. I don't understand how just reading somebody's ramblings can make a person seem alive. Doesn't seem healthy to me; might be better to get this book away from her now."

Jason slowly picked up the leather-bound book, turning it over as he thought of what he and Andy had already read together.

"I promise to take care of this, Sam. I know you'll want it returned to your family to save as a keepsake - family history and all. Thought Andy was still working on her roping? She'll get over being mad at you. Everything else okay?"

"Have you seen Charlie Tucker around town lately? He's been gone from the ranch for about four or five days. He was supposed to come into town for our feed order, but I just checked with them before coming here and they haven't seen him."

Jason sat upright, his feet hitting the floor. "No, can't say as I have. Does he have a lady friend he visits here or down in Laramie? I never saw Charlie hanging around the local bars, but he could be just on a binge some place. Is he fond of his booze? I'll ask Mac if he's seen him around town."

"Charlie Tucker has worked for us over five years and I have never seen him drunk. I'm worried. It isn't like him to stay away from the Circle-D this long. If he's got a girlfriend, I've never heard him mention it. No… something's not right," Sam voiced his concerns.

"What's he driving, Sam? I'll put out a BOLO on the vehicle across the county. Maybe we can turn up some news on his whereabouts."

"He's got an old red Dodge Ram, think it's an '81 model. I don't know what the tag number is."

"That's OK; I can check with motor vehicle and come up with his registration. This is enough information to get started on a search. Don't worry, we'll find him," Jason tried to assure Sam as he quickly jotted down the pertinent facts.

"Let me know if you hear of anything, Jason." They shook hands and Sam headed back to the feed store and his parked truck.

Jason picked up the bound journal again and thumbed through the handwritten pages, skimming over various dates and words, stopping at an entry made in August of 1885. He began to read the details of the Dunlap family and the birth of the Circle-D.

CHAPTER 20

August 4, 1885

The sun in this new land seems to remain higher in the sky and burns twice as hot as what we knew in Scotland. I know that it is just my imagination, but surely the summer heat was never this hot or the days as long back home. Only late at night is there any relief.

I spend the hours of my day digging in my meager garden, harvesting the carrots, onions and potatoes from the dry soil. The animals eat or destroy my precious vegetables and I must always be on the alert. I work from dawn to dusk and still all the chores are not finished. There is wood that needs to be chopped and stacked for the coming winter months, food stuffs to be salted and cured and stored in the newly dug root cellar. James and Michael were so proud of their accomplishment when the cellar was finally dug and lined with wooden planks to keep the dirt from caving in. I was glad to see James happy again; but his pleasure over the finished cellar quickly turned to his usual scowl when he saw my smile. He suspects my every thought and seeks to turn my words against me if I so much as wish him a good morning or voice my hopes for our future. He'll never forgive me for caring for Cody Jarvis. Sometimes it seems too futile.

James and Michael rode into town again today. James did not return until hours past sunset; I was surprised he could find his way home in the pitch-black night. I allow myself the luxury of lighting one lantern for a few hours each night to see to do my sewing or write in this journal. Now in this dim light, I watched him stagger into the cabin. I wouldn't have needed to see him to know that he had been drinking; the liquor smell was stronger than the grime of sweat and horse on his clothes.

He dropped his hat on the table and struggled to kick off his boots, cursing as he hopped on one foot trying to maintain his balance. I clapped my hand across my mouth to stifle any sound, but he heard my small gasp and turned in my direction. His eyes glared anger and hatred for me, his mouth twisted into a snarl that turned his face into a cruel mask. This evil shadow of the man who was my husband loomed in front of me. Where was the man that I married? Was he gone forever?

"What are you looking at? Still scratching in that damn book?" James sneered, "Think you're so smart, well you just wait… people are going to respect James Dunlap. I'm going to make this ranch bigger than Canavan's or even Logan's place. And I found out how to do it all legal like too. Just need to stake out parcels of land for every one of my sons, and you madam are going to provide them."

I stared at him dumbfounded. He must have been thinking of this idea for some time, but my mind rejected the notion of our sharing a loving bed again. James had not come near me since before mid-April and the loss of Anna. I couldn't believe he was planning a family and a future for us. A moment later, I was right to doubt his *loving suggestion,* there was no love in his expression as he approached the bed and threw me onto my back.

"Spread your legs whore, like you did for Jarvis. I'm going to take what is mine. By God, I need a son and you're going to give me one if I have to take you every night."

His rough hands shoved my nightgown up about my hips; dirty fingers painfully groped my flesh, spreading my private parts as I screamed my protest. I pushed against his chest and twisted and turned but my thrashing only seemed to excite him more.

"Go ahead and scream. Who do you think will hear you?" He laughed drunkenly, enjoying my panic and fear of him. His meaty fist connected with my left cheek and eye, pain shot though my head making the room spin and I began to black out just before he thrust into me - again, and again.

I don't know how I am going to endure this nightmarish marriage. To be raped by your own husband night after night until your body is numb and your mind unfeeling. I am nothing more to him than a brood mare or one of his precious cows. Is this to be my punishment for giving my love to another? I've been physically faithful to James although he will never believe me, but God knows I cannot control my heart.

September 22, 1885

A baby… a thing of wonder, a blessing. That's what a baby should be. How can someone so innocent be conceived in such violence? I am as certain as a woman can be that I am indeed pregnant again. James has succeeded in his plans for more land. I only pray that now he will leave me alone. If we survive the winter, my baby should arrive sometime in June. I can only wonder what our life will be.

Jason tucked the journal into his top desk drawer and mulled over what he had read. No wonder Andy is becoming so emotionally attached to her great-grandmother's story. What a harsh life she led and the cruelty of her husband. Hard to believe, the poor woman. Jason shook his head and thought of what he would have done if he had lived back then.

Jason looked up at the sound of the office door opening as Mac strode across the room. Mac tossed his car keys onto his desk, picked up the current notices from his in-box and scanned the current BOLO listing.

"Hey Boss, anything happening? I've been out on patrol. It's pretty quiet out there. I did the perimeter roads of town and plan on cruising county route 25 north and then south as soon as I take a short break, grab something to eat."

"Good job. Platte County deserves our full attention. Keep an eye out for Charlie Tucker as you make your rounds; he drives a red Dodge pickup. Sam Dunlap told me Charlie hasn't been on the job for a few days and Sam is worried about him. I think he may be off visiting a lady friend that he's got on the side."

"Well, if he's got somebody, she must live outside Deer Springs. But I'll watch for his truck; see you put out a BOLO on him. Is he a suspect or just missing?"

"Just missing. It's odd though that we don't know much about Charlie. I don't recall him ever hanging out in the local bars or socializing – just stays at the Circle-D and doesn't have much of a life otherwise. Strange for a guy his age. Almost seems like he is hiding out on the "D". I may do a search through NCIC to satisfy my curiosity."

"OK. Are you making any progress on Ben's case?"

Jason withdrew a brown folder from his bottom desk drawer and spread the contents on his desktop. "Take a look at this statement, Mac. I got this from Goshen National Bank."

Mac studied the column of figures then handed the bank statement to Jason.

"Ben made several deposits into the account and the dates all coincide with our calendar notes. Ben was on the take, and I think it was Brent Logan who bank rolled him. I found Logan's private telephone number among Ben's stuff at the house. It looks pretty obvious that Ben was keeping tabs on Brian Dunlap's whereabouts."

"Whoa, why would Logan need to tail Dunlap? Can't believe that old Ben was dirty. Do you think that's why he shot himself?"

"Ben wasn't a bad man. I think his conscience finally got the better of him. Maybe he just couldn't look that face in the mirror any more. Or maybe Logan wanted more than Ben was prepared to deliver. I don't know. I just wish he had talked to me, confided in me. I think I could have helped him," Jason said sadly.

"So what was so important that Logan needed to know where Dunlap was going? I don't get it. What's Logan up to?"

"That's the other half of the puzzle, Mac. I'm still trying to put those pieces together. I've got an idea, but no proof yet. We'll find it; just a matter of time."

"Well, if anyone can figure it out, you can. Tell me what you need me to do, Boss."

"Thanks Mac. Just keep things running smooth in town and keep your ears and eyes open. Let me know if you run across anything out of the ordinary."

Andy closed the flaps of the cardboard box and reached for the second empty carton. She emptied the last of her mother's clothes from the closet and placed the pile on the bed. Her fingers traced a collar or smoothed the fabric of a favorite sweater. She breathed in the faint scent of her mother's perfume that still clung to a dress. Loving hands folded the garments and packed them into the carton. It was a chore that had to be done and had been delayed far too long. Sighing, Andy dragged the roll of tape across the flaps, sealing the boxes for storage.

She planned to carry the boxes up to the attic storage until she and Gramps could decide what would be the best way to dispose of her parent's clothes. She had selected some of her mother's garments that she wanted to keep and could wear and had put those aside, but the other things would probably get donated to the church or Goodwill. There was plenty of time to decide. For now, Andy was just feeling a sense of accomplishment for completing the task.

Andy walked into the kitchen looking for her grandfather. "Hey Gramps, I've got those boxes packed. Can you give me a hand with taking them up to the attic?"

"Sure. Give me a minute," Sam answered her as he put his hot cup of coffee on the table and turned off the pot. "Alright, let's see what you've got."

Andy and Sam returned to the second floor and Sam tugged on the overhead rope of the concealed attic stairs. The coiled springs of the suspended attic steps groaned as Sam put his foot on the bottom step to lower the ladder in place. He turned as Andy pushed several cartons into the hallway near the ladder.

"You climb up there and I'll lift the boxes up to you."

Andy scrambled up the sturdy ladder steps. She glanced about the large space. Dust motes swirled in a shaft of light shining through the small window. The bright afternoon sun illuminated the room. Several boxes of Christmas ornaments and decorations were stacked close to the stair opening. A large steamer trunk rested against the east wall. More boxes and barrels were crammed into the eaves and knee wall spaces. Dusty sheets covered old chairs and a large mirror.

A collection of old paintings caught Andy's attention. Some were framed, others were just canvases tacked to wooden stretcher strips. Andy remembered her mother's painting attempts when she had spent a summer taking art classes at the junior college in Laramie. She moved some of the frames and poked among the oil painted canvases. A landscape that looked like the north pasture of the ranch filled one frame and a blue vase filled with white daisies adorned another. Andy recognized her mother's signature in the corner. She smiled, recalling her mother's pleasure at dabbling in the arts.

"Andy! What are you doing up there? Come on gal, grab this box."

"Sorry. I haven't been up here for so long, that I couldn't resist exploring a bit," she replied as she reached for the first carton.

Sam stood on the second step and extended the box, reaching the top platform and Andy's waiting grasp.

"I'll just stack these against this back wall. Hold on a second." She slid the box into place and leaned over the stair opening to grab the next carton. In less than ten minutes the task was finished, and all four cartons of clothes were stored away.

"What's in that old trunk, Gramps? Is it locked? Gosh, I remember playing up here when I was little; seemed awfully spooky then. Now it just looks crowded and dusty."

"I don't think that trunk's locked. If it is I sure don't know where the key is. You can look through it, just old family stuff, clothes and books probably. I'm going back down and finish my coffee. You alright up here?"

"Oh sure, go ahead. I'm going to poke around," Andy called down the stairs as she began testing the lock and prying the large trunk lid open. Two moths escaped as she lifted the lid higher and gingerly poked among the brocaded silk fabrics. Andy raised the bodice of a brocade gown, finding the tiny waist closed with hook and eyes. She moved aside some striped silk cloth and found a beaded bag next to a pair of high buttoned shoes. Andy speculated that such an elegant ensemble must have belonged to Gramp's mother. She rummaged through the other contents and found a book of poetry, some sheet music and several papers rolled and tied with a narrow ribbon. A small square wrapped within a black velvet material caught Andy's attention. As she picked up the velvet covered shape, she pricked her finger on a sharp corner. She lifted the fabric and stared at a miniature tintype portrait.

Andy gathered up the rolled papers and the tintype portrait and carried them downstairs to share her treasures with Gramps. Maybe he could tell her the identity of the beauty with the sad expression in the portrait. The woman's dark hair was drawn back in a severe style, but her gown appeared youthful. Andy laid the items on the kitchen table to examine them more fully.

"See what I found."

Sam turned from the window where he had been watching Frank and Bill near the corral. He pulled out a kitchen chair and reached for the miniature, examining it in the light.

"Andy, meet the author of the journal that you've been reading. This lovely lady is my grandmother, Margaret Dunlap."

"Oh my! Is it really? She's so beautiful but looks so unhappy. How old do you think she was when this was done?"

Sam studied the tintype again, rubbing his forehead with reddened finger tips; he stared into space, trying to reach into his memory.

"I remember my father talking about his mother Maggie. She had already passed away before I was born, so I never knew her. If this photograph was taken around 1890, then that would make her about twenty-seven years old.”

“I wonder what she was thinking when the camera shutter clicked. Do you think her melancholy expression was due to her husband James or her lover Cody?” Andy speculated.

“My grandmother never had a lover. What are you talking about?” Sam defended his grandmother’s reputation, surprised by Andy’s comment.

“Oh Gramps, I’m just referring to Maggie’s reference to Cody Jarvis in her journal. She wrote that she loved him; but I don’t know if anything more came of it since you took the diary away from me and won’t let me read what happened! Where is the journal anyway?”

“Humph. The journal? Jason’s got it. He needed it.”

“Jason has it? When did he come get it? I haven’t seen him here,” Andy questioned.

“No, well I took it to him a few days ago. You’ll get it back soon. Don’t worry about it.”

“Well that hardly seems fair; he gets to read it and I can’t. It’s my grandparent, not his. He thinks it has something to do with mom and dad’s crash, doesn’t he?” Andy persisted.

Sam raised an eyebrow in surprise, “What do you know of it? Jason just said he wanted to check some facts; that’s all.”

“I knew it. I just knew there were clues in that book – I would have found them too if you had let me continue reading.” Andy tried to look petulant but couldn’t hold her sense of indignation long as she recalled the scrolls that she had also found in the attic. She handed one of the ribbon-tied parchments to Sam, "What do you think of these?"

"Where did you find these papers, in that old trunk?" Sam asked as he pulled the end of the ribbon to untie the scroll.

He carefully unrolled the document and spread it across the tabletop, placing a sugar bowl on one corner to hold it in place. He held the other edge with one hand as he read the description and facts displayed.

"This appears to be a certificate of marriage between Margaret Doherty and James Dunlap. See here? This line says where the ceremony was held, the Presbyterian Church of Glasgow on November 2, 1883."

Andy studied the swirling penmanship on the aged sheet of parchment. She pointed to several lines of signatures. "Okay, I can read Margaret Doherty's name on this line and the line above seems to have a Reverend Thomas McDougal but where is James' signature?"

Sam examined the signature lines again and then tapped his finger on a mark next to Margaret's name.

"See that X. James Dunlap's name is printed next to that mark. Evidently, he didn't know how to read and write. He must have made his mark and the Reverend witnessed it. The other signatures are witnesses too."

"Oh, you're right! Margaret even mentioned in her diary that James could not read and write. I've never seen that before. Look at the date. They must have left Scotland right after their wedding to be able to travel to America and start the trek west."

"I imagine they had a rough time of it too, traveling across the Atlantic in winter months. Had to be desperate to want to risk such a trip," Sam surmised.

"Let's look at the other papers." Andy was excited about her discovery. She untied a second rolled sheaf of documents. Several pages were printed and appeared to be legal documents. One page contained a hand drawn map with compass points and measurements indicated along vertical lines. An attachment to the map showed names and signatures and once again James Dunlap's name was printed next to a large X.

"If you study the shape of that map, you can see the outline of the Circle-D property lines. Look here; the northern boundary includes the Sarasota Valley, and do you see the drawing of the Little Turtle Creek that runs through the eastern perimeter? It's not a formal platt map, but considering the age of the drawing, this map is a pretty accurate description of the ranch. I'd say this is the original land grant that was registered to James Dunlap in 1884," Sam exclaimed.

"I can't believe these were hidden in that old trunk all this time. Wow." Andy shook her head in wonder. She picked up the third set of papers and unrolled them. "This looks like another set of land grants for the ranch. Maybe they made two copies."

Andy and Sam examined the property lines drawn on the second map and placed the map next to the other drawing, lining up the edges and landmarks. Sam was the first to speak as he looked at the map and then at Andy's expression of disbelief.

"This isn't the same drawing of the Circle-D; this is a different piece of land. I think this is a parcel west of our boundaries."

"This document is dated July 4, 1886. Read the names on this land grant. It says Alexander Dunlap and also James Dunlap but no signatures, just the letter X again. Who is Alexander Dunlap?" Andy questioned.

"That's my father's name. There was supposed to be an allowance in the Homestead Act that permitted a family to file for additional parcels of land under a child's name if the land parcels were adjacent to the original acreage. It looks like James Dunlap filed for a grant under Alexander's name, but I don't understand what this means. We don't own this land now. What happened to it?" Sam read the document again and picked up the map, holding it to the light to see all of the small details.

"Wouldn't there be a deed recorded in the courthouse? If the land was sold later, wouldn't there at least be a record of the sale or something? What do you think, Gramps?"

"I may speak with Jason about what we've found. He told me that your father had been researching land records in Laramie and Cheyenne; these papers may be important. Right now, we better keep this to ourselves."

CHAPTER 21

The intercom squawked as Mac's voice came over the station's two-way radio. "Unit two to Sheriff; come in J.C, over."

"Go ahead Mac. Where are you?" Jason thumbed the open mike, answering his deputy.

"I'm out on county route 25 northbound near mile marker 265. You better get out here; I've got a code 10-79. I think I found Charlie Tucker."

"I'm on my way. Stay with the body. I'll call the coroner. ETA fifteen minutes," Jason replied as he checked his watch and grabbed a forensics kit.

He slipped on his jacket and was already out the door as he punched in the county coroner's number on his cell phone. "Hey Doc, we need you out on route 25, mile marker 265 north. Mac just found a dead body. Yeah … I'm on my way."

Jason floored the Explorer, racing out of town with lights flashing in the early dusk. The setting sun made the western sky glow in shades of amber and indigo. Jason could just make out a pair of buzzards circling overhead in the darkening sky as he approached the location of Mac's cruiser. A red pickup truck lay on its side, off the road in a deep gulley. He pulled in behind Mac's car, leaving the overhead lights flashing, and strode toward his deputy.

"I was just about to turn around and head back to town when I spotted the buzzards and decided to investigate. The body's in bad shape, been here awhile from the looks of it." Mac climbed up on the surrounding boulders and pointed his flashlight into the cab of the truck and shined the light down onto the corpse.

Jason carefully walked the perimeter and inspected the area and ground near the crashed truck.

"Well that's Charlie's truck, sure enough, but I don't see any skid marks or signs of him trying to stop. Looks like the truck drove straight toward the gulley and then rolled. We'll have to wait on Doc Brown to determine the cause of death."

"Gonna be hard getting the body out of the cab. Maybe we ought to try flipping the truck back on all four wheels?" Mac suggested.

"Let's leave the crime scene as it is until the coroner gets a good look. I don't want to disturb anything. Put out some flares on the roadway so Doc Brown can find us. Sun's going down quick and it'll be completely dark soon."

As if to confirm his actions, headlights shone in the distance approaching their location marked now by the burning orange flares. A few minutes later the white mini-van stenciled with Platte County Medical Examiner pulled up alongside the sheriff's Explorer. Doctor Ronald Brown and his assistant walked slowly toward the crash scene.

"Body has been here for a few days by the amount of decomposition in evidence. Do you know the identity?" asked the coroner.

"Mac and I think it's Charlie Tucker. We had a BOLO out on his truck and Sam Dunlap reported him missing about five days ago. What can you tell me about COD?"

"Well, from what I can see, there doesn't appear to be much blood in evidence. If he died from the crash, I don't see it. I'll know better after we get the body out of the truck. Harry, make sure you get plenty of pictures."

Doctor Brown climbed onto the higher rocks, peering into the truck's cab as he attempted to examine the slumped body lying across the bench seat. Harry's camera clicked and flash bulbs illuminated the night as he photographed the body and every angle of the crashed vehicle.

"Okay boys; let's get this truck back on all four wheels. Harry, let's get this door open and see if we can get him out."

The four men pulled on the rolled truck, rocking it back onto its axels and setting it upright. Brown's assistant tugged on the driver's side handle, trying to pull the cab door open. The dented door protested and appeared unmovable.

Mac pried a crowbar into the door hinge and indicated to Harry to try again. Their combined efforts finally succeeded as the door swung open and the body was lifted from the crushed vehicle and placed on a waiting stretcher.

"I can give you more information after I examine the body thoroughly, but at closer inspection now, looks like a gunshot wound to the head. Look at the damage to the back of the skull. I don't believe I am going out on a limb by saying cause of death was a gunshot.”

“Thanks Doc. I’ll need to know what caliber bullet when you can. I’ll meet you back at the morgue,” Jason told the medical examiner as he watched the body loaded into the van.

Jason handed the forensic kit to Mac, “bag and tag anything you find in the truck cab.”

Both lawmen searched through dirty rags, papers and various items. An empty coffee cup, a book of matches, a crumpled pack of Camels all went into the zippered bags for later inspection.

“I think we’re done here. Let’s get Smitty out here tomorrow to tow this in.” Jason carried the evidence bags to his truck and grabbed a roll of yellow police tape. “Give me a hand with this stuff; let’s rope off the crash area until tomorrow.”

“Okay, meet you back in the office,” Mac agreed when they were done.

Jason headed back toward town. He knew he was going to have to inform Sam Dunlap about Charlie, but he wanted to have all the facts first. He pulled up next to the ME’s office, noting the van parked next to the side entrance. He walked into the building, heading straight for autopsy and maybe some answers.

“What’s it look like Doc?”

“Just like I said; single gunshot to the head. I just dug out the bullet – a 9 millimeter. By the looks of the decomp, body’s been dead at least five days. I can’t be more specific in time than that.”

The coroner handed the sheriff a glass specimen jar containing the bullet fragment.

Jason held up the jar, shaking it lightly as he thought of who would carry that size weapon. It was obvious from the type of wound that Charlie Tucker was definitely executed, but why and by whom?

"Thanks Doc. I'll let you know when you can release the body for burial."

He drove back to the sheriff's office and logged in the evidence bags that he and Mac collected at the scene. They had a murder on their hands now, not a simple auto accident. Deciding he had done all he could for one day, Jason turned over the office to the night shift deputy and headed for home.

The lights of Cedarhill were a welcome sight as Jason pulled into his family's drive. He closed the door behind him and tossed his hat onto the rack by the door. Ingrid watched her son as he entered the great room. He seemed distracted and tired, activating her motherly instincts.

"Hello son. Can I get you something to eat?"

"Thanks Mom, maybe something light. I'm more tired than hungry, I think. Is Pop home?"

"Yes, he's in the den. You go ahead in and I'll bring you a sandwich," Ingrid suggested.

Jason found his father reclining in his favorite leather chair and engrossed in a book. Jarrod Hartman looked up as his son entered the room then watched him plop down into a comfortable chair, propping his feet upon an ottoman. He studied his son's face and also noted the lines of worry and fatigue.

"What's wrong Jason?"

"Nothing and everything, Pop. It's this case that I'm working on; tonight, it just got more complicated."

Jason ran his hand through his hair, squeezing his eyes shut as he tried to see clues that were just outside his reach. It frustrated him that he knew he was missing a key point and didn't know where to look.

"Is there something that I can help you with? Sometimes having a sounding board helps. Want to tell me about the case or the problem you're having?" Jarrod offered.

"I've been investigating the death of Brian and Sarah Dunlap."

"But wasn't that an accident? The plane crash, I mean. Are you saying there was more to it?" Jarrod trusted his son's instincts and knew he would not make any accusation lightly.

"Well, the official report says it was an accident, but I've found some evidence that says otherwise. The Circle-D ranch is mixed up in some other problems and tonight I found their foreman, Charlie Tucker, dead. Nobody knows this yet, but I don't imagine you're going to advertise the fact."

Jarrod laughed half-heartedly, "Well thanks for your vote of confidence. I take it that Charlie didn't die of a simple heart attack?"

"Wish he had; would make my life a lot simpler. No, somebody offed him with a 9MM shot to the head. Nasty stuff. Mac found the body in his truck crashed out on the prairie."

"Well… I can see why you're worried. You think they're tied together, the plane crash and Tucker's murder?"

"Yes, I do. Hey Pop, what can you tell me about Brent Logan? I know he's among your friends, but what do you really know about him?"

"I'd hardly call Brent Logan a friend; he's more like an acquaintance. I've had some business dealings with him. We belong to the Rotary Club and are members of some other organizations. Why?"

"Brent Logan stays on just the right side of the law when it's convenient to him. I don't trust the man. I think he's mixed up in this, but I can't prove it yet. How's he make his money?"

"As far as I know, the Logans run cattle like the rest of us, plus he's got oil and some other mineral rights on his land. I think he's done some real estate deals too. All legitimate business deals, as far as I can see. He does always manage to get the best price for his real estate purchases. Surely that's not a crime?" Jarrod asked.

"Yeah, I've heard about some of his real estate deals. There've been rumors that he scooped up some properties with a little help from the foreclosure courts, and maybe some banker payoffs. Like I said, I don't trust the man. He's building his empire at the cost of too many others."

"Brent once told me that it was very important to him to protect his family's legacy and to build his personal wealth to pass onto his own heirs. I believe that's all he cares about."

"I can understand ambition in a man and the need to provide for your heirs, but what did he mean by 'protect his family's legacy'? Protect it from what? Is there something there that's not quite right? Maybe I'll dig a little deeper in that direction. Like I said, this case keeps getting more complicated."

"But you still think it's all tied together?" Jarrod persisted.

"Yes, I do. More than ever, I think. Pop, thanks for being my sounding board."

CHAPTER 22

Gray clouds filled the morning sky as a steady rain fell to earth. Jason turned up the collar of his yellow rain slicker and adjusted the brim of his Stetson as he walked toward his truck. He'd been up and about for three hours, tending to stock and overseeing the final construction details on the kitchen of his own home. The house should be ready by next month. Jason was looking forward to moving into his own place; a new home for a new chapter of his life. He was thinking of the interior details that he had inspected and wondering if Andy would approve. All of his efforts and work would mean naught if he couldn't convince Andy to be a part of his life. He was determined if nothing else.

He drove toward the Circle-D entrance as he focused his thoughts back onto the case at hand and the unpleasant task ahead. Parking near the house, he walked briskly to the kitchen door and rapped lightly. Jason smiled as Andy opened the door and welcomed him inside.

"Good morning. Wet one out there today," Jason greeted as he removed his raincoat.

"Haven't seen you in such a long time; I was beginning to think you had abandoned us." Her eyes drank in the sight of him while a thousand thoughts flitted across her mind – where has he been, who has occupied his time, why hasn't he called? She hated feeling jealous, it was such a foreign emotion to her and it angered her to think she was not in control. Why, she was acting no better than Veronica Logan and that was a sobering thought!

Jason had no idea of the warring emotions struggling behind Andy's calm manner. He was just happy to have this moment to simply enjoy the sight and scent of her, filling his senses. He knew he was really delaying the unpleasant news that was his true mission.

As if on cue, Sam came walking into the kitchen and greeted the lawman, noting the tangible tension in the air.

"Ah young love; these two sure make it difficult," he thought and smiled. He motioned for Jason to take a seat at the table and Andy poured cups of coffee for everyone as she too sat down and waited expectantly. It was obvious that Jason was here for a purpose.

"I've got some bad news for you folks. I'm sorry to be the one to tell you, but yesterday, we found Charlie Tucker's body. He's been dead for a few days."

"I knew there was trouble! I told you Charlie wouldn't just go off and leave us. How did he die, Jason?" Sam questioned. He saw Jason hesitate to say more in front of Andrea. "It's okay, she needs to know, go ahead."

"Looks like Charlie was murdered; shot in the head. Our office is investigating but we don't have much to go on." He watched both Sam and Andy's expressions as the details sunk in.

Andy's eyes filled with tears; jumping to her feet, she looked toward her grandfather and then to Jason. "Why would anyone want to kill Charlie? It's my fault, isn't it? If I hadn't insisted on digging into the plane crash, reading that journal and now someone else is dead."

Acting on instinct, Jason enveloped Andy within his strong arms. He hugged her to his chest, tucking her head beneath his chin. His eyes met Sam's and both men nodded in silent communication.

"You listen to me; nothing you did or said caused this. Charlie's death may or may not be connected to what's going on but that's not your fault. I'll get to the bottom of this; you can trust me."

"I'm scared Jason. I don't know what to do now." Andy stayed within the circle of his arms, feeling secure for the first time in a long while. She was reluctant to move.

"Do you really want to help me? Give up this foolish idea of entering the rodeo. I can't protect you there and you would be too vulnerable."

"It is *not* a foolish idea. You don't understand; I have to enter that contest. Hey, I really resent the idea that you think you can come in here and boss me around!"

"Andy, I know about the prize money and why you need it. I'm not trying to boss you; I'm just worried about you and want to keep you out of harm's way. Will you at least promise to wait until I tell you that it's safe? Sam, can't you reason with her?" Jason threw up his hands in exasperation.

"He's right honey. Give Jason a chance to solve this thing before putting yourself at risk. You know I wouldn't be able to stand it if anything bad happened to you," Sam pleaded.

"Oh, all right. I can't fight both of you, but I'm going to go crazy if I don't have something to do. You've got to let me help somehow." She looked between one man and the other, hoping they would relent.

"Well if you promise to stay out of trouble, you could try to read more of your grandmother's journal. I've been reading parts of it, but now with Charlie's murder, I won't have the time to devote to it. I still think it contains an answer for us and I'm hoping we'll recognize it when we read it, but we've got to keep digging. Can you do that?"

"Yes, I do want to read more of the diary. Maybe it will help to explain the documents that Gramps and I discovered the other day too."

"What documents?" Jason's interest turned to this new subject.

"Oh, wait until you see. I found some documents rolled up and stored in an old trunk in the attic. They look like land grants for the Circle-D. Come on."

Andy grabbed Jason's hand and led him to the attic stairs. She was anxious to show Jason the precious papers, tucked away again in their secret place. "We thought it best if we kept them hidden up here. No one knows they're here."

Jason and Andy climbed the attic stairs and Andy led him to the steamer trunk hidden in the attic corner. She lifted the lid and pushed aside the yards of fabric and photo albums covering the tied scrolls resting in the bottom of the trunk. Andy held the precious documents and gingerly untied the frayed ribbon holding the scrolls in place.

"I saw these when I was up here storing mom's boxes of clothes. I was just snooping in the trunk and didn't realize what I had until Gramps and I examined the papers. Look at the maps and these dates." Andy pointed to the handwritten notes along the paper's margin. "It appears to be two separate land grants, but you know our ranch doesn't include this parcel. What do you think it means?"

Jason inspected the land grants, noting the signatures and names of James Dunlap. "Well, there are undeniably two land parcels defined here and both appear to belong to James Dunlap. Maybe he sold one of the tracts or maybe one of your other family members did. Does Sam have any papers from his father or does he remember any family talk about the land? There should be some kind of record."

"That's what we thought too, but Gramps doesn't think so. It's so strange."

"Hmm. Hang on to these and keep 'em safe up here. I found some records of land grants when I was in Cheyenne; it would be interesting to compare those with these tracts. Maybe we can do that. Meanwhile, I'm going to come back later and bring the journal."

"All right Jason. I'll expect you later."

"Great. How about we make it a dinner date?"

"Is six o'clock okay? Should I dress up or are we being casual?" Andy wondered what he had in mind for dinner, he sounded so serious.

"You can dress comfortable. Six it is," Jason agreed as they descended the attic stairs and headed back to the kitchen area. He waved to Sam and left for the office, thinking of the documents that he just viewed and the other information that he had found from following Brian Dunlap's flight log.

Mac and Jason sat examining the contents of the evidence bags they collected from the previous night. Jason cut the yellow tag on one small bag and dumped the items onto his desktop. He picked up a Camel cigarette package, set it aside and flipped open the book of matches, noting a number four scribbled on the inside cover.

Jason read aloud the matchbook cover, "Gate's Motel, reasonable rates. Ever hear of that one, Mac? Doesn't sound familiar to me."

Mac set aside the bag he was opening and reached for the matches. He read the same printed advertisement and turned the book over to find an address for the motel.

"It must be off the interstate. Isn't Hancock Road that little access road near exit twelve of I-25? Remember when the highway cut through a couple of those small towns and pretty much diverted all traffic away from them, actually blocked off a few roads? I seem to recall Hancock dead ends into the highway ramp; just a little whistlestop up that way now."

"I believe you're right Mac. You've got a good memory for details. How do you think old Charlie got hold of a pack of their

240

matches? Maybe he had a one-night stand at that motel; sure would be one way to keep the town gossips from knowing your love life. Tomorrow let's take a drive up to the Gates Motel and see if anyone remembers him. Let's see what else we have from his truck cab."

Mac and J.C. sifted through gum wrappers, empty Styrofoam cups, balled up hamburger and French fry containers, more discarded cigarette packs, crumpled invoices and feed bills among the pieces of assorted trash.

"Looks like he lived in this truck; what a mess."

"I agree. Hey Mac, hand me those feed bills and old invoices. I'll return them to the Circle D when I see Andy tonight. Bag up the rest of this trash and we'll just tag it until the investigation is done. I don't think we're going to find anything worthwhile in this junk."

"Okay, J.C.; no problem."

"Let's review. So we know Charlie was shot with a nine millimeter and the M.E. says he's been dead about five days. If we can retrace his movements, maybe we can find out who he was with and where. We've got to find the crime scene 'cause we know he didn't die in that crash; there just wasn't enough blood and I really doubt he drove there with a bullet in his head."

Jason glanced at his notes again and looked at the evidence bags, tossing the feed bills in one pile and stacking the sorted garbage in another.

"Mac, I need you to talk with Smitty. Charlie's truck was towed into Smitty's garage and he should be finished with his inspection by now. Write up a report on his findings and that should do it."

"What time do you want to leave tomorrow to drive up to the motel?" Mac asked.

"I'll be in the office by 7:00am; let's plan on going around nine. I want time to read your report on the truck first and see if there is anything else from the medical examiner."

"All right J.C.; tell Andy I said hello." Both men gathered up their notes and the evidence bags and packed up for the day.

Andy studied her image in the mirror for one last time, smoothing her hair and checking her lipstick. Jason had said to dress casually, but she wanted to look nice for him tonight. She had taken extra care with her appearance, hoping he would approve her choice of wool flannel slacks and the soft angora sweater both in a matching lavender color. The decidedly feminine outfit clung to her curves and was so different than her usual wardrobe of jeans and work shirt. She smiled at the girl looking back at her as she fastened the clasp of a silver chain about her neck and added a pair of small silver hoop earrings; nothing to do now but wait on his arrival.

She sat in the living room leafing through pages of an old magazine, keeping an eye on the mantel clock. *This is silly*," she chided herself. She was feeling excited and anxious at the same time and couldn't explain why. It was just Jason.

Gramps smiled knowingly as he watched Andrea toss the magazine back onto the coffee table and jump up to pace the floor.

She was lovely tonight and her mother would have been so proud of the soft woman standing before him.

"Got a date with Jason?" Gramps asked, already certain of the answer.

"Yes. Well, it's really just dinner. He said he would bring back the journal and we were going to grab some dinner out. You don't mind, do you?"

"No, you young folks go have a good time. You deserve it. You've been cooped up for too long and involved in the ranch worries. I'm glad to see you take some time for yourself."

The sound of gravel crunching and a vehicle engine drew her attention as she parted curtains to peer out. Jason was here. Her face lit up as she turned from the front window and hurried to pick up a jacket. Sam was already opening the front door and greeting Jason as he stepped into the room. He quickly scanned the surroundings until his gaze found Andy and he whistled softly at the sight of her.

"Wow! Andy you're beautiful." His eyes drank in her appearance, appreciating every curve. Andy blushed as she felt his hot eyes on her.

"Humph … well maybe you two better get going."

"Right. Here's the journal, Sam, and some other papers that belong to the Circle D. I'll just set them on the table; you can look 'em over later." He turned to Andy to help her on with her jacket as they walked out into the cool autumn night still damp from the morning rain. "Are you real hungry? I thought we'd go out of town for supper tonight. OK with you?"

"Wherever you want to go or do is fine with me. I'm all yours."

"Now that's a statement that makes a body grow warm!" Jason smiled warmly at her and gave her a quick kiss as he opened the car door. "I'd like to make you all mine," he said as he lifted her hand to his lips in a gallant gesture.

Andy watched him as he walked around the front of the Explorer and climbed into the driver's seat. She tried to read his expression; was he being serious or just playful? They drove down the lane and through the gates of the Circle-D onto the county road heading west out of town. Silence filled the truck cab as they both sat lost in their own thoughts. Andy fidgeted with the zipper on her jacket as she thought to break the awkward moment.

"What kind of papers did you bring with the journal?"

"Just some invoice copies and receipts that we found in Charlie's truck. Circle-D name is on all of them; thought you might want to keep them."

"Thanks. I'll look at them tomorrow and see if we've got them recorded already or not. I've been meaning to get back into the books anyway; it's hard keeping up with the book-keeping for the ranch with so much else that has to be done. I don't know what we're going to do without Charlie; Gramps relied on him for handling a lot of the Circle-D's business."

"Well maybe you can hire someone or delegate some more duties to Frank or Bill?"

"I don't see how I can hire anyone with our cash flow being so low. Know anyone who will work for peanuts? The guys stay on because they're like family and have lived with us for so long. I'll talk to Frank and Bill though, maybe your idea will work if they can help with more responsibilities for ordering feed and supplies."

Jason switched on the radio and adjusted the volume as Kenny Rodgers' voice crooned a tender love song. "Feels good to just relax for a bit, doesn't it?" he asked Andy as he reached for her hand and gave it a small squeeze. "It's been a busy couple of months, and it isn't over yet, but maybe for just a few hours we can try to pretend that everything is normal."

A short time later Jason pulled into the parking lot of the Buckhead Inn. The two-story stone structure stretched out in two directions from the center double wide doors and portico. The doors swung open to reveal gray slate in the foyer that gave way to thick colorful Indian rugs scattered across polished hardwood floors. Small round tables covered with snowy white linens were arranged to create an intimate dining atmosphere. Tall windows climbed the height of the two-story structure and provided spectacular views of the mountainside scenery. A large rustic fireplace built of gray sandstone and red granite boulders was topped with a rough-hewn wooden mantle and contained a blazing fire that warmed the expansive room to create a cozy setting. A portrait of an Arapaho Indian chief hung above the mantle.

"My goodness," Andy exclaimed as she gazed about the dining room. "I've never been here; this place is beautiful."

"Buckhead used to be a stagecoach stop and inn for the pony express riders. Now it's a restaurant on the first floor and lodging on the second floor and wings. I was hoping you'd like it. They have great food."

They were seated at a table near the fireplace where they could feel the warmth from the huge hearth. Andy scanned the menu, trying to decide between the rack of lamb or roast duck from among the delicious entrees listed. "Everything looks so good, it's hard to decide."

"Hmm, I think I'm going to try the venison. I told you they have good food here; I've never had a bad meal yet. Mom and Pop liked to come here on special occasions so as kids Jessica and I were dragged along for birthday and anniversary celebrations, but as an adult I've come to appreciate its uniqueness."

"Well thank you for bringing me here even if it's not a special occasion."

Within a short time, their waitress brought their chosen entrees of roast duck and venison and they proceeded to enjoy the meal. They spoke of the weather, the upcoming winter months and the end of the drought … everything and nothing. Small talk passed two hours of time and helped to lull both into a comfortable complacency. Jason watched Andy over the rim of his glass then made his decision.

"I want to show you something before we go home. It's important to me."

"All right Jason. I don't have to be back by any special time." She was intrigued by his request but knew she could not deny him. If it was important to Jason, then it would be important to her too.

"Just give me a few minutes in the ladies' room and I'll be ready to leave."

"You go ahead and I'll take care of the bill." Jason signaled the waitress then retrieved their coats and waited by the entrance.

Andy joined Jason within a few minutes. He stepped behind her to hold her jacket as she slipped it on. He folded his arms around her shoulders and leaned down to nuzzle the back of her neck, breathing in the teasing scent of her.

"Did you have a nice time tonight?" he whispered in her ear.

She nodded yes; the nearness of him sending shivers down her spine. She looked up, turning her head, and Jason seized the moment to brush her cheek and ear with his lips. "Guess we better go."

The clear night sky glistened with stars as they began their drive back to Deer Springs. A brisk chill filled the evening air, a harbinger of the frosty season to come.

Andy rubbed her hands together to warm them. "Brrr … I'm not sure I'm ready for this. It feels like it was just yesterday when we were fighting the summer heat on the trail. I think we're in for an early winter."

Andy watched the familiar sights of Deer Springs slide by as they drove into town and back out. She recognized the road leading to Cedarhill but then was surprised to find Jason turning on an opposite lane. She turned to him in silent inquiry.

"Do you remember my telling you that I was building a place of my own? Well, the house and buildings are almost done. I haven't named the ranch yet, but I've started to buy stock and hope to move in soon."

He drove slowly onto a circular drive, stopping in front of a stone and timber one story sprawling ranch house. A wide veranda wrapped around the front of the home and contained a pair of Adirondack chairs and a welcoming glider bench. Four flower baskets hung from the porch roof waiting to be planted. Jason paused to allow Andy time to take in the appearance of the structure before he opened the front door.

"Come on in. Have a look around." He waved his arm in a gesture to point out the great room with its high ceilings and massive stone fireplace with stove insert along one wall. A butterscotch tan leather sofa sat adjacent to the fireplace and opposite two sage green recliners. A green, gold and brown patterned area rug defined the seating space atop gleaming hardwood floors. The walls were void of art work while bare tables sat waiting lamps or finishing personal touches.

Andy wandered about the room and entered the doorway leading to the dining room and kitchen. She moved about the large kitchen in wonder. The dark cherry cabinets filled walls above and below a green and white tiled backsplash and speckled white quartz counter tops with sparkling clean white appliances. A center island provided ample workspace and seating with green glass pendant lighting fixtures above. It was a bright and cheery room that showed purpose and careful planning.

Jason stood in the doorway anxiously watching Andy's expression as she inspected his home. "What do you think?" He had chosen everything with her in mind and now hoped she would approve his choices.

"It's beautiful! The kitchen layout is wonderful, such a huge amount of workspace and storage. I'm very impressed. Did you design all of this yourself?"

"Um, most of it. I had some help. Do you think you could see yourself living here Andy?"

"Jason Hartman, are you asking me what I think you are?"

He clasped both of her hands and pulled her toward him. He kissed her once gently and then again with passion, drawing her body against his in a crushing embrace. His hands caressed her back and touched her silken hair. He held her tight against his body.

"Will you marry me Andrea? I love you with all my heart." Jason searched her eyes, looking for his answer, his heart pounding in his chest as he waited for her to speak.

"I love you Jason, you know that, but please don't demand an answer from me now. I need time to think." Tears threatened as she sadly shook her head and beseeched him to understand. Her loyalties were torn between father and lover and the result was confusion.

Disappointment filled his mind, closing out her words. He was so sure that she'd say yes to his proposal once she had seen the house. Now he dropped his arms from her and turned.

His hurt feelings colored his words causing him to speak more gruffly than he intended, "Time for me to drive you home."

"Fine! I've got a busy day tomorrow," Andy said in a huff; she could be just as stubborn as him.

"Good!" Jason replied angrily; started the ignition and dropped the truck in gear.

Their romantic and perfect evening ended in a deafeningly silent drive back to the Dunlap spread. Jason stared at the rode straight ahead while Andrea sat looking out the passenger window, tears blinding her to any sights until the lights of the house came into view. As soon as Jason pulled to a stop, Andy leaped from the truck and ran into the house. She didn't wait for Jason to walk her to the door or even say goodnight. Rapid footsteps carried her upstairs where she flopped across her bed to cry out her sorrow alone.

CHAPTER 23

The next morning Andy's eyes were still red from crying and lack of sleep as she spent the wee hours thinking of Jason's marriage proposal. If only the uncertainty of the Circle-D wasn't hanging over her head or the questions concerning her parent's death, then maybe she could think clearly and know what to do. And then there was her father's warning… didn't she have to honor her promise even in death? Where can she turn for answers?

Her feet dragged as she entered the kitchen and prepared a light breakfast. Food didn't seem to matter, nothing did. She knew she was just going through the motions as she poured mugs of coffee.

Sam watched his granddaughter with a heavy heart; knowing she was suffering but not knowing how to ease her pain. He saw her red rimmed eyes as she sat silently staring ahead.

"What's wrong honey? Is there anything that I can do?"

"Jason asked me to marry him last night, Gramps."

"Well, that's good news, not a reason to be crying," Sam exclaimed. "Aren't you happy? Jason loves you and I rather thought you loved him. I don't understand where the problem is."

"Oh Gramps, I don't know what to do! I don't want to break my promise to my father, but I do love Jason. How can I even think of marrying him? And how can I consider leaving you when the ranch is struggling? What should I do?"

"Well for starters, you just stop worrying about me and this ranch. I'll be fine and so will the Circle-D; it's not up to you to save

251

the ranch. Andy, we started this investigation about your parents, and you owe it to them to finish it; beyond that you don't owe anybody or anything. This promise you keep talking about to Brian, well that's just hog wash and I won't hear of it."

"But Gramps …" Andy began to protest but was cut off by Sam as he held up his hand.

"No butts. We take one thing at a time and I'm going to help you. We'll get to the bottom of this if it's the last thing I do. As for today, I'm going to try and make some sense out of that mountain of paperwork on the desk and you're going to read that journal."

"All right. I did say I would keep searching for clues in the journal. Maybe I can look for the dates that match the land grants, start there and see what happened. I just feel like I should be doing more than reading an old book."

"Jason thinks it's important and so do I, so don't think you won't be helping, 'cause you will. Now enough of this moping around, it's not like you and I don't like seeing it."

"Guess I know when not to argue with you! I'll start on the journal as soon as I clean up here. Think I'll start a small fire to help warm the house too if I'm going to be curled up with a book, might as well be comfortable."

June 18, 1886

It was a difficult birth, and I was relieved to have a doctor attend me instead of the mid-wife. The labor lasted for hours and the pain was almost unbearable until I heard my son's strong cries. He let out a lusty wail when the doctor slapped his behind, filling his little lungs with air. I cried for joy – a strong healthy boy, thank God.

"You're all torn up inside, Mrs. Dunlap. I don't like to see this much blood. I'm going to pack you and see if we can stop the bleeding. I want the mid-wife to check you tomorrow. I can't come back out here again."

I could feel myself drifting into a black hole; I tried to stay alert to understand what he was saying, but it was no good. Thank goodness Rose Canavan stayed by my side. I heard her ask the doctor if I was going to die as my eyes closed and sleep over took me.

June 19, 1886

I finished nursing the baby and had just laid him down when James stumbled into the cabin. He walked over to the cradle and lifted the blanket to peer at his son. James' hair appeared wet as if he had bathed in the river in an attempt to sober up, but I could still smell the whiskey on his breath and his clothes reeked of tobacco.

"We need to name him. Do you have any ideas?" I asked James.

"He looks mighty small. Are you feeding him right? I got big plans for my boy."

"The doctor and Rose both said he's healthy and looks like any normal baby. I'm taking care of him the best I can. It would help though if I had more fresh milk to drink. Can't you find time to at least milk the cow while you're home?"

"Are you going to nag me again woman? I'll get your damn milk when I can. Do something useful; put down this name in that book of yours … Alexander John Dunlap. That's what I want him called."

"Alexander … I like it. All right, we'll name him Alexander John."

"When are you getting out of that bed? Who's going to cook my supper?"

"Rose made you food; look in the pie cabinet, she left you a plate. The doctor says I have to stay in bed until the bleeding stops, James. I'm not well."

"Humph, just acting high and mighty if you ask me. Don't think you're going to be pampered like some duchess; you're still nothing but a whore in my eyes."

James grabbed his plate and slammed the cabin door as he stormed out. The baby began to cry. I cuddled him to my breast to calm him.

June 25, 1886

I am finally out of bed but moving slowly. Rose removed my packing and says the bleeding is normal now and will stop soon. The midwife does not think I will be able to have more children; I dread telling James, not that he is ever sober enough to understand. Alexander is a joy and truly my reason for living. Does every mother feel this way, I wonder? Every day I see him do something new; today he smiled for the first time.

Life on the ranch continues the same. Chores fill every hour of my day; feeding chickens and collecting their eggs, milking the cows and tending my garden. I've learned to bundle Alex in a swathing and strap him to my back while I work, looking like an Indian squaw carrying my papoose. I drop into bed each night exhausted, but still my life seems satisfying thanks to Alex. I have not seen Cody in months and I've banished all thoughts of him from my mind to preserve my sanity.

June 30, 1886

James has come home from town with a packet of papers to show me. He says he will claim another parcel of land in Alexander's name. He struts around the cabin and exclaims how big and important he will be with these extra hundred and sixty acres as a landowner in the territory. He keeps talking about making his mark on this wild land and people showing him respect. I can't help but think that people would show him more respect if he would stop being a drunk. I look at the dirty man before me smelling of whiskey and feel no level of affection or respect for the stranger that he has become. I remind myself that he is my husband, and I must honor my wedding vows and for the sake of my son, I know I will do so, but I see very little happiness in my future. Sometimes I dream of Cody and think 'if only ....'

July 4, 1886

It's official, we own more land now. James filed his land grant for Alexander and intends on planting as many fruit trees as he can. He was told he must make some kind of improvement to the land, either buildings or tree plantings, to satisfy the grant and make it legal. James thinks growing fruit trees will be less work than constructing some type of building and less expense. I think he always seeks the easy way out. Lumber can be costly if purchased from the mill in town and back breaking work if you cut down your own trees and split the wood. James has found a local farmer with some apple tree saplings that he is willing to trade for a steer.

I don't know how we would survive if we could not barter for our supplies. Cash money is at a minimum. Last month I was able to purchase canned fruit and twenty pounds of flour at the general store in exchange for two dozen eggs and the fresh butter and thick cream that I made. Our chickens and few dairy cows are both a blessing and a value. James can keep his old Longhorn beef cattle on the range, but these few Guernsey cows provide precious milk that my baby and I need. More than once I have traded eggs or butter for much needed supplies.

July 23, 1886

I've packed up my jars of cream and the wrapped butter pounds and am waiting on James to hitch up the buckboard wagon to drive us into town. For once the weather is mild and not overly warm and I want to take advantage of this temporary coolness. Alex is napping peacefully, and I am trying to let him sleep as long as possible before I have to disturb him for his first trip into town. I swear, I have begun to look forward to these rare rides into Deer Springs if for nothing else than to hear another person's voice. The ranch can be so lonely at times; I crave conversation or just a friendly word to two.

"Well? Let's get a move on", James commanded as he carried my basket outside.

I hurriedly picked up Alexander and joined him outside. The morning sun was high in the sky as we began our trek. I covered the baby's face with a thin cloth to protect him from the swirling dust kicking up along the well-worn trail. With luck he won't need to be nursed until after we arrive.

I swear I am always surprised each time we ride into Deer Springs; more new buildings and many more people. The town is growing in leaps and bounds but not all for the good I see. I counted two more saloons, a mining office and yet another structure painted bright red that can only be described as a bawdy house of ill repute; several men lingered near the door laughing and making crude gestures. Sounds from an off-key piano and loud music poured from the entrance. As we rode past, a scantily clad woman opened the

257

door and pulled one of the cowboys inside. I tried to look the other way, but I felt my face blush a heated scarlet anyway.

It's obvious that Deer Springs has turned into a rough and tumble cow town and not a family community. As we neared the mercantile store several boisterous men stumbled from the wooden sidewalk and nearly fell into the path of our wagon. They cursed violently and shot pistols into the air as James jerked on the reins to guide the horse and wagon away from them. I screamed and the baby began to cry, adding to the bedlam. My composure was shaken badly as I started to climb down from the rickety buckboard. I stood a moment on the walkway, clutching Alex against my left shoulder, juggling my bag and market basket with my right hand while I took deep breaths to calm my fright. Just when I thought I had my emotions under control and could take a step forward, I looked up to find familiar blue eyes staring at me, drilling into my very soul. His penetrating gaze took in every inch of my appearance. Did he see the lines of worry and stress now etched about my eyes and on my face? Would he care?

I stood frozen, unable to think, as I watched Cody Jarvis saunter toward me. He seemed to take in the scene with some amusement, a small smile curving his lips; but then I saw his right hand resting atop his gun holster and I realized that he was ready to spring into action as he studied the drunken cowhands. Satisfied that no harm was imminent, I watched him visibly relax and turn his attention to the baby still crying in my arms.

"How old?" Cody inquired of Alex as he reached out to remove the blanket from the baby's face.

"My son, Alexander, about a month old." I jostled him back into position on my shoulder, still encumbered by my other burdens.

Cody quickly perceived my dilemma as he lifted the market basket and tote from my hands, relieving me to comfort my son properly. I patted Alex on the back and he found his fist to suck on as he quieted down. I saw Cody watch my ministrations and he smiled again, this time more warmly and the smile reached those incredible blue eyes. I suddenly averted my own eyes lest he think I wanted his attention.

James strode angrily toward us. "What do you want Jarvis? He's not your brat, I made sure of that."

"James! Please, people are beginning to stare," I tried to reason with him as my embarrassment grew and I feared an awkward moment would turn into something ugly and dangerous.

"Well Dunlap, I see time has not changed you any, still as even tempered as usual." Cody turned to me and quietly asked, "Are you well Maggie? Do you need anything?"

"I'm fine. Please… I think it best if you leave." I looked into his eyes, silently begging him to understand and not provoke a fight. I had no doubt he would be the victor, but could I live with myself if I was the cause of James' injury or death? Or worse, could my heart bear to see Cody hurt?

He nodded ever so slightly to me and I saw his decision before he announced it. "Don't push me Dunlap." He stood facing me a moment longer, regret showing in his eyes as he touched the brim of his hat and spun about on his heel to walk away.

James gave a harsh laugh as he picked up my basket from where Cody had set it and then grabbed me by the elbow propelling me forward. "Well, I guess I told him! He can't push me around— not James Dunlap. He's not so tough. And I better never see you cozying up to him again."

"I did no such thing. He was only politely asking about the baby."

"Yeah, well I don't want him sniffing around you again. Get about your business, Margaret. If you want time to do your shopping, you best get to it. When I say we're leaving, you better be ready or you can walk home."

I nodded to Mr. Morgan as I entered the general store and turned to witness James push open the swinging doors of the nearest saloon. I made a small sigh of despair, knowing he would be in a nasty mood during the drive back home. It didn't matter that it was early in the day; James drank whenever the mood struck him, and it appeared that he was in the mood now for his whiskey. No doubt he'll want to glory in his triumph over Cody Jarvis. God help me to understand how a man's mind works and their ridiculous sense of pride.

September 6, 1886

If James thought it would be easy planting rows and rows of little trees, he was sorely mistaken. My back aches from the hours spent bending over as we all labored to plant apple trees on the new parcel of land. Mike Canavan is certainly a dear friend, so loyal and helpful. He and Rose worked side by side with me and James to complete the orchard. We were so lucky when we met these wonderful people. Once again, they have come to our rescue.

James wants to pledge the troth of our children in marriage. Little Alexander will be a fortunate man to marry into such a fine family with Rose's daughter Katie. I know it is a tradition of the old world rather than the new to arrange marriages for your children, but I am hopeful that my son will find happiness in his future. Maybe I would have been happier if I had obeyed my parents' wishes in my own arranged marriage. Sometimes I wonder what happened to Albert Pennington; perhaps he transferred his allegiance to my sister Ann. I suppose I will never know.

September 9, 1886

James is beside himself with joy. I've never seen him this excited. He hasn't even taken a drink of whiskey today, so absorbed in his new discovery.

"I'm going to be a rich man Margaret! Would you just look at this silver? I tell you we struck a vein and a deep one! You should have seen Michael's eyes when his pickaxe splintered that large rock and the silver shined beneath!"

I watched him rub the stone and polish it some more to see the sparkle of the ore. Digging in the earth to plant trees has yielded more than apples. James is deliriously happy and yet I worry when I see the greed shining in his eyes and his growing obsession with the silver.

"You need to share that silver with Michael Canavan; after all it was his efforts that found it."

"It's my land so that makes it my silver. Do you think I'm daft, woman, to be giving away my riches?"

"You owe Michael; it will make up for the money that I know you stole from that poor man. He's too loyal to you to ever accuse you of cheating at cards, but I've seen you James."

James' hand shot out quickly and I felt his knuckles graze my cheek as the full impact of the back of his hand slapped my face.

"How dare you accuse me of being a cheat? It's not my fault if a man does'na keep his wits about him with cards in his hand and stakes on the table. He knows the risk; I didn't force him to play."

Tears stung my eyes and my cheek burned as I moved away from him to the far side of the cabin. It was best not to provoke James and suffer his cruelty again. My blackened eye just recently faded to yellow and is still recovering from our last "family discussion".

CHAPTER 24

Jason and Mac drove past the crash site of Charlie Tucker's truck as they headed north toward Hancock Road and the Gates Motel. Jason sat reading over the garage report on the condition of Charlie's truck while Mac drove the cruiser. According to Smitty, the truck was old but mechanically sound; brakes were in working order. Nothing indicated any reason for an accidental crash.

"Hmm, just as I suspected. I thought maybe Charlie had been behind the wheel and then shot, but the evidence points elsewhere."

"I take it that Smitty gave the truck a clean bill of health?"

"Yep, nothing down that road."

Mac turned off the interstate and pulled into the small parking lot in front of the Gates Motel. A window in the far left building held a neon sign blinking "office". Mac and J.C. stood by the cruiser, scanning the property and looking for any signs of movement. Jason noted the row of small, weathered bungalows that faced the roadway and then angled to the right. Rooms contained narrow grimy windows that probably hadn't been washed in months and doors were stenciled with red faded room numbers on peeling white paint.

Jason spied movement behind the window blinds of the small office. Someone was peeking through the broken slats. He motioned to Mac and they turned in unison, to walk briskly toward the office door. It opened as they approached the dimly lit interior.

A slightly built man with graying hair and sporting a heavy five o'clock shadow stood to one side of the portal. His faded khaki work pants were frayed at the cuffs and one knee was worn so thin it looked like it would tear if he bent his leg. A wrinkled shirt hung over the loose-fitting pants. Harry Booker glanced nervously at the two lawmen.

"Howdy. Are you the manager?" asked Jason as he entered the small space. Mac stood by the door, keeping an eye on both office and parking lot while he listened to Jason question the man.

"Yeah, I'm the manager, Harry Booker's the name. My missus and me run the place. What do you want?"

Jason pulled a copy of Charlie Tucker's driver license photo from his pocket and handed it to the man. "Ever see this man? He one of your customers?"

"Can't say as how I remember him. Don't know. Why?"

"Sure he wasn't here about a week ago? His name was Tucker and he drove a red Dodge pickup."

Booker walked behind the counter and reached for a bound book lying atop a narrow shelf. He shoved the guest register across the surface toward the sheriff.

"You can look for yourself. See if his name's here."

Jason flipped through the few pages covered in various pencil and ink signatures. The motel serviced more truckers than tourists; not exactly a thriving business so there weren't too many lines to review. A brief inspection confirmed the manager's statement. No Charlie Tucker name and signature among the guests.

"All right, thanks. Mind if I poke around a bit anyway?"

"No, go ahead. Suit yourself."

"Thanks. Are the rooms open or do I need a key?"

"Ah, I um think my wife's cleaning today so they're unlocked."

"Fine. Thanks for your time and help."

Jason and Mac walked outside and down the sidewalk toward the line of room doors. The rooms closest to the office held high numbers and went down in sequence as they walked further away from the office. Jason pulled out the book of matches and read the number written inside the cover. He stopped in front of door number twelve and entered the poorly lit room. The furnishings weren't too inspiring; matted dark brown carpeting covered the floor while a gaudy brown and orange flowered bedspread and faded matching curtains completed the décor. A mirror, a small chair and chest of drawers completed the basic furniture. Jason peeked inside the bathroom door that stood ajar. Nothing fancy that's for sure.

He closed the door behind him and continued walking past a few more rooms then randomly stopped again. "Go ahead Mac, let's check this one out, room number eight."

Mac did the walk-through this time and found more of the same: brown rug and flowered bed cover, same furniture arrangement and room size; obviously the motel had bought wholesale lots of furniture and linens when it originally opened for business. They opened two more rooms until they turned the corner and approached door number four in the rear of the property.

"Let's look around inside this one," Jason directed as he and Mac entered the empty room. Jason turned on the light switch and immediately he and Mac noted that the flowered bedspread in this room was missing. Only a blue blanket covered the bed. Dirty orange and brown flowered curtains draped the window just like all the other rooms but what happened to the bed?

"Mac, make a note of anything that looks different or out of place. Charlie had this room number written down for a reason." Jason inspected the bathroom then peered into the narrow closet. He opened chest drawers and pushed aside the curtains as he closely examined the room.

"Hey J.C., what do you think that is?" Mac pointed to the blackened smudges on the painted windowsill. He scraped the marks with the side of his car key and picked up small granules. "Could be ash from a cigarette or cigar."

Jason studied the black marks and agreed they appeared to be ground ash. He stooped down and looked under the chair and bed, feeling about with his hand. His fingers touched the short stub of a cigar. He gingerly retrieved the butt and dropped it into a small Ziploc bag.

Jason pushed aside the garish curtains, noticing some dark spots mixed among the orange flowers on the material. He sniffed the spots and detected a distinct metallic smell that gave evidence of blood overspray. He grabbed his Kodak digital camera and captured some close-up images of the curtain stains.

"Mac, yank down this curtain. I want to send it to the state forensic lab for testing on this blood. Did you find anything else?"

"No. Place is so dirty, it's kind of hard to see anything out of the ordinary. Do you think if they changed the bed stuff that maybe there was blood on it? The bed does sit right next to the window."

"That's a strong possibility. Think the blood soaked through? Let's strip this bed and have a closer look," Jason said as he and Mac grabbed the blanket and slid it off the mattress.

Another quick pull of the sheets and thin quilted pad exposed the mattress ticking beneath. Nothing. Jason was so sure they were going to find something. He stood staring at the bed then snapped his fingers as a thought occurred.

"Help me turn this thing over. I just wonder…"

A dark blotch stained a large portion of the mattress cover.

"Well, we certainly have some evidence, but of what? Snap some photos of this, the other room furnishings and window ash."

The sheriff handed the camera to his deputy and reached into his pocket for his pen knife. He ran the blade along the edges of the stained mattress ticking and proceeded to cut out a square block. He carefully lifted the square and slipped it into another plastic evidence bag for further investigation.

"Maybe the guys at the state police lab can give us some help. Meanwhile, let's go talk to Mr. Booker again and see if we can jog his memory of who occupied this room."

They gathered up their baggies and camera then headed back to the front office. Booker was nervously watching from the doorway as they approached. He shifted from side to side as Jason neared.

"Anything you want to tell me about room number four? What happened in there? We've got evidence of blood splatter and I want a name from you."

"I don't know nothing about that. That room hasn't been rented in a while."

"Mac, better read 'em his rights and put on the cuffs. Mr. Booker's going to take a ride."

"Hey! Wait a minute. You can't do that," he exclaimed as Mac jerked his arms behind his back and started snapping on the first handcuff.

"Buddy, it looks like we can, unless you can prove to me otherwise. Start thinking real hard. Who was in that room last week? Why did you remove the bed covers and try to hide that bloody mattress? I need some answers."

"Sometimes people just sneak into our rooms for a quickie, you know? Especially the ones in the rear, maybe the door was unlocked, perhaps somebody just came in. I don't know, I tell you. I can't see everything that goes on. This place ain't exactly the Hilton, you know."

"I'm not talking about a pair of teenagers playing around. We're talking a homicide investigation and right now you're smack in the middle of it. Want to try another story?" Jason nodded to Mac and jerked his head toward the car.

Mac clasped Booker's cuffed wrists and pushed him out the door. He opened the rear door of the cruiser as he bent the suspect's head and guided him onto the back seat. Jason placed the evidence bags in the trunk then started up the engine as Mac slid into the passenger seat. He looked over his shoulder at their prisoner; Booker's face had turned pale and he was trembling as they drove away and headed back to Deer Springs.

Sam read through another stack of feed bills and invoices, shaking his head and scribbling figures on a scratch pad. He grabbed the crumpled invoices that Jason had dropped off and headed for the barn and store room.

"Frank, how many bags of oats and Triple Crown horse feed do we have on hand? How about salt blocks and minerals? I've got invoices from Cooper's and I don't recall seeing this stuff."

"Let me see that paper. We don't have any of this on hand. Charlie brought in a truck load of supplies last month, but I don't know where it is now. In fact, now that I think about it, Bill was mentioning to Charlie that we were low on Triple Crown. I don't get it."

"Well we've been paying Cooper's bills and I can't find what we've been paying for. No wonder we're broke. How the hell can we have used this kind of feed quantity? And here's another thing," Sam handed Frank a second statement, "since when did we buy an automatic feeder for the bottle calves? We don't even have any young calves right now? Look at the price on that!"

"I don't know what to tell you, Sam. Charlie always did all the ordering and I guess I just assumed that you or Brian approved it."

"I want a full inventory done. I've got to find out what we have and what we don't. Get Bill to help you and start right away. I've got to get to the bottom of this."

"Why would Charlie cause all these expenses? What happened to all of it?"

"That's what I'm going to find out. Either Charlie was selling our supplies behind my back, or we paid for things we never received, either way, he was stealing us blind. I trusted the man, treated him like family! That's what's killing me. Why'd he do it, Frank?"

Sam clenched the documents and stomped back across the yard toward the house. Wind whipped across the open field as Sam peered at the darkening clouds and speculated on how long it would be before the impending storm broke. There was a storm coming all right, but not necessarily from the sky.

Brent Logan stood with his arms folded, studying the large framed Platte County map hanging on the wall behind his desk. The Diamond Bar ranch borders were boldly outlined and shaded in a green color on the map; spreading it dimensions across a wide expanse of the county. Brent picked up the marker and highlighted several smaller parcels with the green color then surveyed his work with satisfaction. The Logan empire was growing. He smiled and thought of his father and how proud he would have been.

"It hasn't been easy", Brent thought, as he recalled the last deal and expense to secure the Tarrington's foreclosed spread. That one had cost him more money than he had intended but he wanted their land and the timber on it. Brent ground the end of his cigar into the glass ashtray as he recalled Wilson demanding a bigger cut in the deal. The man was getting difficult; something would have to be done about that. A scowl spread across his face as he studied the property lines of the last two ranches that he couldn't get his hands on – Cedarhill and the Circle-D. He was no fool; he knew Cedarhill was out of his reach; Jarrod Hartman was too good of a business manager to let his finances get into jeopardy. But failure didn't sit well with him; it left a bad taste in his mouth as he thought of how close he had come to owning the Circle-D. If the Dunlaps hadn't made that damn mortgage payment, he'd be seeing a foreclosure on their land and it would be his by now. Goddamn Wilson didn't handle that matter right and now with all this snooping going on…. can't risk another accident.

CHAPTER 25

January 9, 1887

James is complaining of being cooped up, I believe I have heard it referred to as cabin fever. He is determined to ride into town. Today there is a break in the weather. I too am relieved to see the sun shining and the temperatures slightly warmer. I'm taking advantage of the respite from our winter cold to wash our clothes and hang them outside to dry while I can.

James is anxious to be gone and I cannot say that I will miss his constant grumbling and ill moods. It will be good to have the day to myself with him out of the house. Even little Alex senses his father's anger and seems happier when he can crawl about the room without James shouting at him.

I haven't ventured into Deer Springs since before Christmas, not wanting to risk taking the baby out in the bitter temperatures and heavy snow. I have rationed my supplies and pray they last until next month when I can perhaps go shopping again. Thank goodness we still have eggs and milk from our own farm and that allows me some peace of mind knowing we won't come close to starving like past winters. I feel rather proud about that. It's my efforts that feed the chickens and care for the cow. I have to chuckle; I've become quite the frontier woman; my own mother would not recognize me now.

James did not come home last night. No doubt he found a card game to his liking or became too drunk again to ride the distance to our ranch. I had just finished feeding Alex his breakfast when I heard the pounding on our cabin door.

Expecting to see James stumble in, I was surprised to find Michael Canavan standing with his hat in hand and two horses tethered close by. I studied his expression and knew he was the bearer of bad news. I quickly turned to the waiting horses, seeing for the first time the blanket covered body draped across the saddle.

"Is that James? Is he sick or just drunk?" I asked Michael, but in my heart I knew different.

"I'm sorry Margaret. James is dead, shot down by that murdering thief Jarvis!"

"No! You're wrong! Cody wouldn't do such a thing." Shame washed over me as I realized that my first thoughts were of Cody Jarvis and not my husband lying dead. I looked at Michael and then at the draped form. Tears slid down my cheeks as I lifted the blanket from my husband's face, his eyes open and blank, and I reached to gently close his lids.

Michael helped me carry James into the house and laid him on our bed. My mind was numb. What am I to do? How can I manage on my own? What happened? Why would Cody shoot James? It made no sense. I had no answers to the questions swimming in my head.

I stumbled to a chair and collapsed into it. Cradling my face in my hands, I cried softly, rocking my body in a slow motion to help calm my jangled nerves. Michael sat silently allowing me to grieve and to come to grips with the situation. I finally raised my eyes to his.

"You better tell me what you know."

"Well," Michael began his tale, "it seems James had come into town yesterday and met up with some of the wranglers from the Diamond Bar. There's always a card game going on at the Silver Spur saloon and it didn't take James much time before he was seated at a poker table." He hesitated and I could tell it was awkward for him talking to me like this.

"It's all right Michael, you aren't telling me anything new. I've suspected over the past year that he's been gambling heavily."

"I guess he stayed at the table for hours and into the night. I wasn't there. I only rode into town this morning to pick up some dry goods for Rose. I heard of the gunfight from Morgan in the store and I rushed over to the saloon to see for myself."

"Was James already dead when you got there?"

"The room was filled with gun smoke, hanging above the card tables and stinging my eyes as I tried to find James. It took me a minute to get used to the dark and then I spotted James lying on the floor and surrounded by a group of men and dance hall girls."

"Did you see Cody Jarvis?" I had to know if he was involved and yet dreaded hearing any confirmation that he was.

"Um, no, but when I pushed aside the cowpokes standing around James' body, they were all from the Diamond Bar and everybody knows that Jarvis does Logan's killing. He's the hired gun. So, it had to be him that shot him. I hear tell there was a lot of money at stake riding on that poker game; James had bet the ranch on that last hand."

"What do you mean he bet the ranch? I don't understand. Am I going to lose my home? Oh my God, I can't believe this is happening! It's a nightmare."

"I only know what I heard Margaret. I did see some papers on the table, looked like James had signed something, but I can't be sure."

My mind tried to come to grips with this latest horror. Suddenly, I knew what I needed to do.

"I am going into Deer Springs and to speak with the sheriff. I want some facts. Michael, can you please ask Rose to come and stay with little Alex while I go into town? I'll do what I can to prepare James for burial and then ride into town come morning. Can you please bring Rose back here in the morning?"

"Yeah, sure. We've got a pair of young boys boarding with us and working the farm, I'll bring them back with me to help dig the grave."

I thought of the monumental task that lay ahead of me. How was I to cope? How could I raise my child alone? Was I in danger of losing the ranch and our home? Endless questions screamed in my head. I stared at the wintry landscape out the window. James' burial

- how can a grave even be dug in this frozen earth with all this snow? Once again I felt so grateful to the Canavan family as I heard Michael ride away.

Morning came too soon as I watched the faint dawn light filter through our small window. The hours had sped by as I labored through the night, washing and dressing James' body. I did the best I could. His one clean shirt and ill-fitting jacket will have to do as he goes to meet his maker. Now I needed to tidy my own appearance before Michael and Rose Canavan arrive to herald the beginning of my hellish day.

January 11, 1887

Rose knocked on the door with one hand as she turned the knob with the other and entered the cabin. Michael, carrying baby Katie, and his two ranch hands were close behind her. Our little cabin was suddenly very crowded.

"Where do you want the grave dug, Margaret? We brought shovels and our pickaxes and I guess we can hammer together a coffin from whatever wood we can find in the barn."

Alex began to cry to make his presence known. I lifted him from his cradle and hugged him close as my mind digested this latest detail. The baby was wet and needed a clean diaper as well as a bottle of milk. I turned and handed Alex to Rose's waiting arms as she laid Katie in his now empty crib.

"Can you feed and change him Rose while I go outside with Michael? I'm so glad you're here."

I draped my woolen cloak about my shoulders and led the men outside to a spot away from our cabin but on the edge of the flower garden I had planted last summer. It would be a fitting place for James' grave. I liked the idea of knowing there would be fresh blooms gracing his resting place. It gave me comfort.

Michael and the two boys rummaged in the barn, pulling off a few loose planks to use for coffin lumber. Their hammers rang out in the still morning air. It only required a few minutes to complete the task. The men didn't need me to watch them dig the snow-covered ground, so I waited inside the warm cabin until it was ready for the burial. Finally, it was done.

The men slowly lowered the wooden casket into the cold earth, sliding it down long ropes like a pulley. When they finished, we all stood there silent. A hawk screeched as it soared overhead breaking our reverie. Rose produced her Bible and started reading the Lord's Prayer. I wish we could have had a minister to say a few words, but Deer Springs didn't include a church when it experienced its growth spurt during the past year.

"Thank you Rose. We better get out of this frigid air. I need a few moments to get ready before riding into town."

Rose turned to Michael, "You need to ride in with Margaret. It isn't safe for her to go alone."

I felt such affection in that moment for these kind people. My baby would be well cared for with Rose and I would definitely appreciate Michael's company and protection.

We rode in silence to Deer Springs and stopped in front of a row of one-story clapboard buildings. Michael helped me down from the buckboard wagon and tied the two horses to the hitching rail before we proceeded to the marshal's office. I nervously opened the door; my resolve abandoned me. Unsure how to start or what to say, I approached the lawman seated behind the small desk.

"Sheriff Conner, my name is Margaret Dunlap. I need to find out what happened to my husband James."

He waved toward a pair of rickety chairs and indicated for me to sit. I sat on the edge of the hard wooden seat, my hands clasped in my lap. I glanced at Michael Canavan standing near the door. He nodded to me, reassuring me as I waited for the marshal to answer my inquiry.

"What is it you want to know? All I can tell you is that the man was shot during a poker game. He was drunk and cheating at cards and one of the men at the table didn't take kindly to that."

"Do you approve of that kind of behavior? A man gets shot for cheating at cards," I said, horrified by his callous words.

"Excuse me Sheriff, if you could maybe explain how it happened or give Mrs. Dunlap more details…she has a question about her ranch," Michael interjected.

The sheriff turned his attention to Michael. "Who are you?"

"Michael Canavan, sir. I'm neighbor to the Dunlap family."

"Humph, well I wasn't there of course. I entered the Silver Spur after I heard the gun fire. Your husband was drunk, Mrs. Dunlap, and pulled a gun on young Jimmy Ryan when he was accused of cheating."

"That just doesn't make sense. Oh, I can imagine James drunk all right, but not starting a gun fight. So was it this Jimmy who shot him?"

"No, it was someone else, one of Zach Logan's men. There were several at that poker game playing with both Mr. Logan and your husband. All you need to know is that I ruled it self-defense. It was a fair fight. I'm sorry for your loss." The marshal sat back in his chair, looked at Michael and me then folded his arms across his chest as if to indicate the matter done.

I sat in silence, stunned by his words. My eyes burned with unshed tears. Such a waste. This violent land we had come to, and now what? Am I to stay and build a life for my son and I or should I return to Scotland in shame and disgrace? No, as soon as the thought entered my mind my heart banished it – I won't beg my parents for a home, that door was closed. So here I am and here I will stay.

"What about my ranch, sheriff? I was told James had pledged a deed to our land at this poker game. Is that correct? Can such a thing happen?"

"You're new to our country Mrs. Dunlap, so I can see where you wouldn't understand that money and land often change hands when men gamble. It's common practice. If your husband ran out of money he probably bet the ranch; he'd been bragging all over town

279

about the rich silver vein he struck on that land. I don't know who has the deed. Maybe Mr. Logan can help you."

"And where would I find this Mr. Logan? I'd like to see some proof that James signed over our ranch. I can't believe that even in a drunken state James would do such a thing."

"Well, Ma'am, if that's how you feel, maybe you better wait on the arrival of the territory circuit judge. He'll listen to your case if you don't believe me in the matter of your ranch. I reckon he's due here next month some time."

"I think I will do just that, marshal. Thank you for your time." I nodded my head to him and rose to leave when his parting words stopped me in my stride.

"You do that; of course, since he's Logan's brother, I don't think it will matter much."

His last words made me pause as we stepped outside, and I tried to collect my emotions. The brisk wind lifted my cloak and stung my face; bringing me back to my stark reality. I glanced about as a few people hurried across the wooden sidewalk, women entering small shops and the men heading for saloons. I did not recognize very many faces. I felt so alone; I was being swept away by a tidal wave of events that I had no control over.

I sat quietly next to Michael as we made the long ride back to the ranch. The prairie looked so barren in winter; it reflected my own thoughts and future. I shook my head to clear the dismal musings filling my mind.

Smoke spiraled upward from the cabin chimney, a warm welcoming sight that helped to lift my spirits a bit. My son lay sleeping in his bed, safe and sound, unaware of the traumatic change to his little life that was about to begin. How will I explain to him where his father has gone? He's so young. Will he even remember his father as time passes? Would that be a good or a bad thing?

Rose and Michael studied my face; I fear they were watching for signs of hysteria. I don't know what they expected but my calm resolve seemed to surprise them.

"Michael, how can I go about hiring a ranch hand like you have? Do you think there is a young lad who would work for me and live here for room and board? I won't be able to pay much until spring when we have some crops and animals to sell. I intend to work this ranch and live here until that circuit judge forces me to leave. This is my home. I'm staying."

"We'll help you all we can Margaret. Jacob has a cousin that may be able to help you; he's still living with his parents and they have a large family. I'll ask. But Margaret, won't you be taking a chance that Zachary Logan will put you out? If he owns the land now, what can you do?"

"I'm going to fight him, that's what I'm going to do. I plan to speak to this so-called judge, even if he is Logan's relative. The marshal said James was shot in self-defense. But Michael, I cleaned the wound, James was shot in the back."

February 16, 1887

I received word that the circuit judge had arrived at Deer Springs. I must speak with him. I cannot live with the uncertainty of our ranch hanging over my head. Every day during the last month I jumped whenever I heard a sound or someone knocked on the door.

Michael Canavan kept his word by having a young lad from Jacob Yoder's family come visit me. Jacob's cousin Aaron has agreed to stay and help with the cattle and animals on the ranch. He promises me that his brothers will help with the spring plowing and seeding when the soil thaws and our last snow is gone. So at least I have some future plan and that gives me some hope and sense of control. Aaron is a quiet lad and I hardly even notice him in the house; he spends a lot of his time outside in the barn. His hands are always busy mending some leather strap or sharpening a plow blade; such an industrious young man. I count him among my blessings, to be sure.

Tomorrow I'll ride into town and have my day in court. I only hope my nerves will calm down long enough for me to sleep tonight; I'm so anxious.

February 17, 1887

Several men stood outside the Silver Spur saloon talking and milling about and I had to push past them to enter the place. They laughed at me as I did so and I had to pretend not to notice but I know my face blushed red in my embarrassment to be in such an establishment. The Silver Spur has been turned into a courthouse for the day; I was relieved to find the absence of the dance hall girls and bawdy music. A large table had been placed along the back wall with a single chair behind it. Other chairs created three rows in front of the table; an open aisle in the center space. I slowly walked up the aisle and took a seat in the front row, waiting on the arrival of the circuit judge. I sat quietly as more people began to fill the empty seats. I noticed that one man even brought some livestock; two goats were tethered to a rope wrapped around his left hand.

Marshal Conner touched the brim of his hat and nodded toward me as he approached the head table. "All right, quiet down everyone. The Honorable Judge Thomas Logan presiding."

With that announcement, I watched a tall, lean man stride across the room and take his position behind the table. He opened a worn leather case and withdrew two thick books, placing them to his left on the table. I could clearly see the word Bible etched along the spine of one book. I studied the features of this man who would be deciding my fate. Would he treat me kindly or harshly? I almost jumped as he loudly banged a wooden gavel upon the worn makeshift desk.

"Come to order please. The first case on the docket this morning is Henry Jones versus Robert McFadden. Will Mr. Jones and McFadden please stand? Now then, Mr. Jones, what seems to be the trouble?"

I sat listening as the man complained about the sheep grazing in his pastures and why he felt justified in shooting the animals. Then

Mr. McFadden jumped up to argue that his sheep were not taking grass away from Mr. Jones' cattle and he demanded payment for his slaughtered sheep. I waited while Judge Logan appeared to be weighing the concerns of each man then spoke.

"Mr. McFadden this is cattle country. I am restricting you to only grazing your sheep on open range. Mr. Jones, you are within your right to remove the sheep from pastures within your ranch boundaries but must compensate McFadden for the killed sheep. I fine you an amount of thirty dollars for the dead animals."

He rapped the gavel on the hard surface, wrote some notes on a piece of paper then looked at a gentleman sitting in the corner that I had not noticed before.

"Next case is Logan versus Dunlap. Who's here representing Dunlap?"

The suddenness of hearing my name called startled me and I raised my hand to indicate my presence. I felt the color wash out of my face and my firm resolve left me as I saw the judge study my face and look me up and down. He nodded in my direction then spoke again.

"Zachary Logan, I see you are in possession of a deed transferring ownership of a parcel of land? What can you tell the court about this transaction?"

Zachary Logan stood by his chair and touched his finger to the brim of his hat in respect to the judge as he began to speak. I noticed his calm demeanor and the tailored coat that he wore. He did not fit my image of the typical ranchers that I had met in this land, nor did he match the villainous character my imagination had conceived after listening to Michael Canavan's tales or even James' past remarks. So this was Zachary Logan that everyone was so afraid of? Hmm. I admit I was mesmerized until he spoke.

"Judge, the land in question is two parcels that I won during a poker game with James Dunlap. Unfortunately for Mr. Dunlap, there was a disagreement during the game and a gunfight that sadly caused Mr. Dunlap's demise. Marshal Conner can provide you with the details; it was a fair fight in self-defense with plenty of witnesses."

"That's a lie!" I blurted the words as I jumped to my feet. I didn't plan on verbally attacking the man, it just happened.

The judge turned to me as he said, "And you are? Mrs. Dunlap, I presume? What is your version of what happened?"

"Your Honor, my husband was no gunfighter. I cannot believe that James would pull a gun on Mr. Logan. I have asked the marshal for details but have not been told who even shot my husband; just that it occurred during some poker game."

"My condolences to you Mrs. Dunlap, but since you were not present and I was, you will just have to take my word for what happened. Your husband was cheating all during the game. When my foreman accused him, he pulled a gun. Naturally the man had to defend himself."

"What about the deed; when was that transaction completed?" Judge Logan questioned.

I was curious about that too. I still did not believe that James would bet our ranch on a turn of a card. I waited to hear what Zachary Logan had to say.

I thought it odd that Logan still did not name the shooter. I didn't know any more facts now than before. My heart wanted to believe that it wasn't Cody and he had not broken his promise to me. But I must not think of that now, not when it was still uncertain whether I would have a roof over my head come morning.

"Well sir, I believe the round of cards just before the shooting was when Dunlap pledged his ranch against a bet and when he lost, he signed a paper transferring the ownership. He probably wanted to get his land back and started cheating. I don't pretend to know what he was thinking; the man was drunk and angry."

"Do you have the signed deed with you now?" asked the judge.

I watched as Zachary Logan handed a rolled document to the judge. He sat back down and stared at me in such a way that I felt chilled. Now I could see why men feared this man.

"Mrs. Dunlap, what do you have to say in this matter?" Judge Logan turned his attention to me.

"My husband did drink and could become angry. I admit that to be true, but I do not believe my husband would pull a gun on someone. He was not that brave. A wife does not like saying that, but it's true. May I see the papers he signed?"

I stood and approached the judge's table. I reached for the document, but he pulled it open and laid his hand on the paper, keeping it displayed on the tabletop.

I examined the words on the paper, reading the description of our ranch and saw to my horror that both parcels were listed; the one with our home and the one claimed under Alexander's name. My eyes widened as I clearly read the name 'James Dunlap' in a small crimped signature. Zachary Logan's name appeared in a strong swirling script and two other men had signed as witnesses, both Logan's ranch hands, no doubt.

"My husband never learned to read or write. That is not his signature. I cannot accept this deed as true."

"Mrs. Dunlap, I can understand that you are upset about the loss of your ranch, but this court only has your word on whether this is your husband's signature. Do you have any proof to your claim that he could not read or write? Mr. Logan says this is a valid deed and he has witnesses."

I could not think. How could I prove that James was illiterate? I shook my head and stammered, "It wasn't self-defense like this man says. James was shot in the back."

I heard a murmur pass through the courtroom spectators at my words. Evidently, no one had ever dared to defy Zachary Logan before, and I realized that I had just called him a liar for the second time.

The judge and his brother exchanged looks and I saw the judge motion to Logan to stay seated. Once again, he turned his attention to me and smiled slightly.

"Again, Mrs. Dunlap, do you have proof that your husband was shot in the back? It's not what the marshal says, and Mr. Logan has witnesses."

"I buried my husband so of course I don't have proof unless you dig up his body. What was I supposed to do, keep him on ice until you came to town?" My raised voice sounded strident to my own ears. Now I was angry; I didn't care what Zachary Logan or his brother thought.

The judge pounded his gavel once more and I sat back in my chair awaiting his next words.

"I think I have heard enough facts in this case. I believe I can make my ruling now and all parties will be bound by my decision. The matter of the shooting of one James Dunlap will remain as a justified shooting in self-defense, since the marshal of Deer Springs did testify to that fact and I have no evidence to the contrary. As for the disposition of the land parcels, I believe a compromise is in order.The parcel of land containing the homestead and ranch buildings will remain in the Dunlap name, but the unimproved parcel of land will be forfeited as legal gambling winnings as indicated by James Dunlap's signature and shall be transferred to Mr. Zachary Logan's ownership. Are you both in agreement to this?"

"Yes, your Honor. I have no desire to see a widow and child put out in the cold. She can keep the ranch land. I'm satisfied keeping the other parcel as my just due."

Both men looked at me and waited for my answer; as if I had a choice. Justice was not done here today but at least I still had a home.

I tried to appear meek while my blood boiled and nodded, "Yes, thank you judge."

Zachary Logan rose and left the courtroom. His lips curled slightly into a smug smile under his walrus mustache; he got what he wanted. The land and the silver vein were his, all nice and legal in appearance. He'll have to remember to buy his brother dinner as a thank you for his ruling.

CHAPTER 26

June 5, 1887

Sprouts of corn poked through the plowed furrows and in an adjacent field, barley waved its head as the gentle wind created ripples through the grasses. It would soon be time to harvest our spring toil. This season would see whether I prosper or fail working the ranch as a lone woman. God help me if I fail.

I need to drive into town tomorrow. I have eggs and butter to sell at the store in exchange for much needed seed and other food supplies. I hope to handle the wagon and horse myself; Aaron is busy with caring for three young calves that were born last week. He is bottle feeding them and with all his other chores I simply cannot ask him to accompany me. I'm confident I can drive the rig and I must learn to do for myself now. Little Alex is big enough to sit on the seat beside me if I tie him secure with a blanket.

June 6, 1887

The sky is clear and a bright blue this morning but not too hot, a perfect day to make the drive into Deer Springs. I'm looking forward to speaking with Mr. Morgan in the general store. Hopefully I can get into town and back home before the hour gets too late.

Alex is excited and waves his arms about as he babbles in that baby talk that only a baby can understand. He's such a good boy; I'm so blessed to have him. He seems content to sit in his blanket swaddling, wedged between me on one side and the large market basket on his other. If we don't hit any big bumps or go too fast he should be all right.

It's been almost four months since my last visit to town and now I wonder what new buildings I'll see. There always seems to be some change, but as I have witnessed in the past, not always for the better. I pulled up on the reins and managed to bring my buckboard wagon close to the wooden walkway in front of the general store. I climbed down from my wagon and stepped onto the elevated platform before turning to untie Alex and lift him into my arms.

Just as I turned, I felt a hand on my elbow steadying me; I smelled the scent of him, my pulse quickened from his touch, before he even spoke. I'd recognize Cody Jarvis in a dark room filled with a hundred men; he filled my senses. I stood still a moment, trying to calm my emotions before I raised my eyes to his.

"Hello Maggie."

I felt his warm breath caress the nape of my neck as his softly spoken greeting reached my ears alone. Such simple words, but I heard the strain in his voice, the emotion held in check.

"Cody! I need to talk to you," I answered him in the same hushed voice, glancing about to see who witnessed our exchange.

"What are you doing in town and alone?"

"I have business to attend. Is there somewhere private where we can meet?" I already felt curious eyes on me and knew we were drawing attention the longer we stood there.

"The Silver Spur has added hotel rooms upstairs and some dining tables in the side room. Meet me there when you're done with your business, in the side room", he whispered to me then stepped back and made a show of touching the brim of his hat to me in salutation and walked away.

I'm not sure how many onlookers we fooled by our little charade. I jostled Alex in my arms as I lifted my market basket and entered the general store. The bell tinkled as I closed the door, announcing my arrival in the store. Mr. Morgan climbed down from his ladder where he was stocking shelves and moved behind the large counter.

"Good morning, Mrs. Dunlap. What can I help you with today?"

"Hello Mr. Morgan. I've got some fresh eggs and churned butter that I'd like to sell. I am in need of sugar, flour and perhaps some dry goods in exchange if we can agree on a price." I placed the basket on the counter and shifted Alex onto my other hip.

"See you have the little fella with you today. Let's have a look in your basket. How many eggs do you have?"

Mr. Morgan tickled Alex under his chin, smiling at the child, as he poked among the wrapped butter molds and counted out loud the eggs in my basket. "Hmm… I make it three dozen eggs, if I haven't missed my count."

"Yes, that's right. I was keeping my fingers crossed that none broke during my ride into town. I tried to cushion them as best I could. What do you think?"

"Well ma'am… how about three dollars? That ought to buy enough supplies for you."

"Can you do three dollars and two bits? Those are really large eggs and the butter is freshly churned. I'm sure your customers will appreciate the quality." I bartered for a better price; Mr. Morgan seemed to expect some haggling before agreeing on a mutual bargain.

"You drive a hard bargain, Mrs. Dunlap, but I agree. You go ahead and scoop out how much flour and sugar you need and whatever else you want. It's a pity your husband didn't have your business sense."

"What do you mean by that remark?"

"Oh, just that he would not have lost your ranch, that's all. I didn't mean no insult."

"I still own my ranch Mr. Morgan. Only our extra parcel of land was deeded to Mr. Logan, not that it's any of your business." His attitude surprised me. Is that what folks in town were thinking?

I sat Alex on the floor to toddle about as I went about the chore of filling sacks with the food stuffs. My thoughts kept returning to the store clerk's comments as three more customers entered the store. I recognized Mrs. Fitzhughes from the newspaper, but not the two gentlemen.

One of the men poked his friend in the ribs and pointed to me as I reached into the flour barrel. "Isn't that Jarvis' whore? Lookee there, his brat is crawling under foot," he laughed.

"Yep, spittin' image of him. I hear tell she had Jarvis kill her ole man too," the friend sneered.

I stood there speechless. My outrage was rising like a thermometer on a hot day; I couldn't believe the cruel falsehoods that were being spread. I spun about to confront the two men and stomped my foot on the wooden floor.

"How dare you say such lies about me and my baby? Urgh!" My frustration was such that all I could do was sputter in anger and stomp my foot again. The result was only more laughter from the two filthy cowhands.

I turned my back on them and placed my parcels on the counter. Alex sat whimpering, frightened by the shouting and commotion. I scooped him up and cuddled him against my breast. "It's all right sweetie. Mama's here."

"I'm sorry Mrs. Dunlap. If you say those lies ain't so, then I believe you," Morgan tried to reassure me but there was doubt written all over his face.

"Just give me my purchases, Mr. Morgan. Good day sir." I knew my face was blazing as I left the store. I placed the sacks under the wagon's seat and strode down the sidewalk in search of the Silver Spur.

Might as well add one more humiliation to my day by entering a saloon; and the very one where James was killed. How could Cody suggest such a location? I avoided the wide swinging doors in the front of the saloon and headed for a more private side entrance at the corner of the building.

The room was dimly lit and it took a minute for my eyes to adjust to the darkness. Cody was seated at a small table in the rear and I headed that way, nervously glancing around to see if I was being watched. He stood as I approached the table and I noticed the chair he held for me would place my back to the saloon patrons. Well, at least there was some comfort in that. Alex sat on my lap, content to study this strange place and the man across from him.

"He's getting big." Cody commented as he smiled at the baby and lifted his eyes to mine.

"Are you aware that people in town are saying he's yours? I just had a very disagreeable run in with some men in the store. They called me a whore!" I shook my head, trying to stop the tears that threatened to spill.

I could see Cody's expression turn angry then he shrugged it off. "I'm sorry Maggie. I can't control what the scum around here are saying. I wouldn't worry about it."

"Easy for you to say, I have to live here. What will happen when my son is old enough to understand these cruel barbs and questions me about his father? Should I tell him he was conceived by rape or let him think he's a gunfighter's bastard? A poor choice, don't you think?" I wiped away tears that I could no longer control with the back of my hand. I hugged Alex closer and kissed the top of his head; his dark hair so much like James' and so much like Cody's.

"I don't have an answer for you. What would you have me do?" Cody questioned.

"Nothing. Anything you do now will only add fuel to the talk around town. Just tell me one thing… did you shoot James?" I had to know. He had promised me in the past, even when provoked by James, that he'd walk away. I sat waiting for his answer now.

"No, I did not. Believe me or not, your choice."

"I've heard people say you were there; that you were the shooter."

"I wasn't. I can't tell you where I was that night. You'll just have to trust me."

Now it was Cody's turn to give me an ultimatum. Did I trust him? I reached for his hand across the table. My eyes searched his; I tried reading the expression on his face, but he had on his stoic look. I hated that look I had seen so many times in the past; when he shut me out to his feelings and thoughts.

"If you didn't do it, why won't you tell me where you were?" I kept probing for details; my mind and heart were at war with each other. I needed to know the truth, but I so desperately wanted to believe this man that I loved.

Cody pulled back his hand, breaking my grasp. "I can't and I won't. You know how I feel about you Maggie."

"I must think of my son and his future. I cannot build a life with someone who may have murdered his father. If you can't tell me the truth of what happened to James, then I never want to see you again. I'm sorry."

I stood to go, turning back to beseech him one last time, but his eyes had turned cold ,and his face wore the look of the gunfighter I had come to hate and fear.

"Believe what you must Maggie. I'll only say this once. I do love you and will always be there for you if you need me."

"Goodbye Cody."

I watched him as he remained seated and withdrew a packet of playing cards from his vest pocket. He calmly started shuffling the cards as I walked away.

CHAPTER 27

Andy adjusted the straps on her saddle once more and shook out her lariat. Buttercup stood patiently and snickered to her owner as Andy rubbed the palomino's nose. The mare nodded its head up and down as if in agreement to the quietly spoken words exchanged between horse and rider. Satisfied, Andy took a deep breath then led Buttercup to the holding pen as she waited the call to begin.

The Frontier Day parade had ended earlier in the morning; Andy and Gramps enjoyed watching the elaborate Indian and Cowboy costumes on the trick riders and sampled chili from the chuck wagon cook offs. In years past Andy would have entered the barrel racing event that is primarily a rodeo contest for women and youths. She was always able to maneuver her horse through the clover leaf pattern of barrels in a few seconds' time. The barrel racing required all her horsemanship skills to successfully cross the finish line with the winning time; a collection of blue ribbons hanging on her bedroom wall were evidence of Andy's accomplishment. But barrel racing didn't pay a purse and Andy needed to win some money. The bank's deadline was looming. She just had to win.

Frontier Days featured exhibits and rodeo events to attract both tourists and locals alike and now they filled the grandstands as everyone cheered the riders preparing for the calf roping event. Andy tugged on the blue cloth displaying her contestant number five across her back. The announcer's microphone squawked as he described the next rider's name and hometown. From her position outside the corral, Andy studied the cowboy's technique as he proceeded to catch the calf by throwing a loop of rope from a lariat around its neck, dismounted from his horse and ran to the calf, restraining it by tying three legs together. She looked over at the clock with its seconds ticking away as the cowboy raised his arm to signal that he was finished.

"Hmm, not bad, 8.57 seconds," thought Andy as the official time was recorded. She'll need to step up her game to beat that time. Andy hoped the hours of practicing at home would pay off. She glanced around until she found where Gramps was seated and tried waving to get his attention, but he was looking elsewhere and didn't see her.

Jason and his deputies patrolled the arena and grounds. Several other law enforcement officers from neighboring counties were present helping with crowd and traffic control. Jason casually greeted a few people as he moved about the crowd, scanning faces and watching for any signs of trouble. The Governor sat in the stadium's executive sky box with several celebrities and businessmen, so security was high.

Jason approached Mac as he made his rounds, "Everything okay? Sure wish the Governor had skipped this year's rodeo. We've got enough going on without having to worry about someone taking a pot shot at him. Well, just a few more hours and it'll be over."

"Have you seen Andy yet? Did she really enter the calf roping?" Mac asked as he shook his head in disbelief. "By the way, Sam's over in section B, about the third row center, if you need him. I just spoke to him a few minutes ago."

"I'm heading over to the pens now to see her. They just started the roping; don't know where she placed in the lineup, but I guess she'll be riding soon. Keep your eyes open and I'll check in with you later."

"Right. Tell Andy I said good luck."

"I'll do that," Jason replied as he moved toward the corrals near the south end of the arena.

Andy spied Jason walking toward her. This was their first meeting since the night of his proposal and Andy smiled nervously. She had talked to him on the telephone two days ago when he had called to inform them of Harold Wilson's and Paul Cooper's arrest for fraud and embezzlement, but seeing him in person and this close made her insides feel like Jell-O.

Jason reached her in two long strides and wrapped his arms around her waist as he pulled her into a tight hug. He kissed her on each cheek then found her lips as he planted a thoroughly scorching kiss that left Andy breathless.

"Whew!"

"I've wanted to do that for days. God, I've missed you. You don't know how much," he whispered into her ear.

"I've missed you too. I started to drive over to Cedarhill several times but couldn't get up my courage and swallow my pride long enough to do it. Forgive me?"

"There's nothing to forgive. I love you Andrea Dunlap and when all this business is done, I'm going to hold you to an answer of that question I asked. Right now, I just wanted to wish you good luck on the roping. You be careful out there."

"All right Jason. I promise."

"That's my gal. Go show them how it's done. And Andy… you're a winner in my book no matter what the outcome of the rodeo is."

The couple embraced for another smoldering kiss, clinging to each other in a fierce hug before parting while another face in the crowd watched from afar; eyes narrowed in hatred and a snarl twisting the mouth as a vengeful plan formed.

Jason left the holding area and made his way back to the grandstands to watch with Sam as Andy prepared to compete. He scanned the crowd, noting the position of his deputies, the state policemen and the Governor safe in his sky box. He signaled to Mac walking the inside perimeter of the public viewing area.

"Okay Andy, you're up," the chute operator called. "Let me know when you're set."

Andy and Buttercup moved into place behind the barrier in their box. Andy tugged her gloves on tighter and placed the piggin string between her teeth as she gripped Buttercup's reins in her left hand and her coiled lariat in the right. She signaled to the operator with a nod of her head and watched for her cue as he released the calf from the pen.

The barrier came up as Andy urged Buttercup into a full gallop and chased the calf across the open space, tossing her lasso about the calf's neck. She hit her mark and pulled back on the reins to halt the mare as she quickly hopped down. Andy ran to the small calf and flipped it on its side; grabbing three of the calf's legs together she used the piggin string to tie them together with a half hitch knot. Buttercup stepped back slowly as she had been trained, maintaining a steady tension on the long rope as Andy threw up her hands to signal "time" and for the clock to stop.

Andy walked back to Buttercup and mounted the mare, moving the horse forward to lessen the tension and provide some slack in the rope. Just as she turned to look at the clock with her official time, a shot rang out and Andy felt the sting of a bullet grazing her left shoulder. Andy slumped forward onto Buttercup's neck, wrapping her hand in the yellow mane to keep from falling as dark spots swam before her eyes and she heard her name being called from a distance.

Mac pushed through the crowd and ran toward the spot where gun smoke still floated in the air as Jason leapt the corral fence and ran toward Andy, catching her as she slid to the ground unconscious. Both men caught their women just in time.

Mac grabbed the revolver from her hand and clamped handcuffs on a struggling and cursing Veronica Logan. He walked her back toward the gate and waiting police cars while she screamed obscenities and told him what she thought of his parentage.

"You just wait until my father hears of this. You can't treat me this way. That bitch Andy got what she deserved. I hope she's dead!"

"I wouldn't count on daddy bailing you out of this one Ronnie," Jason advised as he joined Mac and watched the paramedics load Andy's stretcher into an ambulance.

"Good job, Mac. You were right on top of things, partner. Can you get that hellcat down to the jail okay? I'm going to ride along with Andy to the hospital."

"Yeah, no problem. I've got it under control."

"Good, I'll get back to the station as soon as I can."

Jason and Sam rode in the back of the ambulance watching the paramedics tend to Andy. Both men smiled in unison as she stirred and opened her eyes.

"Welcome back," Jason whispered in her ear as he pressed a light kiss to her forehead.

"Girl, you just scared ten years off my life! How do you feel?" Sam questioned as he quickly wiped a tear from the corner of his eye.

Andy looked from one man to the other and indicated for the medic to remove her oxygen mask. "What was my time?" she asked.

Sam laughed and squeezed her hand. He couldn't believe the only thing that mattered to her was the competition. "In all the excitement, I didn't even pay attention. Did you see the clock J.C.?"

"You little scamp; yeah I saw the time. You finished at 8.19 seconds, might just be the winning score; pretty fast time for a girl," he teased.

"What do you mean for a girl? You just try and match that time, mister hot shot cowboy," Andy declared with a cough and grimace of pain.

"I think she's getting her strength back. Don't you think so Sam?" Jason remarked as the ambulance arrived at the entrance to the emergency room of the hospital.

Both men jumped down and helped the medics lower the stretcher. The medical personnel hurried to roll Andy through the open doors.

"We'll take good care of her from here boys. You'll need to wait outside. She'll be going into surgery to remove that bullet," the doctor on duty informed them.

A smiling nurse with a kind face patted Sam on the arm as she said, "I'll come get you as soon as she's out of surgery. Why don't you go get a nice cup of coffee and try to relax? She'll be fine. I promise."

"Thanks, nurse. I'll wait right here," Sam informed her as he took a seat in the waiting room. He looked at the clock on the wall, worry etching lines across his face, as he prepared to wait for word of Andrea's recovery.

"I'll go rustle us up some coffee, Sam. I've got to call Mac too. Be right back."

"Thanks, J.C."

Mac answered the ringing telephone and cupped his hand around his ear in an effort to hear better over the screams and shouting coming from Veronica's jail cell.

"Hey J.C., how's Andy doing? She badly wounded? No … that's good."

"What's all that noise in the background?" Jason asked as he listened to the uproar through the phone.

"That's just Ronnie. She's throwing a fit about being locked up."

"Well, don't let her go. I don't care how many lawyers or what kind of bail money Logan produces. I should be back in about twenty minutes."

"No problem. Guess word got out quickly about the shooting. Brent Logan has already called and threatened us with a lawsuit for unlawful arrest."

"Hmm, I think we have enough witnesses to disprove that. If he gets there before I get back, don't let him bully you."

"OK Sheriff. Uh-huh, right." Mac agreed as he listened to further instructions.

He hung up the receiver and walked down the hall to the cell blocks. Veronica jumped up from the cot when she saw him approach.

"You'll be sorry for this. I tell you, I'll have your badge, you moron!"

"Keep talking Ronnie, makes no difference to me. I imagine your daddy's lawyer will be here soon and he can talk with the assistant district attorney. We'll just see what happens then."

"You think you're so smart; you just wait," she spat.

Mac turned his back on Veronica's complaining and moved to the next cells to check on the other prisoners. Paul Cooper sat on his bunk, his head in his hands, looking as dejected as any man could. Harold Wilson stood looking out the small window of his cell, staring at the snowcapped mountain peaks in the distance.

"You boys need anything?" Mac questioned the prisoners as he checked on their status.

"When's my lawyer supposed to get here?" asked Wilson. "I know my rights. I need to talk to counsel."

"The sheriff is expecting your lawyer and the others to arrive with the district attorney real soon. Don't worry Wilson, you'll get to talk to him as soon as he gets here," Mac informed the fired banker.

Both Sam and Jason jumped to their feet as the doctor entered the waiting room. The doctor smiled as he reached to shake Sam's hand.

"You must be Mr. Dunlap? Your granddaughter is going to be just fine. She's lucky; the bullet just grazed her shoulder and had a clean exit, no bones shattered," Doctor Watters explained.

"That's good news. Can we see her Doc?" Sam asked the surgeon. "I'd feel better if I could see for myself that Andrea isn't in any danger."

"She's still in the recovery room and sedated. She'll be sleeping for at least another hour and then we'll move her back to her own room. You can see her then."

"Why don't you go home for a bit and get something to eat or take a nap, Sam? You look all done in. You can come back to see

Andy later," Jason suggested. "Now that I know she's okay, I'm going to get back to the station."

"I hate to leave her, but I guess it won't hurt to get a little shut eye. I am worn out, that's for sure." Sam rubbed the heel of his hand over his eyes, trying to massage away the tiredness. He faced the doctor again needing reassurance, "you'll call me if there's any change, if she needs me?"

"Absolutely, Mr. Dunlap, but I'm certain that she's going to be asleep for some time yet."

Jason and Sam walked out to the hospital parking lot together, looked about and then started to laugh in unison.

"I kinda forgot we both rode in the ambulance; seems we're going to have a long walk back to the fairgrounds to pick up our vehicles."

"Well," Sam paused as he rubbed his whiskered chin, "want to share a cab? Let's call Bobby over at Acme and see if he can come get us."

"Sounds like a plan. I think I've got his number saved on my cell phone." Jason quickly scanned his address book and typed in the number. "Great, Bobby. See you in a minute."

"Guess we just need to sit and wait," Sam told Jason as he sought a spot on the bench outside the hospital entrance.

CHAPTER 28

Assistant District Attorney Ron Carter stood quietly in the corner of interrogation room number one as he observed Sheriff Hartman question Paul Cooper. Cooper was obviously nervous and kept wringing his hands together.

"You do realize, don't you Cooper, that if you cooperate and answer our questions that things might go easier on you?" Jason suggested to the man.

Jason opened a large folder and took out several invoices and bills of sale, spreading the papers across the table in front of Paul Cooper.

"We've got evidence of you receiving stolen goods. The invoices here and sworn affidavits prove you're guilty of fraud. Tell us who you were working with; you aren't smart enough to come up with this scheme on your own."

"Charles Tucker, he made me do it," whispered Cooper.

"You want to say that a little louder? I didn't quite hear you," prompted Jason. He glanced over to the D.A. to see his reaction and received a nod to go on with the interrogation.

"I said, Charlie Tucker. He told me what to bill the Dunlaps and he's the one that sold their inventory on the black market after we invoiced them. He was trying to make them go broke."

"Uh-huh, and who did Charlie Tucker get his orders from?" pressed Jason. "Who wound up with the money that you two stole?" Jason waited for an answer; none came. He looked over toward

Carter and nodded again. "All right Cooper, do you know that Tucker was found dead recently? That makes you an accessory to murder; unless you tell us who your partner was."

"What? I didn't have anything to do with that. You can't prove anything," exclaimed Cooper.

"I don't need to prove anything. You already confessed that you and Tucker were working together in fraud and theft. The way I see it, you must have wanted a bigger slice of the pie and killed your partner or had someone kill him for you," Jason stated and watched for a reaction from the man.

"Tucker came to me; I didn't want to get involved but he made me. I don't know for sure, but I think Charlie got his orders from Logan. I'm not taking the fall for Charlie's death. I had no part of that," Paul Cooper insisted.

"Will you write down the facts like you just told me and sign it? I want to see on paper that you and Tucker committed fraud and grand larceny. You do that and I think the D.A. will drop the accessory charges. Isn't that right Mr. Carter?" Jason pushed a legal pad of paper and pen toward Paul Cooper and instructed him to start writing.

"Yes, Sheriff, since Mr. Cooper is willing to cooperate, I believe our office will limit his charges to just fraud and theft," answered Ron Carter, satisfied with the confession of this suspect. Now on to the next one.

Ron Carter and Jason left Cooper to his writing and opened the door to the second interview room. Harold Wilson sat drumming his fingers on the tabletop; trying to look bored and unconcerned but the sweat beading across his forehead said otherwise. Wilson's lawyer waited with him and now sat more upright, his demeanor alert and anxious to hear what kind of deal he could get from A.D.A. Carter.

"Afternoon, Ron," the lawyer greeted; hoping to set a friendly mood in the room.

"Hello Jeff," returned Ron Carter. He took a chair next to Sheriff Hartman across from the pair and made a show of opening his briefcase and removing a thick accordion file folder. He thumbed through several sheaths of paper until he found the file name he wanted.

"Mr. Wilson, you've got some serious charges to answer to, not the least of which is fraud, embezzlement and malicious intent to defraud investors. What do you have to say for yourself?" Carter queried.

Jason watched the banker squirm in his seat as he conferred with his lawyer and they exchanged whispered comments. It was time to fire the next volley of charges.

"Platte County is also prepared to charge you with conspiracy to commit murder unless we receive your full cooperation," Jason stated solemnly and looked Wilson straight in the eye.

The banker visibly blanched and gulped water from the glass setting before him. His expression was clearly worried now, all pretense of boredom dropped.

"What evidence do you have to support such charges?" questioned Wilson's attorney.

Now it was Carter's turn to dangle the bait that he and Jason had agreed upon in hopes of catching the bigger fish.

"There are several properties that have recently been sold on short sale. The foreclosure process appears to have been short-cutted with speedy sales to a waiting buyer. Wyoming's state banking commissioner has quietly been performing an audit and investigation into these sales and the results are disturbing. Wilson, you've left a paper trail a mile wide that wasn't very smart of you. Interest rates raised, balloon payments demanded, appraisal figures changed, and several strong arm treatments to folks holding mortgages with your bank forcing them to sell out. Do I need to go on?" Carter stated.

"What tactics did you try using on Brian Dunlap? He didn't scare so easily did he? Was it simpler to kill him to get him out of the way so you could deal with a grieving young girl and an old man?" Jason slammed his fist on the table and his voice rose in anger as he demanded an answer from the banker.

"We've got physical evidence that proves the Dunlap plane was sabotaged; their crash was no accident. It was murder and you're involved up to your greedy neck in conspiracy to commit that murder. You may not have had a hand in tampering with that plane engine, but your hands are dirty," Jason continued.

Harold Wilson was as pale as a ghost and quickly conferred with his attorney before nodding and slumping forward in his chair.

"What do you want to know?" he asked defeated.

"I want to know who was behind the plot to kill the Dunlaps? Bank records show Brent Logan as the buyer of all the current short sale properties. It isn't a crime to buy real estate, but it is a crime if he was involved with the unlawful foreclosure acts and extortion. Will you testify against Brent Logan as to his involvement in these acts? Did you ever hear him say that he would kill Brian Dunlap?"

"Yes, I'll testify. Logan's men applied pressure to the landowners, poisoned their stock, sometimes threatening them to sell once their mortgages were in default. I heard him give orders to two of his men about dealing with the Dunlaps, whatever it took. I don't know what that meant," Harold Wilson admitted.

"When was that; the orders against the Dunlaps?" questioned Jason. He needed to tie Logan to a specific time frame.

"I don't know exactly, maybe some time in July."

Jason handed a pen and paper to Harold Wilson as Assistant District Attorney Carter nodded and smiled grimly.

"You know the drill," Carter instructed the other attorney. "I expect a complete statement with details, time and places or no deal on the conspiracy charge."

Jason's head jerked up as he heard a loud commotion coming from the front office. He quickly walked past the holding cells and into the office space. Mac and one other deputy were unsuccessfully trying to restrain Brent Logan and his army of lawyers.

"What seems to be the problem here?" Jason challenged as he moved to stand with his deputies.

"I demand to see my daughter, Hartman! You can't hold her, you've no right," Logan shouted loudly.

"Oh, I think I do, but I will agree to let you speak with her, provided you'll agree to lower your voice." Jason smiled at the large man, enjoying his discomfort.

"You insolent pup, I told you before about talking to me like that," Brent Logan sneered through gritted teeth.

Jason stood nose to nose with him as he answered, "And I believe I told you then, as now, it's Sheriff Hartman to you. If you want to see your precious daughter, I suggest you do as I say."

"Ah, Mr. Logan, it would be best to calm down. I'm sure the Sheriff has every intention of allowing you to see Veronica," one of the three attorneys in tow advised.

"All right; let go of my arm," Logan jerked free of the lawyer's hand and started toward the back hallway. "Where is she?"

Jason followed Logan toward the holding cells, watching for any reaction as Logan saw both Harold Wilson and Paul Cooper in custody. *"Hmm, a flicker of recognition, but no other outward sign,"* thought Jason. He stood to one side as Logan approached the cell door and reached a hand through the bars to grasp Veronica's outstretched hand.

"Daddy, help me please! Get me out of here," cried Veronica as large crocodile tears slid down her cheeks.

"It's all right baby, I'm here." Brent Logan held his daughter's hand, squeezing it lightly as he looked at the dismal cell and then her tearful face. It tore his heart out to see his precious angel being treated this way.

"Why's she locked up? What did she do?"

"The charge is assault with a deadly weapon. She shot Andrea Dunlap at the rodeo this morning," explained Jason.

"Humph, what happened to the Dunlap girl?"

"Andy's in the hospital; thank God the bullet only grazed her shoulder, or your daughter would be up on a more serious offense. As it is, assault with a weapon is still pretty serious. She's looking at prison time for this little stunt."

"Daddy, daddy, you can't let them send me to prison. I didn't mean to hurt her. I just wanted to scare her," Veronica pleaded. She cried in earnest now as she looked from one man to the other. For the first time in her life, she wasn't sure her father could exert his power to have his way.

Brent Logan dismissed Jason and turned to his group of lawyers. "Well, what are you going to do about this?"

"We'll have a talk with the district attorney, sir, and see if he'll let her out on bail. This is a first offense and I'm confident we can get the charges knocked down to a lesser offense. Just give us some time to work out a deal," one of the attorneys reasoned with his client, hoping to win his approval and patience. Brent Logan paid a healthy retainer to their law firm, and they didn't want to lose it but sometimes it was next to impossible satisfying his demands.

"I want her home by tonight. My daughter will not spend a night in jail. Do you hear me?" Logan boomed, and then turned a gentler voice to his daughter. "Just a couple more hours honey, it won't be long."

Logan and his lawyers marched out of the sheriff's office, slamming the door as they left and climbed into his waiting limo. Jason shook his head in amazement as he watched them go.

He approached Ron Carter as the attorney waited on a call he had placed to the judge. "What do you think? I want Logan on more charges than just fraud or extortion. I want to nail him on murder one," Jason proclaimed.

Carter read the statements in his hand as he considered the evidence in question. "We've got a strong case already Jason. This is going to put him away. I need something else, more facts, before I can get a first-degree murder charge to stick."

"What about the forensics evidence we pulled out of the hotel room? Charlie Tucker was shot in the room, the blood stains on the wall and blankets confirm that. I've got cigar ash and finger prints that put Logan in that room too. That's got to link him to at least that murder. Doesn't it?"

"Yeah, that puts him there but that doesn't mean he pulled the trigger. You know his lawyers will tear that apart in court. We need more," the district attorney explained.

"Okay. Give me some time before you file your indictment, maybe I can come up with something. If we could just get him to confess," Jason pondered as his mind tried to work out a plan.

"If you can wring a confession out of that man, you're a better man than me!"

Jason snapped his fingers as an idea came to him, "Maybe we've got the key to our dilemma back there in that cell."

CHAPTER 29

Andrea reached for the telephone on the night stand next to her hospital bed. She dialed home and was relieved to hear her grandfather's voice on the other end of the line.

"Hi Gramps. Yes, I'm feeling fine. They've moved me into a different room and I wanted to give you the number. Mm-hmm, that's right, room three thirteen. Can you bring me a few things when you come?"

Andrea listened to Sam describe his afternoon in the hospital waiting room and how Jason had stayed with him until she was out of surgery. That bit of information made her smile, *"He cares; even though his responsibilities needed him elsewhere, he stayed,"* she thought.

"Um, Gramps, can you please bring my robe, slippers, comb, toothbrush and also the journal? There are only a few pages left in the back of the book; several pages were torn out, but I'd like to finish reading it. Thanks a bunch. I'll see you in a bit."

A half hour later, Sam Dunlap entered the hospital carrying a bunch of daisies and a small tote bag. Andrea's quick recovery lightened his mood, put a spring in his step and made him feel ten years younger. He gave her a big kiss on the cheek as he produced the cheerful bouquet and surveyed her appearance. The left arm wore a sling and bandages covered the shoulder partially exposed by her gown. She still had an IV tube taped on her hand and a few monitor wires, but otherwise she looked good.

"They're lovely, thank you! Can you ask one of the nurses to bring me a vase so I can put them in water?" Andrea opened the tote and rummaged inside, noting the items that Sam had packed and pleased to see the diary under the folded clothes.

"Did I get everything you wanted? Didn't forget anything, did I?" Sam inquired.

"Nope. You did just fine. I might as well put my time to good use while I'm just lying here; can't do much else so I thought I'd read." Caressing the journal, she asked, "how do you think those pages got ripped? I wonder what was written on them. Guess I'll never know."

"Did you have your evening meal yet? My backbone is starting to rub my belly reminding me that I haven't eaten since breakfast. I think I'll visit the cafeteria downstairs. How bad can hospital food be? Will you be all right while I go eat?" Sam asked Andrea as he filled a glass bottle with water for her daisies.

"Oh sure. The nurse's aide said dinner trays are coming around. You go ahead and get a hot meal; it's been a long day for you." She smiled broadly and wrapped her uninjured arm about him in a big hug as he leaned over to kiss her on the cheek again.

Andrea was anxious to read more about Maggie and Cody and could hardly contain her excitement as she reached for the tattered journal. She fingered the edges of the torn paper and wondered again who had removed the pages and why.

I am growing weaker every day. I don't need a doctor to tell me that my time on this earth is short. Some days my fever rages like the fires from hell; other days I shake with chills and no amount of blankets can keep me warm. I only pray that Alex will stay healthy and I beg him to not come too close to me. I must try to protect him, my precious son.

The sky is clear and blue as only a cold winter day can be. I lie on my sick bed and enjoy watching the clouds float by my small patch of windowpane, my only view of the world these past weeks.

I think I'm going mad as my mind drifts and recalls angry words spoken and then quickly regretted; too late to dismiss. I see James standing in the corner pointing his finger at me, accusing me of being a harlot. Then I peer into the shadows and realize it is not his ghost but a mere memory.

I ache for Cody; to be held in his strong arms again, to feel his kiss upon my lips would surely be heaven. Oh, how I regret sending him away. I sometimes wonder what our life would have been like if he had been in it. Would we have suffered the town's criticism? Would there have been such a scandal if we had married? Who knows?

I only know for certain the years of toil and depravation that Alex and I have endured as we worked to save our ranch. The years have been lean and hard, but Alex has secured his inheritance. My son will be able to hold his head up with pride and no man can take this land from him.

He's so young and yet at times seems so old for his tender years. I see a man in a boy's body. Michael and Rose Canavan have promised to look after him when I am gone and will honor our pledge of uniting our two families with the marriage of our children. Katie will be good for Alex; I think they will make a good match. They'll start their lives together with so much more than James and I had; perhaps that will give them a chance for happiness.

March 3, 1896

My strength is failing, and I struggle to keep my mind clear. There is so much that I need to tell Alex – where does a mother begin?

He's restless and I can sense his frustration at being so helpless. But a far greater being is in control of our lives, there's very little that we can do to alter the outcome. I see that clearly now.

"Alex, please come sit down. We need to talk while there is still time."

"Mama, don't talk like that. You'll be well soon. Try to eat more, you'll feel better."

"Alex, there are many things that I regret in my life, but I want you to know that you are not one of them. I love you with all my heart and you have been my greatest joy since the minute of your birth. I wish I could do more for you. I don't know what to tell you to guide you through manhood. Don't make my mistakes. When you love someone, love her with your whole being and give her the greatest gift that you can – your trust. Trust her with your heart and your feelings and share your thoughts with her."

"Like you did with Papa or are you talking about Cody Jarvis? When are you going to tell me the truth Mama? When are you going to trust me? I think I have a right to know who my true father is." Alex spoke in such angry words, it surprised me. I never knew he was in so much conflict.

"James Dunlap is your father; who is telling you otherwise? You have no reason to question that fact."

"I've heard Mike Canavan talking about you, James and Cody Jarvis; how the three of you lived together for an entire winter. Jarvis was always threatening James until the day he finally killed him. So you tell me, Mama, why did Jarvis hate James Dunlap so much unless he wanted you?"

"You're wrong Alex! Don't listen to Michael Canavan, he does not know what he's talking about. I'll swear on the Bible, you are James Dunlap's son. Cody Jarvis and I loved each other, that's true, but we never did anything wrong. He did not shoot your father. You must believe me.

I won't have you thinking that you're a bastard. You need to be proud of your family roots – the Dunlap name dates back generations in Scotland and God willing, you will start a new dynasty of Dunlaps here in America."

"I'm sorry Mama. I should have talked to you sooner. It's just that people look at me funny when I'm in town and I hear the whispers behind my back. I've had fights with kids in school when they've called you a whore. I don't know what to believe is true anymore." Alex cried and sat on the floor with his head resting on my chest.

I stroked his hair and patted his back, comforting him as I did when he was a baby. My heart is breaking to learn that I've caused such anguish in my young son's life.

March 7, 1896

Someone is crying. I sleep and wake throughout the day, drifting in and out like a ship bobbing on the ocean waves. Each time I rouse I hear the crying but when I move my head to look about the room, no one is there. My face is wet and I realize that the crying is mine.

Too many shadows cover the room. I cannot tell whether it is day or night; the light is so dim. I hear voices outside, vague and talking low. The cabin door has opened and closed—a man quietly approaches my bed. My delirium has grown worse for my mind has conjured the image of Cody before me.

"Hello Maggie," he whispered as he knelt beside the bed. His warm hands grasped mine and I tried to smile as his lips brushed my cheek, my forehead and claimed my lips.

"I'm sorry I left you alone all these years. I should have followed my own instincts and come back to you. Do you forgive me?" he asked in a hushed voice.

I squeezed his hand to reassure myself that he was not a figment of my imagination. I dreamt of him for so long that I feared my mind now played tricks with me.

"I've missed you so. I should have trusted you all those years ago. I can't decide whether God is rewarding me or punishing me by bringing you to me one last time before I die."

"Hush darling. Don't say that. I love you Maggie Dunlap for all eternity. I swear I didn't know you were ill; I would've come sooner. I've been away and just heard the talk in town today."

Cody moved to sit on the bed and lifted my limp body to cradle within his arms, my head rested on his shoulder. I never felt more content. Thank you God, it was a reward after all.

I touched his arm and raised my face to accept his lingering kiss. I think he tried to share his body's greater strength with mine. If only it could be so… but too late.

"I love you Cody Jarvis. Promise me that you'll watch over Alex. He needs you in his life."

"I will Maggie. I promise."

March 9, 1896

We laid Margaret Dunlap to rest beneath the large aspen tree that was her favorite and among her beloved flowers. Her few friends attended the private burial along with her son Alexander and myself, Cody Jarvis.

I make this entry into Maggie's journal for her. I hope that in years to come, her son and mayhap her grandchildren will find comfort in her words, memories and life story.

I only wish that I had been there for Maggie. I failed her. In my pursuit of Zachary Logan, I deserted the one person on this earth that really needed me. Maybe someday Logan will get what he deserves, but not by my hand. I hope Maggie forgave me.

CHAPTER 30

Jason entered Andrea's hospital room to find her sitting up in bed crying, blowing her nose with a tissue and lightly caressing her grandmother's diary. "What's this all about? Crying? Are you in pain; should I call a nurse?"

"No silly." Andrea waved her hand to signal no as she reached for another tissue. "Maggie died. I just finished reading her journal and I got caught up in the emotion."

"Sure you're okay?" Jason asked again then bent to greet her properly with a kiss. "Hmm, pretty flowers, somebody beat me to it."

"Those are from Gramps. They are pretty, aren't they? Oh Jason, it's all in here," she said excitedly as she pointed to the diary, the flowers temporarily forgotten. "Just like we thought; Maggie accuses Zachary Logan of murder and stated before the circuit judge that James Dunlap was shot in the back, not in self-defense. She also writes about the land transfer as being illegal because it wasn't James' signature on the deed. She just could not prove it, but I think we can with the documents that we found in the attic."

"Whoa, slow down girl. You aren't supposed to be getting this excited. You'll be setting off all those monitor buzzers or bells."

"But don't you see, this is what my father must have seen and didn't know we had the proof right under our own roof," Andy persisted.

Sam returned just in time to hear Andy's last comment. "What do you think Brian was trying to find? Proof of what?"

"Proof that the Logan family swindled land from the Dunlaps in 1887, that's what. Gramps, can't we do something?"

Andy handed the journal to Jason to read the passage describing the circuit court ruling and the subsequent land transfer.

"Well, it all makes sense now. But don't forget who we're dealing with, these are dangerous people. Let me take the lead on this and I'll speak to the D.A."

Jason slipped the journal into his jacket pocket. "Sam, I'll need those documents from that attic trunk. I'm sure Carter will want to examine the papers if we intend to support your claim with them."

"I'll get them out for you as soon as I get back to the ranch. Do you need me to bring them into the office or do you want to pick them up?" Sam asked.

"I'll stop by. I've got several places to go yet and won't know exactly what time I'll be back in the office. Things are beginning to pop!" Jason exclaimed. "Hey, Andy, are you feeling up to company? My folks want to stop by to see you, maybe in the morning?"

"That's very kind of them. Tomorrow morning will be fine. I'm not sure how long I have to stay here; maybe I'll get to go home tomorrow?" Andy replied.

Jason motioned to his deputy as he entered the sheriff's office, "Everything quiet? Any problems while I was gone?"

"No, everyone's settled down, even Ronnie," Mac answered. "Boy it sure has been a long day."

"Well, it's gonna get longer. The judge issued a warrant of arrest for Brent Logan on charges of conspiracy to commit murder. Let's go pick him up."

"Yes Sir!" agreed Mac as he grabbed his hat and hurried out the door.

They quickly drove to the Diamond Bar and stopped the police cruiser in front of the sprawling Logan ranch house. Jason left the take down lights flashing as he pounded on the entry door. A servant cautiously opened the door part way, but Jason pushed the portal wide and strode into the vestibule, leaving the man stunned and speechless.

"What the hell is going on?" stormed Brent Logan as he marched out of his den and approached the two lawmen. "What are you doing in my home?"

"Brent Logan, you're under arrest for conspiracy to commit murder. Turn around and put your hands behind your back," ordered Jason. He grabbed Logan's wrist as he fastened a pair of handcuffs onto the snarling man and jerked him forward again.

Mac began to read Logan his rights as they led their suspect out to the waiting car. The servant regained his power of speech as he questioned his employer, "Sir, what would you have me do?"

"Tell my wife to call my lawyers and get them down to the jail. You tell them I said they better be quick about it too," demanded Logan.

Brent Logan sat quietly watching the landscape slide by as the group drove back into Deer Springs and made their way to the police station. He knew when to keep his mouth shut; better to wait until his attorneys were present and learn what kind of evidence the sheriff had to support his charges. He wasn't fool enough to give him anymore.

As Jason and Mac led Logan toward an empty cell, they saw two black luxury sedans come screeching to a halt out front. *"Logan's lawyers follow orders very well,"* thought Jason. Briefcases in hand, both men rushed into the office and headed straight for the lawmen.

"We demand to see our client," stated Mark Simpson, senior partner of Simpson, Bowles and Long.

Harvey Long stopped short of running into his partner as he too confronted the sheriff. "Under what warrant did you charge Mr. Logan?"

"Gentlemen, the room's going to get a bit crowded, I propose we all move into the conference room. Assistant District Attorney Ron Carter will be joining us shortly; ah, here he comes now," Sheriff Hartman informed the pair of lawyers as they entered the larger side room.

The two attorneys faced the D.A. and the sheriff then demanded an answer, "You still haven't produced your warrant. I want to read the charges."

"Certainly, I assure you everything is in order. Brent Logan is charged with conspiracy to commit murder," Jason stated as he complied with Mark Simpson's request and handed him a copy of the arrest warrant. He watched the attorney quickly scan the document with a blank expression. He turned to his deputy, "Mac, escort Mr. Logan into the conference room please."

D.A. Ron Carter and Jason took seats on the right side of the long conference table and the attorneys awaited their client as they sat opposite, leaving an empty chair between them. Brent Logan glared at Jason as he entered the room, rubbing his wrists from the now removed handcuffs.

"All right. Let's get started, shall we?" the district attorney began. Copies of the warrant were placed before the sheriff and the defense attorneys. "Brent Logan you are under arrest on several charges; conspiracy to commit murder, accessory before the fact for fraud, and aiding and abetting grand larceny with receipt of stolen goods," Ron Carter concluded as he removed his reading glasses and laid them next to the indictment papers.

"And just who am I supposed to have murdered?" Logan demanded arrogantly. His lawyers tried to quiet him, but his anger overrode his better judgment.

"You're charged with the murders of Brian and Sarah Dunlap and Charles Tucker. We've got forensics that directly places you at the scene of Charlie Tucker's murder," Jason stated emphatically. He watched Logan's composure slip a notch; his eyes flickered at the mention of Tucker's name.

"You can't prove any of that. You're fishing." Logan exclaimed but not as cocky as before.

"Well, I'll tell you Brent, Harold Wilson kept very good records on all those bank deals that you two were partners on; you really should have given him a better cut of the action, maybe he would have been more loyal. The state bank commissioner has put a hold on all the foreclosures filed in the last six months and has begun investigating with a fine-tooth comb. I think you know your name is going to be found and then there's always Harold so ready to explain why he evicted all those families."

"Shall I go on?" Jason asked as he flipped over one page after another and continued his narration. "Paul Cooper certainly told us a tale about how you coerced him into stealing from the Circle-D ranch and bilking them for thousands of dollars. Penalties on the accessory after the fact indictment ought to keep you behind bars for a while. But those are just the tip of iceberg, aren't they?" Jason fought to keep his own temper in line and remain cool, but the man sitting before him had destroyed so many lives, it was hard to be unaffected.

"What evidence do you have on the alleged conspiracy charges, Sheriff?" Harvey Long inquired calmly. He stopped in his note taking to hear the next facts.

"The state police barracks down in Cheyenne are holding one of Mr. Logan's employees – good old Whitey Townsend, and he's singing like a canary," Jason told Long as he watched for Brent Logan's reaction and was satisfied with what he saw. "Whitey is the hit man that took out poor Charlie Tucker while Brent here sat and smoked his cigar right next to him, cool as a cucumber."

"And the Dunlaps? They were killed in an airplane accident. What makes you think my client was involved with that?" pressed Mark Simpson.

"Charles Tucker heard Brian Dunlap talk about searching through land records and deeds with the intention of filing a law suit against the Diamond Bar ranch and Brent Logan. Charlie was working for Logan and reported all of Dunlap's movements to Ben Miller; between the two of them they kept an eye on Brian Dunlap, but when Brian got too close to discovering the truth, Logan ordered him killed. I found evidence of the substance used to block the plane's hydraulic line that caused the crash. Charlie Tucker actually sabotaged that plane; the same thick gook was in a can under his truck seat. He caused the death of those good people."

Simpson and Long exchanged looks with each other and then Mark Simpson questioned the district attorney, "What kind of sentencing are you going for? Is there room for a deal, after all, my client didn't pull the trigger?"

"I might be able to argue for a more lenient prison term if Mr. Logan will sign a confession to all of these allegations," suggested D.A. Carter.

"Humph, like hell I will!" snorted Logan.

"Not even for your sweet daughter's sake?" asked Jason.

"What's she got to do with it? My daughter had no part in any of this."

"I never said she did. But she is being charged with assault with a deadly weapon. She's looking at jail time in the women's state prison for her shooting of Andrea Dunlap yesterday," Jason stated and watched Logan squirm.

D.A. Carter picked up on his cue and added, "If you agree to sign a complete confession to all indictments, I believe I can see my way to reducing the charges against Veronica to simple assault. Since this is her first offense, I'll request the judge to show her leniency with perhaps only a short six-month jail sentence. That's the best I can do, after all, she did shoot someone."

"We need some time with our client to discuss this," Simpson told the D.A. and sheriff. The lawmen rose and left the room.

"You've got ten minutes to discuss our offer; after that it's off the table," stated Carter.

CHAPTER 31

Andy reclined on the soft bed pillows; she watched the fluffy clouds float past against the brilliant blue backdrop of the early winter sky. Her mind drifted, memories filled her thoughts as she realized it was four months today that her parents had been killed. It felt like just yesterday and yet so much has happened since that horrible day that it could have been a lifetime ago.

A commotion in the hallway broke her reverie and drew her attention. She recognized Jason's voice and her grandfather speaking before they entered her hospital room, followed by Ingrid and Jarrod Hartman. Everyone seemed happy and in such a light mood; it was such a contrast to Andrea's dark thoughts of a moment earlier.

"What's going on? Have I missed a party or something?" Andrea looked questioningly from Jason to Gramps.

"It's over honey!" Gramps told her elated. "Jason did it." He squeezed her hands and carefully hugged her.

"Did what? I don't understand."

Jason stepped forward to explain the happenings of the night before. "Brent Logan has been arrested in connection with your parent's death. He's confessed to everything."

"Wow, let me take a minute to absorb what you're saying. That's it, we proved it?" Andrea asked in wonder.

"Well, things just started falling into place. Sam started the ball rolling when he suspected those phony feed invoices from Cooper's store and confronted Paul Cooper. After that Cooper crumpled and spilled his guts to the entire plot between him and Tucker. I just followed the clues that led me to Harold Wilson and discovered the state banking commission was already secretly investigating him, so we joined forces and shared information that sealed his involvement. Both men agreed to cooperate and testify against Brent Logan," Jason explained to his rapt audience.

He glanced at his parents and pride was clearly written across their faces as they listened to their son relate how he solved his case. Jarrod asked, "How did Brent Logan figure into Brian and Sarah's death? I don't think I understand."

Jason cast a worried look toward Andrea and Sam as he said, "Sam, I hate to tell you this, but Logan ordered Charlie Tucker to take care of Brian and Sarah. It was Charlie that messed with the hydraulics and caused their plane to crash. I'm sorry. I know you were fond of him, but he'd been working for Logan all along."

Andrea had started to cry and Jason went to her to gather her in his arms and try to console her. He laid a hand on Sam's shoulder as that man cursed Tucker for the traitor that he was.

"That son of a bitch, if he wasn't already dead, I'd kill him with my bare hands. I guess he got what he deserved."

Andrea wiped away her tears and broached another topic. "What about the Dunlap land? What are we going to do about Maggie's claim?"

"I showed the land grants to Ron Carter and the journal passage where Margaret Dunlap doubts the signature on the transfer. He's going to do what he can to file a writ for ownership based on fraud.

Maybe we can finally get some justice for your family," Jason explained.

"Jason, your ancestors would be mighty proud of you, I certainly am. Guess it's in your blood." Jarrod clapped his son on the back in congratulations.

"What do you mean?" Andrea's curiosity was peaked.

"Didn't he ever tell you? Jason here comes from a long line of lawmen, all the way back to his great-great grandfather. He was a Secret Service agent and then a Pinkerton man working undercover back in the late 1880's. They did that a lot back then, especially when Wyoming was only a territory, before we gained statehood," Jarrod related.

Sam shook his head sadly. "I wish Brian was here to learn all this. He was always so stubborn when he got an idea into his head. I'm afraid when Brian was only a young boy he was influenced by stories he read written about his grandfather Alexander. Most of his life, my father was a bitter old man who used to talk about how his own father was killed and the man who did it had gotten away with it; the suffering that he went through as a child. I fear he only repeated stories told to him by Michael Canavan, the man that helped to raise him after Maggie died. Canavan always believed that Cody Jarvis shot James Dunlap, and nothing would convince him otherwise. I think Brian thought that too, especially after reading Maggie's diary. He even questioned whether Alex was Cody's son, but in reality, Alex was as sullen as James Dunlap almost to the end of his life," Samuel recounted.

"As they say, the apple didn't fall far from the tree. I'm sorry I never told you this before, Andy, but I didn't know that your dad had transferred his hatred of Jarvis to the Hartmans."

"Okay, my mind must still be in a fog. What am I missing here?" Andrea looked from her grandfather to the Hartman family.

"I think I can help clear things up," Jarrod Hartman began. "Cody Jarvis is my great grandfather. I have letters that he wrote when he left for the Spanish-American War as a Rough Rider with Teddy Roosevelt. He talked about having worked as both a Pinkerton agent and even a Treasury agent, and his regret about not being able to arrest someone named Zachary Logan. That failure seemed to rest heavily on his mind. He was killed in the war shortly after that in 1898."

Andrea laughed and hugged Jason tighter as she held his face in her hands, searching his eyes. "You're related to Cody Jarvis?"

"Of course; what do you think my initials stand for? J. C. – Jason Cody, it's an old family name!" he smiled in return. "Now, about that answer that you promised to a question of mine…"

Andrea's eyes raised to her grandfather's and saw him smile and nod happily, before turning her full attention back to the handsome sheriff before her. "Yes, yes!" she declared as she kissed him with her full heart and being.

Applause erupted from both family members in celebration, disrupting the hospital silence. Ingrid and Jarrod beamed their approval at the joyful couple.

EPILOGUE

Andrea smiled at her image in the mirror as she arranged the soft white veil atop her hair, tucking in a loose curl here and there. Her bridal bouquet lay waiting on the dresser; delicate white daisies cradled in baby breath and fragrant white columbine blooms sparkled in the bright summer sunshine. It was going to be a glorious day… her wedding day, if only her parents were here to see it. The thought saddened her but she knew in her heart that their spirit was here as they looked down from heaven.

From her window, she watched the crowd gathering beneath the large aspen tree and the floral arbor that Frank and Bill had erected for the wedding ceremony. It appeared the entire population of Deer Springs and more were on hand to witness the union of the Dunlap and Hartman families. Andrea lifted her skirts and slowly descended the stairs.

Sam waited at the foot of the staircase and offered his arm to escort his beautiful granddaughter to her groom. His smile stretched from ear to ear and pride swelled his chest.

"Andrea, you are a vision today. I love you so much; I know your mother and father would be so happy for you."

"Thanks Gramps; I love you too."

"Everything has turned out really good. We have Jason to thank for our good fortune, so do a lot of folks around here," Sam commented.

"You're right. He helped several families get their homes back after Brent Logan and Harold Wilson were sent to jail. He told me the state banking commission reversed all those foreclosures and a federal judge repealed the property sales. I shudder to think how close we came to being included in that lot."

"I guess that's why the town turned out today; celebrating your wedding and restoring Deer Springs back to a town we can all be proud to call home."

"Have you given any more thought to what you're going to do with the money from our silver mines that we own now? Circle-D has just doubled in size; you better hire on a few more hands," suggested Andrea.

"There's time enough to make plans for the ranch. I've already told Frank that he's promoted to foreman; should have done it years ago. You know, Jason bought our cattle; he's got 'em on his spread now. He told me he'll give me back some of the heifers and a bull so I can start up my breeding stock again. He's a good lad and if I'm not mistaken, he's chomping at the bit for you to join him under that arbor. Shall we get this shindig under way?" He kissed Andy on the cheek as the music started and they began their walk up the aisle.

Andrea's smile was radiant; tears glistened in her eyes as she focused on her handsome groom waiting patiently. She saw his sister Jessica, pretty in her blue bridesmaid gown, smile shyly at the best man, Gavin McNally; causing him to blush embarrassedly. Andy nodded to friends and well-wishers as she made her way up the aisle to the altar and Jason.

Andrea Dunlap repeated her vows in a clear strong voice as she pledged her heart to her childhood friend, her lover, her husband – Jason Cody Hartman, and the next chapter of her life.

Past mysteries that have woven their webs entangling so many lives have finally been broken. Has fate righted a wrong? Maggie and Cody's eternal love has spanned the generations; we see it today in the eyes of Jason and Andrea.

True love is indeed an Endless Circle.

APPENDIX A

DUNLAP FAMILY TREE
Circle-D Ranch

JAMES JOHN DUNLAP –
Born 1861, Died Jan.10,1887
Married – Nov. 2, 1883
MARGARET DOHERTY -
Born 1863, Died Mar. 9,1896
Son: Alexander John Dunlap - B. 1886
   Daughter: Anna M. - B. 4/12/1885; D. 4/13/1885

ALEXANDER JOHN DUNLAP
Born June 18,1886, Died Oct.6,1945
Married - 1903
KATIE ANN CANAVAN
Born Aug. 2, 1886, Died Jan.8,1944
   Daughter: Peggy Ann, B. 1906, Died 1913
   Son: Alexander J. Dunlap, Jr., B. 1916, Died Oct. 1943
   Son: Samuel J. Dunlap, B. 1920

SAMUEL JAMES DUNLAP
Born Oct. 17, 1920, still living
Married – Mar. 1944
MARY K. BARNES
Born Apr. 4,1922, Died 1989
Son: Alex J. III, B. 1946, D 1946
Son: Brian James Dunlap, B. 1947

BRIAN JAMES DUNLAP
Born Aug. 5, 1947, Died 7/21/1997
Married - 1973
SARAH CUMMINGS DUNLAP
Born Feb. 1, 1949, Died 7/21/1997
Daughter: Andrea Brianna Dunlap, B. 1977

APPENDIX B

HARTMAN FAMILY TREE
Cedar Hill Ranch

CODY JARVIS
 Born 1859, Died Aug. 8,1898
Married - 1896
ROSALYN O'HARA
 Born 1862, Died 1908
   Daughter: Maureen Anne Jarvis - B. 1896

MAUREEN ANNE JARVIS
 Born Dec. 29,1896, Died 1971
Married - 1912
DANIEL JARROD HARTMAN
 Born 1886, Died 1968
   Daughters:
   Deborah A. Hartman- B. 1915, Died 1996
   Patricia Sue Hartman – B.1913, still living
   Son: Christopher Cody Hartman - B. 1919

CHRISTOPHER CODY HARTMAN
 Born May 3,1919, Died 1990
Married - 1941
DIANE M. BECKETT
 Born 1926, still living
   Son: Jarrod C. Hartman – B. 1946
   Daughter: Ruth D. Hartman – B. 1949, still living

JARROD CHRISTOPHER HARTMAN
 Born Aug. 5,1946, still living
Married - 1969
INGRID SCHMIDT HARTMAN
 Born Nov. 9,1950, still living
   Daughter: Jessica Hartman, B. 1975
   Son: Jason Cody (J.C.) Hartman - Born 1972

APPENDIX C

LOGAN FAMILY TREE
Diamond Bar Ranch

ZACHARY LOGAN -
Born 1859, Died Oct.10,1898
  Married - 1878
SARAH MURPHY
Born 1861, Died 1890
  Son: William Henry Logan, B. 1880

WILLIAM HENRY LOGAN
Born Jan 2,1880, Died 1948
  Married - 1905
KATHLEEN MORGAN
Born 1884, Died 1935
  Son: Avery Harold Logan, B. 1915

AVERY HAROLD LOGAN
Born July 3,1915, Died Oct 6,1945
  Married - 1939
CLARA LEE
Born 1923, Died 1983
  Daughter: Annabelle Logan, B. 1940
  Son: Brent Logan, B. 1941

BRENT LOGAN
Born June 2,1941
  Married – 1965
IRIS PARKER
Born Sept. 18,1946
  Daughter: Veronica Lynn Logan - Born 1976

ABOUT THE AUTHOR

Combining a love for travel with the joy of reading romance and mystery novels since childhood, Nancy M. Wade fills her writing with warm characters set in exciting locales.

She and her husband resided in central Ohio for over forty years; now retired, they claim the hills of Tennessee as home. An honors graduate of East Tennessee State University, Nancy studied film and criminology.

Nancy M. Wade's works include western romantic suspense novels: _Endless Circle: A Circle-D Saga_ and book two of _Circle-D Saga, Moment in Time_. A rich family drama, _Reflections: A Sentimental Journey_; a historical romance novel, _Frontier Heart_; plus, a contemporary short story called _Courtship of Laura._ Watch for _Gun For Hire_, the final book in the _Circle-D Saga_ trilogy, coming in 2023.

Nancy also pens an exciting cozy mystery series _A Meadowood Mystery_ with four books _Scarecrows and Corpses, Reunion with Death, Deadly Bones, and Berry Little Murder._

All of her works are available for order in both paperback or E-book formats on Amazon.com, or online in Barnes & Noble Books, Books-A-Million and IngramSparks.

Follow the author on her Facebook page: https://www.facebook.com/authorNancyMWade/ and on her web site https://nancymwade.com .

MOMENT IN TIME

Circle D Saga: Book 2

An American West dynasty tale of struggle and violence as dramatic as *Yellowstone* or Janet Dailey's *Caulder Saga* - the **Circle-D Saga** tells a story of conflict, love, and hate between three families who each staked their claim in the wild west of Platte County, Wyoming. The Circle-D Saga follows tales of love and mystery with generations of three families: the Dunlap, Hartman, and Logan families that span from the late 1880-1890s in wild west of Wyoming through World War II to modern day.

In **Moment in Time,** the **Circle-D Saga** continues... follow the Dunlap brothers from their struggling cattle ranch on the plains and rugged mountains of Wyoming to the green countryside of war-torn England where they experience both the thrill and dangers of serving on the mighty Flying Fortresses of the Eighth Air Force. Their sibling rivalry comes to a head when both brothers vie for the heart of a pretty English WAC. Can Samuel prove himself worthy? Can he measure up to his older, admired brother Alex? Will tragedy or triumph await them as each man struggles to survive the battles of a world at war?

Past conflicts with the sprawling, neighboring Diamond Bar ranch will haunt the young veteran and his new war-bride when they return to the Circle-D ranch. They must confront cattle rustlers and murderers as they fight to save their home and forge a bright future for themselves and generations to come.

MEADOWOOD MYSTERY SERIES

Meadowood is a small rural community with historic old buildings and folks who enjoy the quiet life – that is until murder comes to town. Follow Meredith Gardner, Aunt Fran, and all of Meredith's gal pals: Anna, Colleen, Barbara, Martha, and Carol as they investigate, snoop, and meddle in the affairs of their small rural hometown, Meadowood. If there is a crime a foot, you can be sure that Merry and her friends will be hard at work solving the mystery.

Merry is a busy housewife, Avon cosmetic saleswoman, mother, and cub scout den leader who manages to insert herself in her husband Doug's sheriff department investigations. Nothing stops Merry - a body found in a Halloween corn maze only presents a challenge when Merry has to prove a friend innocent while also uncovering a financial swindle in town *Scarecrows & Corpses*. A high school class reunion turns into an investigation of a murdered woman with Doug the prime suspect until Merry puts the pieces of the puzzle together in *Reunion with Death*. Murder runs in the family when Merry's mother becomes a person of interest in the death of a famous paleontologist with *Deadly Bones* during a disastrous cub scout field trip. And Christmas will never be the same in a *Berry Little Murder*. This cozy mystery series contains plot twists and turns with fun characters you'll admire, laugh with, and root for all within a small town setting.